a kiss in kyoto

the **publishing** CIRCLE

admin@ThePublishingCircle.com
or
THE PUBLISHING CIRCLE
Regarding: Kumiko Olson
19215 SE 34th Street
Suite 106-347
Camas, Washington 98607

A KISS IN KYOTO / Kumiko Olson
ISBN 978-1-947398-23-8
FIRST EDITION
Printed in the United States of America

BOOK DESIGN BY MICHELE UPLINGER

a kiss in kyoto

愛

a story of love in japan

KUMIKO OLSON

Island Nation
of
Japan
KYOTO
TOKYO

chapter 1

NEW HOME

MY FOOT IS BECOMING NUMB as I sit on the tatami mat for my weekly Zen meditation. This week is the same as every other. I try to show patience as my dad recites a sutra.

Today is the start of the last week I will be living with my parents. Freedom! Well . . . at least it's a partial freedom. My parents have agreed to let me live alone on the condition I promise to fulfill the *omiai*, an arranged marriage. I already know my mom will begin to overwhelm me with pictures of potential men. Even so, I am still eager to escape the strict rules of the temple life: no meat, no alcohol, no nights out, no fancy clothes.

A buzz in my pocket diverts my attention. Furtively I check the message. A text from Yuki says, "You want to get together today?" I text back, "I'll be free after the Zen meditation. See you at eleven. The usual place."

Yuki, my best friend and coworker, hails from Nagoya

prefecture where she worked in a branch office of the Industrial Bank. Three years ago, she transferred to the head office of the department of international wire transfers, where I have a position. Being the same age, twenty-eight, and having the same interests, shopping and touring, we clicked right away like best friends from a previous lifetime.

Besides our common hobbies, Yuki fascinates me with her femininity and self-confidence. Her body is slender, delicate, and full breasts make her all the more feminine. She moves with grace and knows how to exploit her body language and facial expressions. She blinks her deep brown eyes often, at times seemingly intentional. Fluttering her curled lashes slowly as she shuts her eyes, she looks as if she's expecting a kiss from a lover. Her makeup is remarkable. Alluring. Tempting. My dad would consider her mannerisms vain and shallow. Although I am the daughter of a monk, I want to look like Yuki.

Coming from a monk's family, my mind has been molded to be selfless, benevolent, and humble. As long as I reside with my parents, I will never be able to live boldly like Yuki.

Finally, my dad stands up. The weekend Zen meditation is over. I dress as elegantly as I can to meet Yuki, then rush to the café in Shinjuku. The Shinjuku station area is always packed with millions of people as this area is one of the largest commercial districts and entertainment centers in Tokyo, plus it's the seat of the metropolitan government and site of premier hotels. Bustling through the crowd, I arrive at the cafe right on time and order coffee. She is late, as usual.

After thirty minutes pass, Yuki appears in a stunning black sheath, three-quarter sleeve mini dress, her hair all tacked in a braided updo.

"Hi Naomi, sorry for the wait."

Her standard greeting. Although perturbed to hear the same

phrase, I say with a smile, "It's okay." With a coffee in my hand, I watch her take a seat.

"So, when is the big move?" Yuki asks in a lilting voice as she pulls her chair in closer.

"Next week, as a matter of fact."

"Cheers! I'll help you," says Yuki, then turns her head toward the waitress to order tea.

"That would be wonderful. Can't wait to be on my own," I say with a full-blown smile. "I'll cook curry rice with lots of meat and have plenty of wine to drink."

She smiles weakly. Perhaps she doesn't appreciate how difficult it was to persuade my parents to agree to my independence.

"Let's travel somewhere for a few days."

I look down.

"Why are you suddenly so morose?"

"Hmmm . . . my parents. Hope they won't bombard me with *omiai* requests."

"Huh, *omiai*!" Looking askance, she raises her eyebrows. "Who does an arranged marriage, these days? It's 2004, the twenty-first century."

"My parents are old fashioned. You know that." I feel my chin jut out at her annoying remarks. "Anyway, that's the condition I agreed to so I can live alone."

"Well then . . . good luck! Maybe they'll find you a rich man."

"Urgh!" I slap the table. "I don't need a rich man. I want to find a man I can truly devote my heart to."

"Sorry." Her tone changes to one of concern. "Don't worry, you'll find the right man." She sips her tea, pinky finger pointing upwards.

"Umm, I hope so." I gaze into my coffee cup. The once lovely heart-shaped cream has morphed into a brown and white lollipop swirl.

* * *

Here we go! Two weeks after moving, my mom sets me up with an *omiai.* Mr. Ishida Norio, the son of a major financial contributor to my dad's Buddhist temple. He graduated from a prestigious school and works at an internationally recognized company. His resume is almost perfect. His picture shows him to be a fine-looking man with sharp features. A slight coldness in his eyes unsettles me, but I decide to meet him for lunch at a French restaurant in Ginza.

On the *omiai* day, I leave my apartment with a gait like an unmotivated dog on a leash. *Meeting marriage material—how would I know if this is the right man for me? I've never had a real boyfriend; my male friends are just co-workers and old school mates.*

My train reaches Yurakucho station and I lumber to the restaurant. As I stand by the *maître d'*, a middle-aged waiter in a black tuxedo with a bowtie approaches and asks my name. He escorts me to a gentleman who is standing and waiving at me with a white handkerchief. He is taller than I expected, and he is indeed a good-looking man.

As the waiter pulls out my chair, Mr. Ishida says with a beaming smile, "My name is Ishida Norio. Thank you for coming today." He bows like a dipping bird, his head and back in a straight line.

I reciprocate the bow. "My name is Ochiai Naomi."

The waiter pushes in my chair and I sit. Mr. Ishida sits back. The waiter bows, then withdraws. I take the napkin from the table and spread it across my lap. My fiddling fingers tug at the edges of the linen. Mr. Ishida's smile looks posed. I assume he has done many *omiai.*

"I'm glad you are here," says Mr. Ishida, placing his napkin on his lap.

I drop my head to bow, then lift my eyes to find his mannequin-like eyes staring at me.

With a quivering voice, I start to say, "I've never done *omiai*, so . . ."

"Meeeee too," interrupts Mr. Ishida without showing any sign of nervousness. "Please feel free to ask any questions. So, in your resume, I see you like traveling. Where have you been?"

"Just on day trips. My friend and I visit often Yokohama, Kamakura, Nikko, and Hakone."

"Eh, no overnight trips?"

Before I answer Mr. Ishida's question, a waiter comes to our table. He recites the special of the day, leaving the wine-colored menu behind. Oblivious to his last question, I glance at the menu. Not knowing what to pick, I select the lowest-priced dish from the lunch entrees.

"No!" Mr. Ishida blurts.

Surprised by his reaction, I squeeze my eyes shut.

"Sorry, I didn't mean to startle you, but what you selected is not that great. Let me order your food."

I nod "yes", feeling annoyance in my chest.

He studies the menu. All the while, I sit up straight, keeping my hands in my lap.

"Do you like pork?" asks Mr. Ishida, pointing to the menu to show me the pork tenderloin with caramelized Granny Smith apples and a Calvados sauce.

"Mhmmm." I nod, thinking it sounds delicious.

"This is really tasty," says Mr. Ishida and raises his arm for the waiter. "We'll have *le filet de porc aux pommes caramélizées, sauce Calvados.*"

As the waiter sails away, I ask, "You speak French?"

"A little. I took French for my college foreign language requirement."

He sounds snotty. "Is that so?" *Me too,* I say to myself, not wanting to let him know that all I remember is the word *"manger"* which means "to eat."

Our meals are brought to the table. Mr. Ishida tries the pork and comments on how tender it is. He continues to critique the food for several long minutes, then finally changes the subject.

"Last weekend I went to the Izu Peninsula, a popular place for diving. I go there most weekends."

"How far is it from Tokyo?" I ask while cutting meat into small pieces, trying to be as polished as I can.

"About two hours. The water is crystal clear," says Mr. Ishida, widening his eyes in memory. "You can see both tropical and cold-water species of fish since currents from the north and south flow into this area."

Raising my eyes from my place, I nod and *hmm.*

"My next major trip is to Hawaii. Wouldn't it be cool to swim with a giant sea turtle? Green turtles swimming through beautiful coral reefs in startling blues, yellows, reds, and purples," says Mr. Ishida. "You know, scientists are learning to decipher the messages these colors convey and how the fish perceive them. Would you be interested in coming with me to Hawaii?"

A piece of meat sticks in my throat and I choke. I can't believe he's already inviting me on an overnight trip.

Feeling mortified, I guzzle some water. The coughing brings tears and he hands me his white handkerchief.

Taking his pressed cotton handkerchief, I say with a small dry cough, "Thank you." I concoct an excuse. "I'm not a good swimmer. Besides that, I cannot take a long vacation." I dab the cloth at the corners of my eyes, hoping he will change the subject.

A crooked smile appears on his face and I can almost hear him thinking, *"I'll find a way to get you into bed."* "Well," he opens his mouth, "please think about it."

His cocky countenance is annoying and impolite and I dislike him, but I smile and hope he will forget about his invitation.

When we finish our lunch, he insists on taking me home. Assuming this is how to end an *omiai* date, I say "thank you" and follow him to his car. As I slide into his shining black SUV with black tinted windows, which reminds me of a small version of a funeral coach, I glance back and see a diving mask and fins sticking out from his duffle bag.

He turns the engine and reaches for the stereo. "Would you care to listen to some music?"

"That'd be nice." I expect a popular station, yet piano with the sound of splashing waves fills the car.

"Do you like Bach?"

"Oh, yes," I say, but I think "not really" would be the truth. Classical music puts me to sleep. I don't know why I cannot be forthright.

Backing the car from the parking lot, he asks, "Where is your home in Shinjuku?"

I give him directions and he deftly negotiates the crowded main street of Ginza.

"My father can't wait for me to be a family man." He laughs hard.

I slouch a little, pressing my hands onto my lap.

"He'll give me half his fortune if I take over his business." Stopping for a red light, he turns to me. "His company is growing."

With a forced smile, I say, "Is that so?"

His eyes look like he wants to hear more from me, but the light changes and he faces forward. I glance through the side window and take a deep breath.

He continues to recount his bright future. I pipe up to point him in the right direction. In a few minutes, he parks the car in front of my apartment.

With his hand on the wheel, he turns to look me over. "I

enjoyed meeting you. Thank you for coming."

"My pleasure." As I bow my head, his hand reaches for my hand in my lap. I raise my head to look into his eyes. My breath stops.

"I'd like to see you again," says Mr. Ishida, holding my hand. Never has a man stared at me so intensely. As he squeezes my hand as tight as a blood pressure cuff, I feel cornered. I lean backward.

He releases my hand. "Can you meet me again?"

I already feel he is not the right person for me. He is too ego-inflated and conceited, but I say "yes," out of respect for how his father supported mine. I tell myself *just one more date.*

"Thank you. I'll call you soon," says Mr. Ishida, raising the corner of his mouth.

*   *   *

The evening of the *omiai* date, my mom calls to tell how much Mr. Ishida enjoyed meeting me.

"Mom, I'll date him, but don't pressure me, please. I'd like to take plenty of time to get to know him."

"Of course, I understand, but I'm glad you decided to see him again."

"Umm," I respond. "I've got to go, Mom. I'll call you soon. Good night."

"Oh . . . ooo . . . kay, good night." Her voice trails off and the line goes dead.

In an instant, the phone rings again.

"Mom! I . . ."

"Hello, Naomi-san, this is Norio."

"Oh! Mr. Ishida. I'm sorry, but I didn't expect you on this line. My land phone is used mostly for family members."

"It's all right. By the way, please call me Norio. I'd like to show you where I go diving. You like the ocean?"

Eyes shut, I take a slow, deep breath. *This is too fast-paced for me.*

As my lungs reach full capacity, I quietly release my breath.

"How about next Saturday?" he continues, as if we already have an established relationship. While I am sizing up his temperament, he offers, "I'll pick you up around ten."

I glance at the July calendar above the phone table. No marks on that Saturday, but I stare at the date until the voice in my head says, *you're taking too much time.* I finally spit out, "Okay."

"Great. I'll see you then." Without delay, the line is cut and I hear a long beep.

I walk across the room to stand by the window, lifting the bamboo shade to gaze at the vivid sunset. A crane flies in a sky that's aglow with the setting sun. *I should talk to Yuki,* I tell myself. *She's more experienced in the ways of relationships.*

Flipping my cell phone open, I push Yuki's number, but she doesn't answer. I leave a brief message telling her how the *omiai* went.

*   *   *

Monday, the bank is always busy and the employees are pressured because of their heavy workload. I notice Yuki is not at the office. She shows up at the office around noon, about the same time our boss, Mr. Yamada, comes in.

I slip over to Yuki's desk. "You are late today."

"Yeah, I wasn't feeling well, but I'm fine now. Sorry not to respond to your text. It seems your *omiai* partner is crazy about you."

"I find him egotistic and insensitive."

"Well, men are like that. You can't judge from just one date."

"You think so?" I ask. I can't help but notice the bags under her eyes. *I wonder if she spent the night with a man? I've seen that kind of languid face before. Does she have a new boyfriend? No stop it,* I tell myself. *She said she wasn't feeling well . . . get back to work—today is a busy day.*

*　　*　　*

Since leaving my parents' home I have been indulging. No more monastic food. Wine, meat, cheese and some fruit dominate my small refrigerator. My consumption of vegetables is essentially zero. My newly purchased loveseat becomes my favorite spot, where I can sink in with my feet on the coffee table and watch movies late into the night. Popcorn dots the couch. Nobody says anything. I love being on my own.

Saturday arrives and Mr. Ishida knocks on my apartment door at precisely ten o'clock in the morning. In his casual outfit, a pair of slim blue jeans and a white shirt, he looks less intimidating.

"You look dashing in your pink dress," says Mr. Ishida, scanning me in my knee length, flared skirt."

"Thank you," I say, as I feel my face grow hot.

We get into his SUV. Our destination is the famous scuba diving point in Izu Ocean Park where Mr. Ishida goes on weekends. As the engine starts, the same classical music I heard on our first date comes on. Outside, heavy clouds blanket the sky, an occasional ray of sunlight penetrating the gloom.

"Hope it doesn't rain today," says Mr. Ishida, looking up through the sky roof.

I nod in agreement. My voice seems to be asleep at the vocal cords. Being an innately shy person, I become quieter in this confined space with a man who may be thinking of me as his future wife. The silence is intolerable, so I brainstorm, hoping some topics will pop into my mind.

Cocking my head, I start. "So, Mr. Ishida, you . . ."

"Call me Norio." He glances over at me.

"Yes." Suddenly I lose my thought. *Find another one.* "What kind of food do you like?" I take a quick breath and quietly release it.

"Anything that's good, but I'm more inclined toward

Mediterranean or French cuisine. Do you cook?"

Not really. My mom cooked, I tell myself, but realizing that does not sound good, so instead I say, "I like cooking. At my parent's house, we ate vegetarian, but now that I'm on my own I eat anything."

"Good for you."

He takes the conversational lead, and our conversation begins to feel like a job interview. I am the interviewee and he the interviewer.

Around noon we pull into the park. The place looks a little desolate. We are still in the rainy season and summer vacation has not yet started. The two wading pools near the shore have few swimmers. A beach hut stage that faces the ocean stands lonely.

Getting out of the car, we enter a dive shop. Dozens of scuba tanks line the wall next to a huge air compressor. A lady stands in front of the tanks. She is dressed in a wetsuit, displaying a strikingly curvaceous body.

He stares at the lady as if I do not exist and I feel a little jealous, even though I do not have strong feelings for him.

"Norio-san," I call. He turns to look at me, but his stare returns to the woman as she reaches for a diving tank.

Rude! I quietly walk away from him toward the door. After a few seconds he catches up to me and says, with no sign of embarrassment, "Let me show you my favorite diving spot."

His impolite behavior, perhaps his usual habit around pretty women, kills my mood. He shows me his favorite diving spots, but my attention is elsewhere and the rest of our date becomes like an unwanted field trip.

When leaving the park, fat raindrops start falling and soon becoming a torrential downpour. We hurry to the car, soaking wet. My chiffon dress clings to my body, accenting my figure. Raindrops run in rivulets down my face. He reaches for a towel from his duffle bag and offers it to me. Although still annoyed by his insensitive behavior, I take the towel and thank him. He turns the heater high and hot air ripples my dress. As I press the towel on my chest, he leans over to kiss me. I push him away and he withdraws. I look into his eyes with a racing heart.

"I'm sorry," says Mr. Ishida, but his eyes show no remorse.

An uncomfortable silence descends as we drive, broken only by the sound of heavy rain impacting the windshield. The sky is heavy with clouds, the ocean gloomy, and the palm trees droop under the torrential rain.

While selecting a radio station, he asks, "Would you mind me asking a personal question?" He settles on a popular station, but the volume is too low to hear the lyrics. "Have you had a boyfriend?"

"Uh-uh, no," I murmur.

His mouth twists.

We stop for lunch and drive back home after that. Our conversation is perfunctory, but we manage to avoid long periods of silence. We part at the door of my apartment. My intuition is that he has no further interest and my desire is for him to resign our *omiai*.

*   *   *

After a few days, I decide to tell my parents how I feel about Mr. Ishida, hoping I can stop dating him. I call my parents' home.

"Hi, Naomi. I'm happy for you," answers my dad. "Norio-san's parents are excited to meet you next weekend. By the way, his father made a large offering to the temple the other day."

Oh no! I close my eyes and struggle with my thoughts. "Dad, it's too early to meet his parents. I'm too overwhelmed right now. I need more time."

"Okay." He pauses, then says, "Oh, you want to talk to your mom?"

"It's okay. Good night, Dad."

Without further ado, we hang up. I sigh, feeling a heavy weight on my shoulders. I stare at my cell phone on the coffee table for a while, then grab the phone and hit Yuki's number.

"Hello," I say, hoping she still wants to do an overnight trip.

"Hey, what's up, Naomi?"

"Yuki, I think I need a vacation. How would you like to go on a trip somewhere far away?"

"I'm up for that. Let's do it!" is Yuki's spirited reply. "But can you go for more than one day?"

"Yes, now that I'm out of the nest, my life is more under my control," I say, feeling contradicted as I think of Mr. Ishida. "How about Kyoto?"

"Sounds great!"

"Can't wait." I sigh, thinking this trip will be a welcome escape from the whole *omiai* thing.

* * *

Yuki and I request two days off to make a three-night, four-day trip. Our boss, Mr. Yamada, reluctantly grants us permission. I phone Mr. Ishida to tell him about the trip. His voice sinks when I say next weekend I will be in Kyoto with my friend. He manages to say, "Have fun," and our talk ends almost instantly.

chapter two

DEPARTURE

FINALLY, OUR VACATION DAY ARRIVES. I have never traveled without my family, except for school trips. I feel like a kid who just got her first bike. Freedom! I'm going to enjoy this trip and forget about the current affairs.

A cerulean sky holds a few wispy clouds that hang high over Tokyo's skyscrapers. There's not a breath of wind—the sun is already intense as I dash into Shinjuku Station to catch the 8:00 a.m. train. Crowds throng the passageways. As I finally reach the platform, the train slows, brakes screeching as it comes to a halt. The doors swish open, and people depart as I step in. Though the train is full, luck is with me. I squeeze into the middle of a long row of riders who share a bench that faces the passengers crammed together on the opposite side of the aisle. Musical chimes play their well-known melody and a calming voice speaks through the overhead speakers. *Tokyo iki, door ga shimarimasu.* I whisper, "Going to Tokyo, doors closing" to practice my English, though I hardly know if I'm saying it properly. I barely have time to situate myself with my bulky duffle bag and we're off. My body sways as the train rocks gently from side to side. Already warm from my dash through the station, the sun hitting my back causes me to perspire and beads of sweat pearl on my forehead.

At the Tokyo station, where I am to meet my friend Yuki, I get off the train and snake through the hordes in the transit center, one of the busiest hubs in Japan. Summer vacation has started for those who attend school, and young tourists crowd the passageways.

I arrive at the *Shinkansen* bullet train platform and easily spot Yuki. A white, broad-brimmed summer hat almost covers her face, showing only her small lips, rouged in crimson. Wearing a yellow summer dress printed with red poppy flowers, she stands out—elegant and attractive. Some passengers stare at her and a twinge of jealousy startles me. I feel pretty today, but my dress, certainly not high couture, lacks sophistication. It is just a straight, sleeveless orange dress. Not even a brand name. Although it is hard to surpass Yuki in fashion or flair, I am proud to be her best friend. Nonetheless, I always find myself competing.

Yuki and I hop on the *Shinkansen*, a futuristic-looking, aerodynamic bullet train. Our destination is Kyoto. For over one-thousand years, Kyoto was the heart and capital of ancient Japan and is filled with national treasures. With hundreds of Buddhist temples and Shinto shrines, palaces, gardens, and museums, we could visit Kyoto for weeks and still see only a small part of the many amazing sites. During our stay in Kyoto, the famous Gion festival will take place—it will be my first time at the festival, something I have wanted to see since I was a little girl. We have decided to stay at a hotel in the Gion district for the first two nights, and then spend one night in Ohara—a tranquil rural village in the mountains north of Kyoto.

The train is full of passengers, but luckily the reserved seats in front of us are empty. We rotate the seat so we both can sit by the window, facing each other. As the train leaves Tokyo behind, the houses and tall buildings give way to green forests.

"It's nice to get out of Tokyo once in a while," Yuki says with her elbow on the window, propping her delicate chin up with her cupped hand.

Her enthusiasm seems forced, but I brush it aside and look down, catching sight of Yuki's French nails. Pale pink glitter is embedded in the acrylic. "Nice to get out," I say, turning away from Yuki to look outside. "Lovely . . . it's picturesque, isn't it?"

Yuki tilts her head toward the window, her countenance rueful.

"What are you thinking, Yuki?"

"Nothing, really," she says, still looking outside. "Look at the grape vines!" she says, changing the subject.

I can't continue to ignore her doleful expression. "Yuki, you look sad. What's bothering you? Can you share with me?"

Keeping her gaze on the landscape, her silence is unbroken. She reaches for her Louis Vuitton duffle bag and takes out an Evian. Finally, her gaze wanders to my face. "Umm . . ." she sighs. "Well . . . to tell you the truth, I . . ." Her eyes hesitate then shift to her lap.

"Please tell me."

A few seconds of silence ensue, then she raises her chin wearily. "I'm in a bad relationship. I want out."

"What do you mean 'a bad relationship'?" I ask, thinking of my own problem.

"I made a mistake. I shouldn't have accepted this man's invitation to go golfing. I was naïve."

"You don't like him?"

"I don't dislike him, but I never intended to develop a

relationship. Besides, he's married." She casts her eyes down and fingers her water bottle.

"Married? Are you having an affair?" I don't intend to sound accusatory, but realize I do.

"It's complicated! You don't understand," she snaps.

"Sorry." I sit back and focus on the scenery going by.

Yuki says gently, "I'm sorry I spoke sharply. Believe me, I don't feel good about myself. You know . . ." she pauses, "about three months ago, there was a close call. His wife suspected I was having an affair with her husband, but I assured her we were not. Feeling shameful, I tried to end our relationship many times. Well . . . it's hard to explain so you could understand. Let's not talk about it anymore; let's try to have a fun trip." With her eyes fixed on me, she gives a slow nod, then takes a lingering sip of her Evian.

"Okay," I say. Neither one of us wants to talk about our current relationships. I certainly don't want to ruin my trip by bringing up the topic of Mr. Ishida.

The mood has suddenly swung from one of joy to somberness. For what seems an eternity, we sit quietly, staring at the passing scenery. Mr. Ishida's face flashes across my mind.

Wanting to break the awkward silence, I reach for my handbag to pull out a chocolate bar.

"Would you like to have some?" I offer, breaking the bar in half.

"Thanks." She takes the offered piece with a sweet smile, as if she too is seizing this chance to soothe our curt exchange.

Two hours after we leave Tokyo, the train enters Nagoya, a major railway station and the only stop before Kyoto. Passengers carrying travel bags are lined up on the platform. As the train comes to a stop, the doors slide open and passengers stream in. A young couple appears at our compartment, looking pointedly at the seat number. I immediately stand up and move to the seat on the aisle side next to Yuki. The young man turns the seat back in the other direction and the couple sits down. The train lurches forward and swiftly gains speed as it heads out of the city.

I start ruminating about who Yuki's boyfriend could be, but no one comes to mind. Her eyes meet mine. I grin and push the thoughts from my mind, not wanting to further sour the mood.

"You know, Mr. Yamada wasn't in favor of us taking vacation together, but I'm glad he gave us permission," I say, biting into a piece of the chocolate.

"At times, I can't stand him," says Yuki in an undertone.

"I agree. He's moody."

"Having such a young wife must take a toll on him. He maybe has neither the stamina nor money to meet her fancy," she says icily.

I chuckle, but am puzzled by her comment. I look at her, trying to determine what she is really talking about.

She closes her eyes and takes a deep breath with her head down. Silently I wait.

Lifting her head as if it weighs a ton, she quietly surrenders. "I've been having an affair with Mr. Yamada."

"Eh! Our boss?"

She nods.

"How long has this been going on?" I say, intentionally keeping my voice soft.

"I really don't want to talk about him." She bites her lower lip.

"I understand," I say, and start feeling sorry about her dilemma. Her life sounds muddled. Well, mine is too, but not as bad as hers. I decide I'll share what's troubling me. Perhaps she'll open up. "By the way, my parents suggested I keep dating my *omiai* partner, so I met with him again last Saturday."

"How did it go?" Her pensive look turns to curiosity.

"Not well!" I almost growl.

Yuki blinks her eyes and says nothing.

"Besides being arrogant, he's rude." I cross my arms. "We went to the Izu Ocean Park last Saturday because he wanted to show me his diving place."

"Yeah?"

"When we were in the scuba shop, a shapely woman, wearing a wetsuit, walked in."

"Yeah?"

"Mr. Ishida couldn't keep his eyes off her the whole time we were there. Admittedly, the wetsuit showed off her perfect figure." I take a wheezy breath in irritation. "But you know, it's disgusting when I'm standing right there, and my so-called date is lusting after another woman. Can you imagine, after all that, he even tried to kiss me in the car? And he wonders why I don't call him by his first name. I don't remotely feel close to him."

The instant I say this, I realize Yuki is not the right person to complain to, as she also steals men's glances.

"Naomi, if you know that much already, you'd be better off without him," she says in a firm voice.

"Right." I nod reflectively, already pondering the thought of canceling the *omiai*.

"Kyoto station, next stop," comes the announcement as the train slows.

Minutes later, we are in Kyoto. The doors open, and we step from the bullet train, following other travelers: young couples, a few elderly couples, and groups of friends like us. Countless tourists swarm like army ants through the passageways of the modern station building, which resembles an international airport.

The huge wall clock shows ten to twelve. Yuki suggests we eat inside the building, so we take an elevator to the food court on the eleventh floor. After drifting around to see the display case at each restaurant, we settle on an Italian café.

Plopping onto a chair, Yuki releases a long sigh. "I'm already tired."

"The heat wave zapped your energy, huh? Lunch will give you a boost."

"It's the humidity. Also, I'm hungry. I woke at five and skipped breakfast."

We order pepperoni pizza and I order a glass of wine. I'm surprised Yuki doesn't order one too. The pizzas are served long after the wine.

"The wine is making me sluggish, but I'm on vacation." I say, shrugging my shoulders. "The more relaxed I become, the more glued I become to this chair."

"Well then, shall we go?" says Yuki, grabbing her duffle bag.

We leave our bags in a locker at the station and go sightseeing.

When we walk out of the station, the humid smell of newly wet asphalt from a summer shower engulfs us. Yuki pulls a lacey, white cardigan from her bag and covers her small shoulders. I slip on a blue sweatshirt, mismatched with my orange dress. At least I won't get a chill by sacrificing comfort for fashion, I think, trying to feel better about my appearance next to Yuki.

There are bus stops for numerous destinations and crowds stand waiting for their buses. We look for the bus station for Ryoan-ji, the Zen temple, and join the tail-end of that line.

Our bus arrives around one thirty. The bus quickly fills with tourists and we are soon buried in the crowd. For twenty minutes, we stand, not talking—only those lucky people who have seats are burbling about the places they want to tour today.

The bus finally reaches our destination. The early rain shower cleansed the air and the sky is a crisp blue with a few brushstrokes of clouds. The temperature is quickly rising to thirty Celsius which isn't surprising since Kyoto lies in a basin surrounded by mountains and becomes unbearably hot and humid in summer.

We shed our outer garments in relief and head for the temple.

Near the Ryoan-ji temple, a few souvenir shops sell Kyoto's famous pickled vegetables and red bean confectionary called *yatsuhashi*. Never turning down a freebie, I stop at one of the pickle shops and sample scarlet queen turnip, eggplant, and cucumber pickles. Other tourists nibble without purchasing.

I step over to Yuki, nibbling on a slice of cucumber, "Ahh . . . these are scrumptious! If I had some *sake* right now, I'd be in heaven. Try some."

"I'll pass. Not my favorite." She twists her cheek.

Why suddenly so picky? I think, then mentally chastise myself for being judgmental.

At last we reach the main attraction of the Ryoan-ji: the Zen Rock Garden. Leaving our shoes at the entrance, we step into the abbot's quarters. The old wooden floor is polished from centuries of human foot traffic. People sit along the long veranda, admiring the rocks in a sea of raked pebbles. I find the view calming. The moss-covered boulders look ancient. Yuki and I squeeze into the line of viewers. The serenity of the garden is meditative, despite the noisy crowd.

Standing up, Yuki taps on my shoulder. "It's already four. We'd better leave soon. We need to pick up our travel bags from the Kyoto station before we go to the inn."

"Right, I totally forgot about them." I jump up and click my camera for one last photo of the garden.

*　*　*

After retrieving our bags, we board the subway to Shijo Station. From the station, we walk a kilometer or so to our accommodations in Gion, the famous geisha district. The inn stands on a hillside, surrounded by lofty maple and cherry trees. Climbing the narrow cobblestone path from the gate to the entry, we pass stone lanterns and bamboo trees. I open the sliding lattice door to the inn and step inside the exposed aggregate entrance. A lady in a kimono immediately appears and greets us in the soft, melodic intonation of the Kyoto dialect. "*Yokoso Okoshiyasu*—Welcome!" She then places two pairs of slippers in front of us and leads us to our room.

After passing the hallway, we approach a narrow stone alleyway, flanked by guest rooms. Wooden lanterns with paper insets set on the floor in front of each room and light our path; the authentic elegance of Kyoto is everywhere. Once out of the main building, we climb the stone steps to the annex building on a higher hill. The maid finally stops and slides open the door to our room. Leaving our slippers at the entrance, we step up into the tatami room. The maid hurries into the back room with short, quick steps, kneels at the table, and reaches for a red, lacquered tea box. She takes out two tea cups and confectionaries and serves us tea.

She intones sweetly, "Enjoy your stay!"

"Thank you," we say.

She puts her hands lightly on the tatami in front of her to bow, almost touching her forehead to the tatami mat, then dismisses herself.

Yuki and I stretch our legs under the low table. Reclining back on the floor chair, we sip our tea.

"Look at this red *oranda* goldfish!" Yuki says, pointing to a delicate fish inside the sky-blue-colored jelly confectionery.

"Pretty . . . it's almost too beautiful to eat," I say, holding my own piece to the light to observe. I put it in my mouth, bite it in half, and chew slowly before drinking tea. The sweets offset and balance the bitterness of Japanese powered green tea. "How do you like Kyoto? I think Kyoto is nice."

"I agree," Yuki says, slicing the sweet with a tiny wooden fork.

I can't help but notice she doesn't bring up the topic of her affair now that we are settled in, staying as mum about the subject as I am.

It is a little early for dinner, so we decide to go to the hot spring. In the changing room, I see her naked for the first time. I wonder how her breasts could possibly be so big while the rest of her body is so small. My small breasts seem like they stopped developing at the age of thirteen or fourteen. I become self-conscious. I try to cover both my breasts and pubic area with the hand towel, holding the towel vertically, but it falls short of covering everything. When I step into the cedar-log bathtub the essence of cedar mixed with steam rising from the tub calms me. Through the glass wall, I look out over a small botanical garden bathed in the summer evening sun.

Tying up her hair, Yuki says, "Wouldn't it be cool to live in Kyoto?"

Her doleful eyes tug at my heart. I realize she wants to escape her current situation as much as I want to escape mine. "Indeed, Kyoto is nice, but I am relishing my apartment. The only downside is my annoying neighbor. She's an old maid who seems to have nothing better to do than snoop on the neighbors," I say, hoping to cheer her.

Yuki laughs.

We get out of the bath. At the changing room, Yuki puts on light makeup for dinner. I too swirl some pink cheek powder over foundation and brush on pale pink lipstick.

* * *

In the tatami dining room, there are twelve black lacquer western-style tables and chairs. The furniture is out of place on the tatami floor, but I realize the tables are there to accommodate foreign guests. The room is already filled with guests, including some Westerners. We take the last table in the corner of the room.

A maid brings dishes to our table, one after the other. Steamed egg custard filled with lily root, fish cake, mushrooms, and a few diced chicken thighs is composed attractively in a biscuit tea cup. A mixed *sashimi* plate is made with thinly sliced tuna, squid, and sea bream snapper. Large shrimp tempura lay in a bamboo basket. A clear broth with pine mushrooms and cryptotaenia, a member of the parsley family, releases a fragrant steam when I lift the lid of a red, lacquered bowl. I glance over the mesmerizing selection and pick up a shrimp tempura with my chopsticks.

"Look at the *Maiko*-san!" I hear other guests exclaim and everyone's attention shifts to the exquisite woman in traditional Japanese attire who has just entered the room. She looks so young. Yuki leans close to politely whisper about the *Maiko*-san's history. I learn from her that *Maiko*-san, a geisha trainee, starts her apprenticeship at age fifteen and achieves *geisha* at twenty. To reach this status, they must persevere through vigorous training to become a great *shamisen* player, which is a three-stringed instrument, and a dancer. No social life, no friends, and with restricted family contact: it must be hard for such young girls to undergo this discipline. *What's on her mind?* I wonder. *I'm enjoying my free time after leaving the temple house, but she'll not have the world commoners can have. The life of a Geisha seems to be an expensive sacrifice.*

Maiko-san's exquisite kimono is embroidered with many brightly-colored threads on white silk. Her orange sash, brocaded in gold, drapes down her back. Her hair accessories are small, colorful fabric flowers. Many ornaments poke out of her raised hair as if her hair were a flowerbed. Wisteria flowers dangle down the left side of her face. At the other side of her face, thin shiny metal sticks swing with her every movement. Because her face is painted so white, and her hair is so starkly black, the colors of the hair ornaments and kimono are strikingly contrasted. Her rose-petal-like red lips are eye-catching. Taken by her beauty, my appetite fades.

Shuffling her sock-covered feet, *Maiko*-san circles the room, serving *sake* to the guests. Meanwhile, a hotel employee hurriedly sets up the stage, putting a microphone and a red cushion in place for the musician. A middle-aged musician appears, dressed in a simple but elegant kimono, carrying a *shamisen*. Kneeling on the floor cushion, she faces the short microphone stand. The *Maiko*-san approaches the center of the stage and freezes into a pose to commence her dance. The *shamisen* lady plucks the strings with an ivory pick a few times and then begins chanting.

Chinton shan . . .

Haaa . . .

Yosanoh . . .

The dancer flicks her silk fan fully open and with quick short steps twirls in a small circle. In her choreographed performance, her head, hands, and legs flow gracefully with each step. Her eyes are the only part of her body that are motionless, as if she were a Japanese doll. Many guests record her performance.

"How flowing her dance is!" I say and meet Yuki's eyes to share my pleasure.

"Umm . . . indeed, impressive." Her eyes slip away to nowhere.

Oh no, I think. Yuki's poor mood has returned.

Dinner will be more delicious if I eat while it is hot, but the *Maiko*-san steals my attention. My chopsticks rarely move, and my wish to comfort Yuki's vexed mind fades. While watching *Maiko*-san dance, I notice a tall foreigner busily clicking the shutter of a sizeable camera that sets on a tripod near the stage. He occasionally aims the lens at Yuki, but she seems not to notice.

When the *Maiko*-san finishes her dance, she kneels on the tatami mat, places her right hand over her left, and delivers a final bow. The audience applauds.

After the dancer leaves, everyone's attention returns to food and conversation. While waiting for Yuki to finish her food, I look around. Everyone has left except the photographer and his partner, a Japanese man. Although the two are talking intently, occasionally their faces turn to us. Yuki seems unaware of being watched.

The foreigner is in his thirties and the Japanese man appears to be in his late twenties. The photographer is tall and slender. I find his blue eyes and high-arched brows appealing; his dark blond hair stylishly hanging over his wide forehead projects virility. The young Japanese man is also attractive. His eyes aren't as large as the photographer's, but they are clear and intelligent looking, and his nose is straight and high for a Japanese. His well-formed body structure and mannerisms exude confidence and amiability.

Yuki finally finishes toying with her dinner. The photographer and his partner finish their conversation and walk away. Before leaving the room, the foreigner turns toward us, gives a tiny bow, and says, "Good night!" in Japanese.

Yuki responds in English, "Good night, gentlemen!"

"Good night!" I say in English, raising my hand up to my smiling face to wave.

When we return to our room, the lights are on and two futons have been prepared by our maid.

While changing into one of the *yukata,* cotton robes, laid out for us, I say, "The photographer was taking your picture, Yuki."

"I noticed that. I wonder what kind of photographer he is?"

"Hmm . . . well, what do you think the other man does?" I roll to my side to look at her.

"Maybe he's a translator, or just his friend."

"He's charming, isn't he?"

"It's getting late. We should get some sleep. It's been a long day," says Yuki as she shuts her eyes.

"Good night," I say, staring at the ceiling illuminated by the moonlight.

I begin to compare the two men—Mr. Ishida and the man with the photographer. Mr. Ishida sometimes appears stern and cold. What I dislike most about Mr. Ishida is his arrogance and insensitivity. In addition, his smiles are paper thin. The man I saw in the dining room has an innocent, friendly smile—his whole face engages in a captivating smile which conveys gentleness and kindness. The more I think of Mr. Ishida, the more I feel he is not the right person. No more dates with him. I'll tell my parents when I get home—and hope my parents will understand.

* * *

Yuki is still sleeping, so I decide to go to the public bath alone. At six o'clock in the morning, the hallway is quiet. No one is in the outdoor bath. The garden is waking up with the morning sun and it is already bright. The bamboos look golden. It's going to be a hot day.

I sink into the hot tub and lean my head on the side of the pool. Mr. Yamada's face flits to mind. *He's cheating on his wife. He has three kids. How could Yuki get involved in this mess? Stop!* I chide myself. *I don't want to spoil this vacation.*

Feeling a bit light-headed, I step from the hot tub and walk into the changing room where I put on a white dress with blue polka dots. Having refreshed myself, I leave the room. At the entry, when I duck through the beaded curtain, I see the Japanese man from last night.

Summoning courage, I say, "Good morning. An early morning bath?" In that instant, my body, already hot from the bath, turns crimson.

"Yes, you too?"

"Yes, an early morning soak in a hot spring is invigorating," I remark. "I wanted to come with my friend, but she is still sleeping."

"My client is also sleeping. He's a magazine photographer from America and still has a little jetlag."

"Is that so?" Desiring to say more, nothing comes to mind. A sweet smile plays about his lips.

As he puts his hand on the curtain to the entrance of the men's side, his eyes lock onto mine until I feel the urge to say something.

Looking over my shoulder, I rack my brains. "Enjoy the hot spring and have a wonderful day. It's going to be a hot day."

"Thank you, and you, too, have a fun day," says the handsome man with a charming smile that draws me like a magnet. The softness of his eyes and his smile etch themselves into my mind.

When I return to the room, Yuki is up and ready for breakfast. She is in a navy blue, short-sleeved, off-the-shoulder dress. Her hair, braided into a fish-tail, hangs loosely down the side of her head to frame her face. Her eyes have been made up to be a glamourous, smoky black.

"Wow, a different look today!" I say, scuffing across the tatami room to the corridor to hang my wet towels on a steel stand, all the while marveling at how she's done her eyes.

"You look chic in your polka-dot dress," says Yuki as she waits for me at the entry door.

"You think so? Hope the men we met last night are in the dining room," I say, finishing up with my towels.

We head for breakfast. Upon entering the room, I see no sign of the photographer and his partner. Yuki's face seems to fall. Maybe she, too, is looking for them. In silence, we seat ourselves at the empty table.

Our breakfast arrives promptly. A lot simpler than the dinner menu, spread before us is a sliced mackerel, an eggroll, cold bean curds, miso soup, and pickled cucumber and red radish.

Wishing they'd come to breakfast, I say, "By the way, I chatted with the photographer's partner at the entry of the public bath."

"Really? What did you talk about?"

"I learned the foreigner is the partner's client. He takes photographs for a magazine."

"Interesting. Is the fellow you spoke with a translator?"

"I don't know. I didn't ask."

"I wonder if they are staying here again tonight?" Yuki looks engaged in pleasant thoughts for the first time since we've arrived.

Raising an eyebrow, I say, "That'd be my wish."

chapter three

GION

AFTER BREAKFAST, YUKI AND I HURRY to the kimono rental shop. We can't wait to mill around in our kimonos at the Kiyomizu-dera Temple complex, perched high atop a mountain overlooking the city of Kyoto.

The kimono store looks like it could be from an earlier century. A wooden building with lattice covering the exterior windows and a gray clay-tiled eave above a sliding entry door impart a traditional touch.

"Welcome to Yumezono. Come in," the lady of the shop says.

"We'd like to rent summer kimonos for the day," I say, mimicking her cheery cadence.

"Certainly." She beckons us to follow her to the back room. As we step into the room, the smell of cypress scented incense and the slow gentle strumming of a *Koto* draws me into the moment. A huge array of colorful silk kimonos and *yukatas*-casual cotton robs hang on racks. Piled high on open shelves in one corner are more formal kimonos with subdued patterns and colors. Three young ladies are looking for *yukatas*. The shop lady lightly bows to the customers as she passes and a few steps further she stops and points out the silk kimonos. "Yours are in this section."

"Wow," Yuki and I say in sync, glancing around.

"Please take your time to find the one you like. We also provide undergarments and accessories." She waits patiently as we begin to look through the kimonos.

Yuki's eyes sparkle when she immediately finds one she likes.

"What do you think?" Yuki asks, draping a mint-green kimono over her shoulder. The bottom is designed as a river flowing with silver and yellow chrysanthemums.

"Lovely," I say.

The lady adds, "It will look elegant on you."

I meander around to find the one I like. "How about this pale pink one with a cherry blossom design? It's my color," I say, pulling the sleeve to my chin.

Yuki and the lady take a few steps toward me. "Yes, it's your color," says Yuki with a grin as the shop lady gives a deep nod.

I smile at them while thinking it would be awesome if the American photographer's partner could see me in this kimono. His intimate gaze this morning, in front of the public bath, flashes to my mind.

"Would you like to try them on?" asks the lady.

"Yes!" We say with one voice.

"Take them upstairs and a lady up there will do the fitting."

Carrying our kimonos, we ascend the stairs into the *tatami* dressing room. *Tatami* mats, woven from soft rush plants, cover the floor, sweetening the air with a grassy scent.

Yuki is first, and I watch her being dressed. She puts on the summer undergarments made of gauze. The fitter, perhaps in her early twenties, ties the soft yarn rope around Yuki's stomach.

"Aha . . . too tight," utters Yuki, exhaling in a long breath.

With a surprised look, the fitter says, "Sorry," and quickly loosens the cord.

I glance at Yuki's stomach and notice a slight bulge. In the public bath, her belly was covered with her hand towel. The fitter rewraps the kimono around her and gently ties it with a sash, obscuring her figure.

"It's done. You look gorgeous." The fitter wipes her forehead with the back of her hand.

"Yes, you look beautiful," I say, wondering about Yuki's tummy bulge.

Another lady takes Yuki into a different room to do her makeup and hair.

"It's your turn," the fitter says, turning to me. She reaches into a cherrywood cabinet to find a sash to match my light pink kimono. "Even though you chose a single-layer kimono, it'll be hot. Did you consider maybe selecting *yukata*, a casual summer cotton robe?"

"I know summer isn't the best time to wear a kimono, but I want to feel like a lady from the last century walking around the ancient city of Kyoto. A *yukata* is too casual," I respond.

In ten minutes, she finishes. She says, "You look pretty," but with less enthusiasm than when she complimented Yuki.

I drift into the salon where Yuki is still on a chair. I beam at her in the mirror; she grins. Her low rolled up-do hairstyle is decorated with only one elaborate tortoiseshell. She looks so elegant.

I wish I could get a super chic hairstyle. Now I regret having cut my hair short.

The beautician hands Yuki a mirror. She takes the mirror, checks the hairdo from all angles, and nods with satisfaction. The beautician calls me over to sit in the chair.

She asks with a puzzled expression, "How should we do

your hair?"

"No hope for a cool hairdo for me?" I mutter.

Unfortunately, my hair is too short to style, but after a moment the hairdresser reaches into a drawer and picks out a long, straight hairpiece. Placing the hairpiece on my head, she blends it with my hair. She next bundles the hair, now long and voluminous, coils it into a tight bun, and sticks a pink-flowered-hairpin through the high bun.

"Whoa. Pretty, isn't it?" she says with a wide smile.

"Yes, indeed. I like it," I say, smiling back, excited with the transformation I see in the mirror.

* * *

Wearing a kimono is exhilarating and it is flattering that people look at us as if we were celebrities. As wonderful as the attention is, it makes me feel self-conscious. Yuki looks at ease. I notice she is beginning to perk up and be more playful. A cute guy aims his camera to take our picture. She puts her hand to her chin as if blowing the wispiest of kisses. I mimic her gesture, feeling in seventh heaven.

With all this attention, I try to project a lady-like figure, walking with chin up and back straight, but wrapped so tightly in my kimono, I am forced to take tiny steps like a turtle, a laborious way to sightsee.

We take a taxi to Higashiyama where the rickshaws are queued up, waiting for tourists. A man in a *happi*, the traditional Japanese straight-sleeved coat, usually made of indigo or brown cotton, and imprinted with a distinctive crest, greets us. His outfit is complete with a conical straw hat and slip-on thong footwear.

"Ladies, you look beautiful," says the rickshaw driver.

"Thank you." I give a tiny bow and an ingratiating smile.

"Are you friends or sisters?" asks the driver.

I grin at his comment.

"We are best friends," answers Yuki.

Yes, we are, despite her earlier reluctance to tell me about her relationship with our boss. I begin to revel in Yuki's companionship as she seems to be enjoying the trip now, apparently putting her issues aside.

The driver takes my hand. I use the other hand to hold up the kimono's train as I step onto a small stool to climb into the two-passenger cart. Yuki follows.

The driver says, "Here we go ladies. Relax and enjoy the ride!"

"The driver lifts the rickshaw's poles, forcing us back into a reclining position. I grab Yuki's arm. She chuckles.

The man pulls the rickshaw effortlessly and the ride is smooth and comfortable. He periodically turns his head back to explain the well-known sights, and his years of experience as a rickshaw driver show in his skill at maneuvering the cart and simultaneously conversing with us.

He enters the south side of Gion, along Hanamikoji street, lined with lovely wooden buildings still functioning as exclusive teahouses where geishas hold court. Just gazing at the wooden lattice windows of the teahouses mesmerizes me. The night scene must be quite exotic, I imagine, with red lanterns hanging above each secretive doorway, lighting the way for the geishas and *maiko* trainees, scurrying to their teahouse appointments.

Foreigners are everywhere, seeking a glimpse of a geisha. I look around, hoping to encounter the American photographer and his partner. My attention is more on looking for them than on sightseeing. I notice Yuki's head also turns when foreigners pass. I wonder if she might be interested in the photographer. The hour flies by, and before we know it, we are back at the rickshaw station.

From the station, we meander along a narrow historic shopping street that changes its name three times—Ninen-zaka, Sannenzaka, and Kiyomizu-zaka—before finally reaching the Kiyomizu-dera Temple. This famed cobblestone road is fringed by two-story buildings occupied by numerous gifts shops. Awnings extending out from the shops expand their space to display unique Kyoto merchandise. Yuki walks at a snail's pace, so I slow my gait to enjoy the beautiful pottery, lacquerware, tortoiseshell hair ornaments, and other crafts on the stands in front of the shops.

Dabbing a handkerchief on her sweating forehead, Yuki pleas, "Let's find a restaurant where we can relax." She seems short of breath.

"Good idea."

We enter a small bistro nestled between gift shops, and order cold noodles.

"You know . . . I don't think it was a good idea to rent a kimono in summer," I say.

"I totally agree," Yuki says, flapping her Japanese fan in front of her face.

The noodles come in ice water, along with a cold dipping sauce.

"This looks delicious," I say as I pick up a few strands of noodles with my chopsticks and dip them in the sauce. Soon, forgetting my manners and kimono etiquette, I scoop voluminous amount of the noodles into the sauce and slurp, raising the cup to my mouth. My long sleeve slips down, revealing my undergarment. "Ahh. The cold noodles are refreshing, aren't they?"

"Uh-huh." Yuki puts the chopsticks down on the table, but half of her noodles still float in the bowl.

"Are you finished? Ready to move on?"

"I guess," she says, with unconvincing eyes.

When I step from the cool, dark restaurant, the brightness and heat daze me. We have a fifteen or twenty-minute climb along the cobblestone road to the temple. I feel it will take forever.

* * *

We finally reach the gate of Kiyomizu-dera Temple, located halfway up Otowa Mountain. At the top of the street, we approach a vermillion two-story gate. As we enter the gate, we can see the stunning compound spread out before us on the mountain terrace. We pass the bright red bell tower. Nearby is the three-story pagoda, also colored in vermilion.

"Stand in front of the pagoda. I'll take a picture of you," I say, waiving my hand for her to go.

"Okay. You're next," says Yuki, shuffling over the pebbled ground.

"Smile!" I shout, backing up to capture the entire image of Yuki and the pagoda. I realize I need a wide-angle lens, so I pull out the lens from my kimono purse, but I don't know exactly how to use my brand-new camera. As I fiddle with the equipment, I sense someone standing behind me.

"May I help you?" says a man.

I turn and break into a smile when I see who it is. "Aha . . . it's you."

"Need some help?"

"I bought this Nikon for the trip. The salesman told me it's a simple camera. But, umm . . . changeable lenses . . . I never had," I say in broken English, feeling inadequate. My face heats.

"May I have your camera? By the way, you look cute in a kimono," says the photographer.

"Thank you," I say, and hand the camera to him, feeling more embarrassed.

With alacrity, he quickly attaches the wide-angle lens and hands the camera back. I thank him. Centering the image of Yuki and the pagoda in the viewfinder, I click the shutter. Standing beside me, he clicks off high-speed shots of Yuki.

"Hi, Mr. Photographer," says Yuki, waiving her hand as she walks toward us, her smile genuine, her voice buoyant. I haven't seen that sort of happy gesture from her in a long time.

The photographer says, "Hi. You look different in a kimono."

"You ladies look gorgeous," calls out his partner as he comes toward us, holding an *omikuji*, a paper fortune, in his hand. He must have gone to one of the nearby shops that sell talismans and paper fortunes.

We step away from the path to introduce ourselves.

"I heard from Taka that you ran into each other in front of the public bath this morning," says the American.

Taka grins at me.

"Yes, we did," I say, shooting Taka a look of "you told him about me?"

Taka gives me an effervescent smile, tiny dimples playing at the corner of his mouth.

"By the way, my name is David," the man says, reaching his hand out to shake first Yuki's hand, then mine. "We're here to capture the beauty of Kyoto for a magazine article. Taka is assisting me."

"My name is Yuki. This is my friend and co-worker, Naomi," says Yuki, pointing to me.

"So, Taka-san, are you an interpreter?" I try to enunciate "interpreter" slowly, wary of possible pronunciation errors.

"I own a company that arranges custom tours for foreign visitors and I sometimes serve as a guide." In fluent English, he speaks slowly, perhaps in response to my own caution with the language.

"No wonder your English is so good," says Yuki.

I feel self-conscious speaking English. Yuki spent three years of high school in London as the daughter of an expat. My English is fragmented. I often cannot even finish a sentence properly, even though my college major was English. David and Taka are patient, never interrupting, and listen with total presence. I already like them.

"What have you ladies planned for the day?" David asks.

"We'll be spending time here until early evening. Then we go to Gion," says Yuki.

"Really? Our plan is the same as yours. Would you like to come with us? Taka can tell you the history of the area. He's my private tour guide—a good one."

"That'll be superb," is Yuki's automatic response.

I nod in agreement, then lower my eyes. Maybe I'm overreacting, but I feel inferior not being able to communicate as well as Yuki.

"You don't look convinced, Naomi-san. Are you sure you want to go with us?" asks Taka in a tender, concerned voice.

Heartened, I affirm at my own slow pace, "Yes, I'd love to."

Taka grins and David drawls, "Goooood."

The four of us amble to the main hall of the Kiyomizu-dera Temple. Upon arriving at the temple, David lightly holds Yuki's hand to assist her up the stairs. Taka reaches his hand out to me. My heart skips a beat. His hand is soft and smooth, but his grip tightens when I stumble.

"Are you all right?" asks Taka, peering into my eyes.

"Yes, sorry." My face flushes with embarrassment.

Once we ascend to the top of the temple, we follow Taka to the large veranda, which overlooks a precipice.

"This temple is underpinned by 139 pillars, each twelve meters long," Taka explains.

"That many?" I near the balustrade. "Look! The Kyoto tower looks like a UFO."

Everyone chuckles.

"It does," David says with a wide smile, then he scans the

horizon. "What a spectacular view." He snaps pictures of the vermilion pagoda with the city as a backdrop.

Glancing down at the trees, Taka says, "It'll be breathtaking in spring with the cherry blossoms, and in autumn with the colorful foliage."

"There are cherry and maple trees along the ravine to the south," says Yuki.

"The cherry blossoms and vibrant leaves will make this place stunning and awesome for shooting photos," David says, smiling at Yuki and me, "but if we had come at a different time, we wouldn't have met the two of you."

Yuki grins and I giggle and shrug my shoulders, feeling shy once more.

Taka continues his tour description. "Not a single nail was used in the construction of this temple. It gets its name from the waterfall within the complex, which runs off the nearby hill."

As Taka leads us to the center of the hall, he says, "The temple houses within it a priceless statue of the Kannon Bodhisattva, the goddess of mercy."

We all, except for Taka, take pictures of the deity statues. When Taka finishes his explanation, David suggests taking a lunch break. It's almost two o'clock. Yuki and I had lunch earlier, but I am already starved.

"It'd be nice to sit down," Yuki says, eyeing the photographer.

"There's a small restaurant," Taka says. "It's located right next to the waterfall."

"Sounds good," Yuki says, not mentioning we already ate. Perhaps she doesn't care whether we eat or not, but is thinking it would be nice to sit and get better acquainted.

"Would you like to stop at the waterfall before we go to the restaurant?" asks Taka.

"To the waterfall first," I sputter, then turn to Yuki.

"Fine with me," says Yuki.

"All right," says David, quickly changing his camera lens.

We walk to the Otowa Waterfall where a small stone alcove is built into the hill. Water, channeled through three separate rock conduits, falls gracefully in front of us from the top of the roof into a small pond below.

"The three waterfalls originate from the same source, but impart different benefits it's said. One is longevity, another knowledge, and the last one, love. You are supposed to make a wish before taking a drink," Taka explains.

I take the ladle hanging next to the waterfall.

"By the way, if you drink from all three streams, it's considered greedy and bad luck," Taka adds.

Yuki and David take a ladle and reach out to catch some water as it splashes from the roof. I take one and only one sip, wishing for romance.

Taka, in the roll of a guide, just stands and watches us.

After giving my invocation prayer for new romance, I hand the ladle to Taka and hope his wish is the same as mine.

He turns to me. With a gleam in his eyes, he takes the ladle and sips the sacred water. I brush stray hair away with the back of my hand as I contemplate the possibilities.

The four of us leave for the restaurant next to the waterfall.

In front of the restaurant, we sit at a trestle table under a large, red, oiled-paper umbrella—a nice retreat from the scorching sun. Soon our tofu is delivered in indigo bowls. It is refreshingly cool, served with a slightly sweetened soy sauce and a sprinkle of scallion. After finishing the tofu, a waitress brings us noodles topped with leeks and a raw egg. A breeze fans the sweet aroma of the soup over the table. I lick my lips and plunge my chopsticks into the bowl.

"The food smells good," David says, his nose hovering over the steaming broth. He raises his head, places the napkin across his lap, then looks at Yuki and me. "Lucky coincidence to meet you again. So, how long have you guys been in Kyoto?"

"We arrived yesterday around noon," says Yuki, taking charge of the conversation as she usually does.

Taka peers at me. "When are you going back home?"

"We are going to Ohara tomorrow for one night, then back to Tokyo," I respond, careful of my pronunciation, grateful he's including me.

"Too bad." David frowns. "We're going there too, but not tomorrow. We're in the Gion area for two more nights."

"I wish we were able to take more vacation time." Yuki releases a heavy sigh as she lays her chopsticks neatly across the rim of the bowl.

I wonder if she is thinking about Mr. Yamada and how he gave us a tough time about approving our vacation.

Taka rests his chopsticks on the soup bowl. "So, you two work for the same company. What do you do?"

Yuki takes over again before I can push a "yes" through my mouthful of noodles. "We work in the Foreign Wire Transfer Department of an industrial bank."

David sips a spoonful of broth, raises his eyebrows, and asks, "An industrial bank, huh? Do you transfer large sums of money?"

Yuki replies, "Yes, we do. It requires our undivided attention to avoid errors. One mistyped digit will send funds to the wrong country." She wags her index finger. "But the worst part is, if you don't realize your mistake quickly, you can't retrieve the money. It's a loss for the bank."

I notice Yuki's habit of gesturing when speaking English. Taka does the same. Normally Japanese people don't do this, except for the occasional peace sign. Yuki must have picked up the habit when she lived in London and Taka perhaps acquired it from working with foreigners.

Wrinkling his forehead, Taka says, "That's scary."

Taka's worried look makes me feel I want to change the subject, so I ask, "Taka-san, where is your company?"

"My office is near the Royal Hotel," Taka answers.

I blink in surprise and look at Yuki's face to see she is also astounded. "Really! We go to that hotel for lunch occasionally," I say.

"Well then, you should stop by my office when you have a chance," says Taka. "It's about five minutes from there." He pulls a pen from his chest pocket and draws a map of his office and the hotel on a napkin.

Taka seems to be genuine and approachable. He is about our age, an amiable person with a distinctive air about him. His white teeth and warm eyes, nestled under balanced, arched eyebrows are pleasing. I like his dimples when he grins.

Yuki asks David about his job and personal life. I do not comprehend the whole conversation, but I do understand he is single, lives in New York, and travels worldwide for his work.

"Do you guys always travel together?" asks David.

"Fairly often, but only for day trips. This is our first overnight trip," Yuki answers. Her chopsticks move to accent her words like a conductor's baton. "What do you guys do in your spare time?"

"I do *kyudo*." Taka rephrases, saying, "I practice the Japanese traditional martial art of archery at a gymnasium near my home."

"Really," says David with admiration.

"Lately, I haven't done much because I started diving again."

"Where do you go?" I ask.

"I went to college in Hawaii for four years, majoring in International Business, so I used to dive in the waters around Oahu island. Since being back in Tokyo, I go to the Izu Peninsula."

A small agonizing knot forms inside me at the mention of Mr.

Ishida's favorite diving site. Trying to hide my agitation, I sip my green tea. As I tilt my head up from my cup, I catch a quick knitting of his eyebrows and wonder if he sensed something was wrong. I shoot a not-to-worry expression at Taka and he smiles back.

His four years in the U.S. explains why his behavior is so different than that of other Japanese men. His animated facial expressions and hand gestures fascinate me. Most of the Japanese men I know suppress emotions and use less body language. Taka is westernized, but still respects Japanese tradition: only a few Japanese people still practice kyudo. And clearly, as a tour guide, he enjoys explaining the history of our country. His eclectic personality intrigues me.

Yuki seems to be finished eating. She wipes her mouth, rests her chopsticks on a stand she had folded from the chopsticks' wrapper, and asks, "David, what do you do in your free time?"

"My work is my hobby. As a photographer, I travel often and visit exotic places like Kyoto," says David. He unconsciously brings his chopsticks in front of his face while he talks, and noodles hang from them, swaying in cadence to his words. "When I have a chance to go to a tropical island, I snorkel."

"It must be awesome swimming with all those colorful fish," Yuki says. Her eyelashes slowly flutter up-and-down like a baby bird opening its eyes for the first time.

Her subtle flirtations hint of Yuki's attraction to David. I must admit, David is charismatic. His calm presence, gentle manners, and good looks remind me a bit of Kevin Costner. It's hard to guess a foreigner's age, but I assume he's in his late thirties. I think his maturity and pleasant appearance appeal to her. I can't help but think of her affair with our boss, but I try to repress my judgement.

Brushing off that thought, I say on a whim, "Snorkeling is something I'd like to do."

I surprise myself. This is a bit out of character, as I don't swim well, but somehow this group of people has emboldened me. Speaking English with David and Taka makes me feel special, as most of the people around us have no idea what we are saying.

"Okinawa is a beautiful place for snorkeling. If you want, you can come with me when I go next time," Taka says.

"That sounds fantastic," Yuki says, before I have a chance to respond.

After some delay, I add, "I hear Okinawa has beautiful beaches."

"Indeed, they do, Naomi-san," Taka responds, his chopsticks almost touching his lips.

"Next time I'm in Japan, I'd like to check it out," David says.

"Sure. You'll find great spots for photo shoots. The islands between the Pacific Ocean to the east and the East China Sea to the west have stunning beaches with emerald water." Taka looks at David while talking, though his eyes animate as he turns and catches my look. The excitement must show in my eyes.

A waiter comes to our table. "I'm sorry. If you are finished eating . . ." He turns to look at the line of people at the entrance, "Other customers are waiting."

Taka says, "Ah, sorry. We'll be leaving right away."

As we leave the eatery, Yuki says, "It's almost four o'clock. We'd better go back to our hotel. Our kimonos need to be returned by six, and it takes forever to move in them."

"Would you like to spend the evening with us?" David asks. "We're going to a restaurant near the Kamogawa River."

"Sure, we'd love to," Yuki says with a quick nod.

"Naomi and Taka, sound good to you?" David asks.

"Umm . . ." I mumble.

"What, Naomi?" asks Yuki.

"How about the Gion festival?" I whisper to Yuki in Japanese.

Taka responds in English, "The Gion festival is held near the Kamogawa River, so we can see the festival after dinner. It gets prettier late at night with numerous lantern-covered floats."

I nod appreciatively.

"What do you say, David? You'll find quite spectacular scenes for your photography."

"Sounds good. Let's meet in the hotel lobby at seven," David responds.

"All right," Yuki agrees, finally looking at me to confirm I am okay with the plan.

I am, but I'm still a little annoyed by Yuki's selfishness and insensitivity about our original plan.

chapter four

GION FESTIVAL

Our hotel will return our kimonos to the Umezono shop as a service, saving us a trip.

We shuffle on tired feet into our room and immediately untie our sashes and peel off our kimonos.

"Phew," I sigh. "I can breathe again!"

"Yes, indeeeed," Yuki puffs.

"Shall we wash off the sweat and treat our sore muscles to a bath before we meet the guys?"

Yuki nods as she folds her kimono into a small square.

After returning our kimonos to the reception desk, we set off for the public bath. A few ladies are bathing, their cheery voices echoing throughout the bathhouse as they talk about places they have visited.

Soaking my tired body in the steaming hot spring, I daydream about our upcoming evening.

"*Onsen*, hot spring, is such a pleasure," I say, laying my head on the folded hand towel I've laid on a flat rock.

Yuki appears trapped in her head; she does not respond. I glance around the surrounding garden which is adorned with tidily sculpted shrubs. I wonder what Yuki is thinking. Is she thinking of the American photographer, or Mr. Yamada?

My gaze drops to her stomach for a second, but before I can see anything, she scoops up a towel and wraps it around herself, then walks to the bathing area where an array of soaps and shampoos are provided. We sit on low wooden stools in front of faucets to draw water and wash in silence.

When finished, we leave the bathing room and go inside the changing room. After dressing, we sit in front of a wall mirror. A long cedar slab, mounted at the bottom of the mirror, holds all sorts of brand-name facial skincare products.

"May I borrow your concealer?" I ask. "I want to hide my freckles."

She studies my face. "Do you mind if I do your makeup?"

"Not at all." I offer my travel makeup kit. "Please, I'd appreciate it."

She brings her bamboo drum-shaped stool in front of me and sits. She spreads out an assortment of cosmetics from her pouch, ignoring my travel kit. She has an amazing set of brushes: a brush for powder foundation, one for brows, one for cheeks, one for lips, and three different brushes just to apply eye shadow. She works quickly, and her touch makes a dramatic change, creating a soft look.

"You like it?" she says. I turn to look in the mirror.

"Umm . . . I look different." Mascara astonishingly lengthens and thickens my eyelashes, and the cherry-red lipstick makes my lips look more full. Staring at my new image, I say, "I like it."

"It's better. A lot better," she says with an affirmative nod.

"Really?"

She nods again, then puts her makeup things back into the pouch. "Let's go. We'll be late."

The clock strikes seven as we leave the room to meet David and Taka in the lobby. As we approach, I notice David's blue eyes are fixed on Yuki.

"Hi, ladies." Taka greets us with his signature smile.

Yuki and I say, "hi" in sync.

"Hello, you two," says David, moving between us to wrap his muscular arms on top of our shoulders to give us a hug. "Naomi, you look striking."

Grinning with pleasure, I shoot a glance at Yuki and she smiles back at me.

We leave the hotel for the restaurant near the Kamogawa River. It is still stifling hot: zero wind with intense humidity. The stagnant air is enervating, but my spirits are high as the sky as I anticipate the evening with these two alluring gentlemen. My head is too busy romanticizing to care about the heat.

*   *   *

Despite all the effort Taka took to make a reservation at one of Kyoto's classy restaurants, we dine quickly and hurry to the festival.

Over thirty magnificent parade floats crowd the streets of the Gion district. Each float is a work of art. Collectively, they are referred to as a "moving museum." Hundreds of thousands of people gather to enjoy the biggest festival of Kyoto. David's finger is clicking away, capturing the giant floats decorated with numerous large cylindrical paper lanterns. The sound of drums, flutes, and the local participants' shouts travel through the air.

An enormous crowd of spectators chokes the roads. We are caught up in the excitement and carried along by the parade. Conversation is difficult in the cacophony, so we fight our way through the crowd. The main road is blocked, but other streets, jam-packed with vehicles, are open. When we cross the street, a motorbike speeds past, almost hitting me. I hear David yell and turn back.

"Oh, my God!" I gasp. Yuki is on the ground. For a second, I don't comprehend what's happened, but soon realize she's been hit. Running to her, I scream, "No!"

I drop to my knees next to her. "Yuki, are you all right?"

Yuki lies motionless, eyes shut. My hand shakes as I touch her body. "Yuki, are you all right?" I repeat. "Yuki, wake up," I cry.

She doesn't respond. I feel I am about to faint. In the distance, a siren wails. Struggling to breathe, I turn to David. His face is ghostly pale.

"Yuki!" He drops down to support her upper body with his arm. "Yuki," he says, his voice breaking.

Yuki's eyes open with a lot of effort, but are vacant. She glances at David as if she has no clue what happened.

People crowd around us. The police and paramedics arrive. An officer pushes his way toward us, saying, "Move out of our way! Please move on!"

"What happened?" he asks as he reaches us.

"She was hit by a motorcycle," says Taka.

While Taka talks to the officer, paramedics rush in to attend to Yuki.

As one of the paramedics checks her pulse and pupils, he asks me, "How long has she been down?"

The shouts of spectators and the police questioning Taka distract me. I struggle to form a coherent response.

"This is the license number I wrote down," I hear Taka say as I manage to sputter, "Ten minutes. She's been on the ground for about ten minutes."

The crowd parts as the paramedics roll a gurney next to Yuki. As Yuki is lifted into the ambulance, a paramedic asks me to come along.

David asks to go too, but the paramedic stops him.

"David, I'll give you a call once we get to the hospital," I tell him.

He manages a reluctant nod.

Taka quickly writes down his cell phone number, puts it in my hand, and says, "We'll be there soon."

The siren screams again, loud and eerie. I hear one of the paramedics say to the radio, "Where's the next available hospital?"

The other paramedic, who is checking Yuki's oxygen level, asks me, "What is her name and your relationship to her?"

"Her name is Okada Yuki. My name is Ochiai Naomi and she is my friend," I answer.

"Okada Yuki-san, can you hear me? Do you remember what happened?" The paramedic asks in a loud vice.

Yuki looks at him, but does not respond. Her eyes close again.

Putting a nasal cannula on Yuki, the paramedic asks me, "How old is she?"

"Twenty-eight."

"Does she have any medical conditions that you know of?" asks the paramedic, then flips to the next page of his form when I murmur "no."

"Is she on any medications?"

Staring at Yuki's face, I say, "I don't know." I wonder if I should mention she might be pregnant.

All earlier romantic thoughts of the evening are dispelled by the horror of possibly losing Yuki. Pressure builds in the back of my throat—it isn't easy to talk. The blaring of the siren and all the medical equipment makes me nervous and I can hardly breathe. Finally, the ambulance reaches the hospital. The doors burst open, and paramedics rush Yuki into the ER. With an uneasy feeling, I follow. Nurses and a doctor run into the room, and the doors swing shut behind them.

A nurse approaches and asks me to wait on the bench near the entrance to the emergency room. "The doctor will see you later to report her condition."

"Yes, thank you very much," I say and bow.

As I rest on the bench, I call Taka. "Hi Taka-san, I'm at the Central Hospital in Kawaracho," I say in a shaky voice.

"Are you all right? We'll be there right away," Taka says in a firm voice.

"Um . . . okay." I nod to the phone and hang up.

It's almost ten o'clock. The hospital is closed for day-only patients and the corridor becomes quieter. Waiting without any news is killing me. I rest my face in my hands, elbows on my lap, running through all kinds of scenarios. Sounds of footsteps echo in the distance. I turn and see Taka and David approaching.

"Naomi-san," Taka calls.

I exhale deeply.

"How's Yuki?" says David. His face is as pale as it was earlier.

"I haven't heard anything."

"She'll be all right," Taka says as he sits next to me and holds my hand.

I offer a rueful smile.

*　*　*

Around midnight, the door finally opens, and an elderly doctor appears.

"Are you Naomi-san?" asks the doctor softly.

"Yes."

"May I talk to you privately?" I follow him, and he opens the door to a small consultation room.

"Please, have a seat," says the doctor, his expression unreadable. His stoicism has me preparing for the worst.

"Is she all right?" I ask.

"She'll be all right," the doctor says. "The fetus, however, miscarried soon after she was admitted. She didn't need surgery or a D & C, but she did lose a lot of blood."

"Yes." I bow.

"According to the X-rays, everything looks fine, other than some significant bruising that can result in acute pain. We gave her some medication and an IV to replenish the fluids due to blood loss. She should feel better soon."

I nod.

"Hopefully, she'll sleep the rest of the night. We'll check her in the morning and if all is well she can be discharged tomorrow." The doctor lifts his spectacles in a salute then stands up.

I stand up and bow deeply. "Thank you very much."

"Oh, do you know if she would prefer to be in a private room or a room with other patients?"

Knowing Yuki, I say, "A private room, please."

I return to Taka and David. They fidget as they await my report. I hesitate, as I do not have the foggiest idea what to tell them, but I think I should not be the one to tell of the pregnancy.

"What did the doctor say?" asks David, frown lines creasing his forehead.

"The doctor said he took X-rays and everything is fine other than bruising. Oh, the doctor also put her on a drip to replace lost fluids and gave her a painkiller," I say weakly and hold my breath, hoping there won't be more questions.

David sighs. Taka's squared shoulders relax. The ER door opens and a nurse pushes Yuki through on a gurney.

"We'll take her to a private room on the second floor," says the nurse.

Taka and I bow and the three of us silently follow the nurse. Yuki's bed is rolled into the elongated service elevator and we squeeze in beside the bed. The room is across from the elevator.

Taka, David, and I wait outside until the nurse finishes with Yuki. David paces, rubbing his forehead with the palm of his hand while Taka and I stand there like wilted sunflowers.

Pushing the gurney out of the room, the nurse motions. "You may go in. Two chairs lean against the wall. I'll bring another chair."

Taka and I bow, and we all enter the well-lit room.

David leans over the bed. "Poor Yuki," he says under his breath, staring at her as she lays motionless in a deep sleep.

"It's late. Both of you look tired. You can go back to the hotel," I offer. "I can manage by myself."

"No. I want to stay until she recovers," David insists.

"Well, let's stay here until Yuki can talk at least," Taka offers.

A nurse brings in a chair, then checks Yuki's IV drip and dims the room lights. "If you need anything, just push this call button," she says, showing us the control before she leaves the room.

No one talks. The three of us sit along one side of the bed with me next to Yuki's head. Time seems to stand still. I close my eyes.

Hours later, my mouth feels dry. "Is anyone thirsty?" I whisper.

"I am," says Taka softly. "I'll get a coffee. Anyone want a coffee? Tea? Soda?"

"Coffee would be nice," utters David.

Taka leaves to get coffee; David inches his chair closer to the bed. He carefully lifts the blanket and searches for Yuki's hand. Her eyelids twitch, then open languidly.

David leans forward in his chair and brings his face close to hers. "The doctor said you'll be all right," he assures her.

Yuki closes her eyes and takes a deep breath. I wonder what she is thinking.

The door eases open and Taka slips in with two cans of hot UCC coffee. Yuki's eyelids part and she turns to look toward Taka.

Dawn begins to illuminate the curtains, creating growing

shadows in the room. Taka hands a can of coffee to David and nears the bed.

"You're awake! Good morning, Yuki-san," Taka says.

"Thank you, Taka-san," says Yuki, as she sits up, "and thank you all." She scoots up toward the steel headboard, pulling the blanket toward her as David helps support her back.

"How are you feeling?" asks Taka.

"Every part of me aches," says Yuki.

"Of course. You were hit by a motorcycle," I say.

Yuki nods a few times as if recalling the incident.

It is almost six. In the shadowy room, flooded with the gray light of daybreak, Yuki's face is sallow with exhaustion, but her eyes are focused.

A nurse enters the room. David, Taka, and I leave the room and I hurry to the restroom. When I return, David and Taka are back in the room, talking with Yuki.

"Naomi, I can take care of Yuki now and you guys can head back to Tokyo," says David.

"Maybe I should stay with her," I say, looking at Yuki.

"I feel okay now, Naomi," says Yuki in a soft, but determined voice.

I bite my lip. "But Yuki! You look so weak."

A warm, strong arm encircles me and David says, "Don't worry. I can take care of her."

I look at Yuki and see her nodding, but I confirm in Japanese, "Do you really feel comfortable with only David here?"

"I do. I'll be fine," says Yuki, then she turns to David.

Are they already in love? As Yuki breaks her gaze, I add, "Your doctor said if things are okay, you'll be discharged soon."

Yuki closes her eyes and nods slowly.

In case she needs to stay one more night, I say, "I'll extend the hotel reservation one more night if possible. If not, I'll find another hotel."

"Naomi, that's not necessary," says David. "I told Taka I won't be able to continue our work here, so he's going home today. Yuki can use his room or stay with me."

Yuki looks at me pleadingly, as if saying, "David can take care of me." Her long earnest gaze overrules my concern.

"Okay, I'll cancel the hotel in Ohara and go back to Tokyo, too."

"Thank you, Naomi and Taka-san. We'll be back to Tokyo soon," says Yuki, her countenance softening.

"Okay, have a safe trip," says Taka.

Reluctantly I say, "Call me if you need any help."

As we walk out the hospital, the taxi Taka ordered is waiting in the driveway. The sunlight is hard on my tired eyes, but Taka shows no sign of weariness. He lets me in first, then slides in next to me. He puts his arm gently around my shoulder. I lean against him and feel the warmth of his body. His tanned arms are firm and sturdy. *Aha,* I think, *I could sleep forever against his shoulder.* But the ride to the hotel is brief.

In the lobby, Taka says, "We can meet here, once you pack your things. Take your time. Call me when you are ready."

"I'll be back soon," I say, and hurry to my room. Once inside, I jump into the shower and quickly bathe. Rushing, I put on makeup, then tidy up Yuki's belongings.

"Taka-san, I'm ready," I say into my cell phone, trying to hide my shortness of breath.

"All right, I'll be in the lobby."

At the front desk, we ask if they will keep Yuki's belongings until she returns, then we leave.

Taka has already called another taxi, and by the time we get outside the hotel the cab is waiting. Things move smoothly with Taka's strong managerial skills. I wish he would let me share the cost of transportation. Having only known him for eighteen hours,

I am beginning to feel indebted and the traumatic event seems to have brought us closer. While I ponder everything that has happened, the taxi races through the city, then pulls to the curb of the huge, futuristic Kyoto Station.

Inside the station, the masses of summer tourists drift in all directions. The atmosphere is oppressive, and my already fatigued body becomes more lethargic. Taka notices my condition.

"Are you hungry?" he asks.

"I'm starving. Let's have breakfast," I say, pointing to a café just ahead.

We settle into a booth. Soon hot Kilimanjaro coffee and a croissant sandwich with egg and ham are set before me. Closing my eyes, I breathe in the aroma of the fresh brew as if it will erase my fatigue. The food and coffee seem to help us relax, and Taka's countenance grows sweeter by the minute. Re-energized by the breakfast, we leave the café and hustle through the station to the Shinkansen platform.

The *Shinkansen* bullet train is crowded. I sit by the window with Taka next to me on the aisle seat.

"If you want to sleep, you can lean on my shoulder," Taka whispers in my ear.

"Thank you." I glance at him and can't help but smile.

I put my head on his shoulder and close my eyes. But my mind is unsettled and I think back to a few days ago when I was on this same train with Yuki. Now I am on this train with Taka. What a surprising change of events. I'm exhausted, but my mind won't rest. David and Yuki might have a romance. What about me? Taka-san is attractive. Does he have a girlfriend? I sit there, musing.

"Shin-Yokohama! Shin-Yokohama!" The announcement echoes at the station, waking me. I turn my head and see Taka reading a history book, but when our eyes meet he closes his book and asks, "Did you get a little sleep?"

"I guess so," I say. "How long have I been sleeping?" I sit straight, pulling back strands of hair from my forehead.

"Maybe an hour and a half."

"I thought you were sleeping?"

"No."

"Is that so?" Feeling foolish, I look out the window.

"Tokyo Station. Five minutes," comes the resounding voice from overhead. With my elbow on the ledge of the window and my face cupped in my hand, I watch the buildings race by. In five minutes, we'll be at Tokyo Station, and he hasn't told me he wants to see me again.

My chain of thought brings all sorts of memories of the Kyoto trip. Leaving Yuki in the hospital with David was disquieting, but they obviously wished to be by themselves, and I had no say about the matter. The doctor did say Yuki would be okay, and David seems to be looking after her. Nonetheless, questions flood my mind. What if David asks more questions? Is she going to tell him about the baby? And her affair with a married man?

I wiggle my shoulder a little to put my neck in a better position. Taka's warm hand reaches out for me and cradles my head.

I look up at him.

"Are you comfortable?"

"I'm just thinking about David and Yuki. Quite honestly, I'm not sure it was a good idea leaving the two of them alone."

"They'll be fine. David is a responsible person. Besides, they are adults."

"You're right," I say, but my head lowers with the weight of apprehension. Taka-san has no clue about Yuki's unborn baby.

"I understand your concern. Are you going to call Yuki-san?"

"Yes, once I get home. Perhaps by then they'll be back at the hotel."

"Please give me a call after you talk with her. I would like to know how she is." Taka pulls a notebook from his jeans' back pocket and starts jotting. "This is my work number." He tears off the page. "I'll be in the office this afternoon."

I take it from him. "But today is Sunday."

"We are open weekends since this is the tourist season."

"Okay. I'll call you."

"I would like to see you again. Let's go out for dinner." He looks into my eyes. "I would like to get to know you better."

"Dinner sounds good," I say, nodding, but I casually look out the window to mask my shyness. The scenery is agricultural with sporadic houses. I spot Mt. Fuji. "Look." I point at the mountain.

"It's beautiful, isn't it?"

The image passes within seconds, but we keep looking out the window at the sweeping provincial panoramas.

"Tokyo Station. Five minutes," comes the resounding voice from overhead.Taka reaches overhead to take down our luggage.

The train reaches its final destination, Tokyo Station. The passengers jam the aisle, and soon the doors open. As Taka and I exit the train to stand on the platform, Taka says in a firm voice, "I'll wait for your call."

"Yes, I'll call." I offer a weighty nod and he does the same.

We part, heading our separate ways, but I can't help but look over my shoulder, watching Taka meld into the flow of people leaving the train before I step off the platform and head to the taxi queue.

chapter five

ITALIAN RESTAURANT

THE STAGNANT, SWELTERING AIR ENVELOPS me as I open my apartment door. I step inside, drop my travel bag, crank the small air conditioner mounted on the living-room wall to high, then crash on the loveseat.

"Two o'clock," I murmur, watching the clock on my bookcase. The doctor's words echo: *If things are fine, Yuki will be discharged this afternoon.* I grab my cell phone and tap out her number, hoping everything went well and she is back at her hotel.

"Hello, Yuki. It's me," I say when she answers.

"Naomi . . ." Yuki takes a deep breath. "I don't know what to do."

"Why? What happened?"

"David isn't with me right now," she says. "I couldn't lie, so I told him," Yuki sobs, then continues, "that I was pregnant with my boss's baby."

"So, you did tell him."

"Yes, I admitted my ambitions to become a manger someday

led me to give into my boss's offer of advancement for sex."

"Yeah"

"I told him I *never* wanted that kind of relationship. I was a fool and hated who I'd become and tried to break up many times. He wouldn't let me go. In fact, he threatened to terminate my job." She raises her voice. "I was thinking of an abortion!"

"Uh-huh . . ." I murmur, feeling her desperation, but not knowing what I can do to console her. "Where is David now?"

"I don't know. He left, saying he has some arrangements to make."

Yuki's crying becomes more and more hysterical. I feel so helpless. "Calm down, Yuki."

"He tried not to express any anger, but it was obvious he was disappointed, which is understandable. I was so naïve." She sniffs.

"You want me to come back?"

"No . . . I'll come home to Tokyo." Through the phone, I hear a door close. Yuki whispers, "David has returned. I'll call you back."

The phone goes dead. In despair, I rub my forehead with my open palm. If we hadn't stumbled onto Taka and David, we'd have only nice memories of our Kyoto trip. I compose myself, then push the number Taka gave me since I promised to update him on Yuki's situation.

"Hello, may I speak to Taka-san?" I ask. I realize I don't even know his last name.

"Mr. Taniguchi is on another line. Would you like to wait or call back later?" asks a female voice.

"Would you tell Taka-san that Ochiai Naomi called?" I ask, pressing my cell phone tight against my ear.

"May I tell him what this is in regard to?"

"I'm his friend," I say hesitantly.

"I'll let Mr. Taniguchi know you called," she says bluntly.

As I start to say, "Thank you," I hear the phone disconnect.

Feeling perturbed, I wonder, who is this lady? She was so impolite. I wait five or ten minutes for Taka to return my call. Nothing. Thirty-minutes pass. He told me to call, so I called. My face becomes hot. How foolish I am to consider romance! I lie on the sofa and close my eyes to quiet my agitation.

I awaken to the ring of my cell phone.

"Hello," I answer after taking a deep breath.

"It's me," Taka says. "I spoke to David. He's going back to New York tomorrow. Do you have any idea why? Have you talked with Yuki-san?"

"Yes! I did. I called you earlier, but you were on another call," I say a bit accusatorially. "I asked the lady, whoever she was, to have you call me."

"Sorry, she must have forgotten."

Still feeling distraught, I continue. "I wanted to ask if you had a chance to talk to David. When I called Yuki, she was crying."

A few seconds of silence follow, then he asks, "Would you like to get together tonight? I know of a cozy restaurant that is quiet. We can talk undisturbed. Do you like Italian food?"

"I'd like to be available for Yuki if she should call when she gets home."

"If she calls, I'll drive you to her," says Taka.

With a deep sigh, I murmur, "Okay."

"Would you like me to pick you up?"

"I'll meet you at the restaurant." My voice still feels strained.

He gives me directions and we decide to meet in an hour.

Taka must feel bad about the whole situation—both Yuki's accident and David suddenly leaving without an explanation. All the good and bad memories of our trip surface, evoking mixed emotions. Ceaseless thoughts slow me down, but I need to speed up to meet Taka. My stomach churns with anxious anticipation, as I stride to the shower. Just as I apply shampoo to my hair, the phone rings. I turn off the shower, jump out and grab a towel, rush to the living room, and snatch my phone from the coffee table.

"Hello," I answer as water pools on the floor around my feet.

"This is David," he says slowly. "I need Yuki's address."

"David! What happened?" I ask, even though I know I will have a hard time understanding him.

"Please, could you give me Yuki's address?" David asks in a soft voice. "I'm not able to reach her. She's not answering her phone."

I want to know what happened but realize he probably doesn't want to explain such a complex matter to someone who doesn't speak English well.

"Please wait," I say, reaching for my handbag to get my address book.

I enunciate the address carefully. David repeats the address back slowly. Relaying her address is quite a long process, as I need to translate from Japanese Kanji to Roman letters. While I recite the address, my stomach twists. *Why isn't she answering his call?*

"Thank you, Naomi."

"You're welcome."

"Naomi, take care."

"You too, David," I respond in a faint voice.

I sense he wants to talk more, but after a few seconds of silence, he hangs up. Saddened, I return to the shower.

I need to hurry. My desire to impress Taka has diminished as I think of Yuki and David. I only put on lipstick and wear a denim summer dress. Grabbing my keys and handbag, I dash for the restaurant.

*   *   *

We meet at the Italian restaurant Taka suggested, which is in the center of Ginza. As I step inside, a waiter greets me.

"Are you with someone, or by yourself?" asks the waiter.

"I have a friend coming," I say and crane my head to look into the room. "He might already be here."

The waiter tilts his head. "Are you Naomi-san?"

"Yes, I am." I nod, wishing I had dressed up.

"Please follow me. Your friend is waiting."

He escorts me to a table in a cozy nook. Taka slides out from the booth.

"Hi, Naomi-san, please have a seat," says Taka, gently crinkling the corner of his eyes. He then turns to thank the waiter.

I slip into the cushy leather booth and Taka sits back down.

"By the way, just before coming here I received a call from David. He asked me for Yuki's address and said that she was not answering her phone. He didn't seem to want to talk further."

"I feel responsible for this happening," says Taka.

"It's not your fault," I mutter, despite thinking Taka could have interceded and prevented David from staying alone with Yuki at the hospital.

He folds his hands on the table and leans forward. "Frankly, leaving Yuki-san like that was uncomfortable for me, but David insisted, and I believed his concern was genuine."

"I felt the same." I cannot help but express regret in my voice.

"I'm sorry. I shouldn't have let David be alone with Yuki-san." He lowers his eyes for one long moment, then ask softly, "Can you think of any reason that may help me understand David's sudden change of mind? His original plan wasn't to go to New York on Monday."

Now the pressure is on. "Well . . ." I gaze down at the snow-white linen-covered table, thinking it's too personal to talk about Yuki's unborn baby. "I—" I start to say something, but thankfully the waiter approaches and hands us a wine list and menu.

Taka flips through the wine list and asks, "Would you like wine?"

I glance down and rub the side of my neck.

"How about a Merlot from Kobe? It has a nice bouquet. You'll like it." He turns to the waiter and orders. "What's today's special?"

"Seafood pasta with shrimp, scallops, and mussels." He stoops lightly over the table with his index finger politely pointing at the menu.

"Naomi-san, how does that sound to you?"

I nod *yes*. I am not in the mood to think about food.

The waiter takes our order and disappears.

Taka's face tightens. "What were you going to say before the waiter came?" His eyes plead with mine and I feel compelled to tell the truth.

"She lost her baby in the accident."

"So, she was pregnant?" asks Taka in a hushed tone. "I'm sorry to hear that." He leans back against the booth and breathes deeply as if lost in thought.

The waiter appears and presents the wine label. Taka gives a nod of approval. The cork is pulled, and the waiter pours a small amount in a glass. Swirling the glass, Taka sniffs, takes a sip, and gives a nod. The waiter carefully pours the wine into our glasses, then withdraws with a light bow.

"So, she has a boyfriend?"

"I don't know that you'd call this a relationship."

"What do you mean? Not really a relationship?"

"I don't feel comfortable talking about Yuki's personal matters. But I can say the guy is a jerk and Yuki wanted to end the exploitation. In fact, she said she tried many times."

"Who's the man?" He stares into my eyes.

I sigh and ponder for a while. Reluctantly, I begin. "Please don't tell Yuki I've told you these things."

"I won't," says Taka, shaking his head slowly. "I just want to help her."

"Umm," I groan, looking aside for a while, then finally I turn back to him. "He's our section chief."

"Really?" Taka sets his wine glass on the table and twists the stem of the glass with thumb and forefinger.

Silently I wait for a response.

Taka takes a sip of wine. "Well, tomorrow I'm taking David to the airport. I'll talk to him about the predicament she is in. Don't worry I'll tell David not to let Yuki know about what I heard from you."

Silence ensues. For a while, neither of us can find a subject to talk about. I surreptitiously glance across the table and notice how his white shirt against his suntanned skin radiates a young, fresh manliness. *How old is he?* He has the fingers of a pianist, long and slender. He realizes I am watching him. I lower my eyes.

The waiter returns, breaking our silence. He places the seafood pasta in front of us and pauses with a tall, slim pepper mill in hand. We have him pepper our food and he leaves.

"Naomi-san, you look cute without makeup."

"Thank you," I say shyly. His stare becomes unbearable. I sputter a haphazard question to fill the gap. "How many employees work in your office?"

"Five people, including myself—three tour guides, a bookkeeper, and a receptionist who makes travel arrangements," says Taka, rolling a fork full of pasta in his spoon.

"Is that the receptionist who answered my call?"

When he finishes chewing his bite of food, he answers. "Yes. I'm sorry she didn't relay your message. She gets busy sometimes."

Thinking he is defending the receptionist, I look down and say nothing. Taka drops the subject. For a few minutes, our conversation stalls, but the silence doesn't really bother me. Candlelight casts flickering shadows across Taka's face.

"Do you like swimming?" asks Taka, grinning, perhaps

attempting to change the mood.

"I enjoy swimming, as long as I can keep my face out of the water."

What a captivating smile he has. Not wanting to appear rude by staring, I avert my gaze to my hand and notice the time on my watch.

"It's almost ten. I need to go, or I'll miss the last train," I say in a rush.

"I agree. It's getting late," says Taka, placing his napkin on the table. "I'll drive you home."

Before meeting with Taka, I was upset over Yuki's issues, but Taka's sympathy and understanding of Yuki's situation eases my mind. He is a genuinely nice guy, and treats me like a lady. Above all, I like how he gazes softly at me.

Leaving the restaurant and walking to his car, I am even more aware of Taka's physical presence. He opens the door, and I slide into his Audi. A faint scent of leather tickles my nostrils. He sits down behind the wheel and turns on the ignition. The blue illumination from the dashboard creates an intimate mood.

City lights reflect on the windshield as we zip down the street between the tall buildings.

"How do you spend your weekends?" asks Taka.

"I recently moved out of my parents' house, which is part of a temple complex. My dad is a Buddhist monk."

He turns to me with a surprised look.

I smile at his reaction. "An ascetic lifestyle is like cooking without spices: no fun. Every weekend in the early morning I had to wipe the temple floor, then meditate. Now that I live alone, I don't need to follow any strict house rules. No dictated waking times. No Zen meditation. No sweeping the garden. I have the liberty to do whatever I want, whenever I want. I can indulge in reading books and can go out with Yuki and my other friends without having to be home at a certain time." My heart sinks when I say Yuki's name.

Taka must sense my feelings. He asks jauntily, "What kinds of novels?"

"Currently I'm reading Haruki Murakami's books, but I also love French literature."

"I wish I had more time to read," says Taka.

His dimples are visible in the faint light. As I am about to speak, Taka asks directions and we focus on the roads. In a few minutes, we reach my apartment.

As he puts the car into park, he turns to me.

"Thank you very much . . . and good night," I say, looking into his warm eyes.

Slowly, his hand envelopes mine and his face becomes serious. My heart is fluttering like crazy. Taka cautiously leans across the console and kisses me. I freeze. With soft caresses, he strokes my hair, and my eyes close involuntarily. His warm lips against mine are as tender as a flower bud. I return his kiss. All those years, I dreamed of finding someone special. Could he be the one? The Kyoto trip was fateful. Then in a flash Yuki's face pops to mind. I open my eyes.

He releases his lips from mine and gives me a quizzical look..

"Are you all right?"

"Yes. I'm just . . . worrying about Yuki."

"I understand. I'll call you tomorrow after I talk to David," says Taka, then nods to himself.

My heart is still beating fast.

He intertwines his fingers with mine and lightly squeezes them, saying, "It's been good to see you. Good night and sweet dreams."

"You, too. Thank you, good night," I murmur and reluctantly slip out of the car.

As I close the apartment door, I hear him drive away. His

tender kiss lingers.

* * *

I awake from a horrible dream of a man breaking into my room. He's dressed in black, wearing a mask, and brandishing a shiny kitchen knife. In the dream, there was no way out. The black shadowy figure reached for me and grabbed my hand so tightly it almost broke my wrist. I wake up, screaming from a dream that's so realistic and vivid that I shudder at the mere thought of it.

Shaking it off, I remember I had promised to call Mr. Ishida. My *omiai* partner is waiting to introduce me to his parents. Perhaps he will call me today as I had told him I would be gone a-four-day trip this weekend. I am going to tell my parents Mr. Ishida is not the right person for me. But first things first. I need to text Yuki to ask how she is doing.

Around noon, my phone rings. Mr. Ishida's monotonous voice fills my ear. "Are you back from the trip?"

"Yes." I use a calm neutral tone.

"How was your trip?"

"Good."

"I'm glad. By the way, my parents can't wait to meet you. Can you come with me to visit them next Saturday?"

I say nothing.

"Why you are quiet?" he asks, his voice sounding strained.

Mr. Ishida is ignoring my desire to move slowly. Whenever things do not proceed as he wishes, it shows in the tone of his voice or facial expression. Blood rushes to my head. *I'm fed up with this. Sunday I'll go to my parents and tell them how I feel about Mr. Ishida.*

"Sorry. Next weekend I'm not available," I blurt.

"Are you upset?" asks Mr. Ishida, raising his voice an octave.

"No," I lie.

"Let me know when you are available to meet my parents. All right?"

"Yes." *If only his father wasn't a supporter of my dad's temple, I wouldn't hesitate to be blunt with him.*

"Talk to you soon."

"Goodbye." I put down the phone with a heavy hand.

*   *   *

Hoping Yuki will come to work today, I get off the elevator on the twenty-fifth floor and hurry to my office. It is almost nine o'clock. She should be here, but she's nowhere in the office. As I run to the bathroom to call Yuki, I hear someone call my name. I turn back and see Mr. Yamada, approaching.

"Do you know why Yuki-san is not here yet?" asks Mr. Yamada with a thin smile.

"I'm sorry. I don't."

"Didn't you two go on a Kyoto trip together?" probes Mr. Yamada.

I wonder how he knows about our trip. Yuki must have told him. Avoiding eye contact, I answer, "We did, but I don't know why she isn't here."

He remains still, so I turn to him with a blank stare.

"Oh, okay, she'll be here soon," Mr. Yamada says, then scuttles toward the men's room.

I see him taking his cell phone from his pocket. Assuming he is calling Yuki, I decide to call her later and return to my desk.

Lunch time comes. On the way up to the company restaurant, my cell vibrates in my pocket. It's Yuki.

"Hello. Are you at lunch?"

"Yes."

"Sorry for not responding to your text yesterday. I slept all day after I received David's call. David was a little different, calmer and kinder. Please say thank you to Taka-san. It was kind of him to have talked to David. I don't know about our future, but it looks like we'll be writing to each other."

"It'll be a good way to get to know each other."

"Yes, thank you, Naomi. I'll see you in two days. I'm not ready for work yet."

"Rest well and don't worry about work. Glad you sound better today. Take care." I hang up and ponder her words, "A little different, calmer and kinder." What did Taka say to David?

chapter six
OKINAWA

Taka phones my office. Without revealing what he talked with David about, he hastily asks if I had a chance to talk to Yuki. I tell him I did, and that Yuki sounded better. He releases a big sigh followed by, "Good." Then he pauses as if lost for words. His voice becomes apologetic. "I'm leaving for Okinawa for a two-week business trip." He goes on to tell me a group of people from England hired him as a guide and interpreter for some sort of marine project. My expectation of spending the weekend with him is shattered. But when he shares that his receptionist will be accompanying him, a pang of jealousy strikes. Because of the kiss in the car, I already feel possessive. I straighten my back and from the corner of my eye catch Mr. Yamada approaching my desk. I quickly end the call.

"You didn't need to hang up your call," says Mr. Yamada, then he looks at me with a simpering smile. "Were you talking to Yuki-san?"

I shake my head. "No," I say.

"Yuki-san called the office and left a message. She'll be taking tomorrow off too, but she didn't give a reason."

"Well . . . she might have some urgent business," I say, thinking what a selfish, manipulative man he is.

"I wonder if she may be sick," Mr. Yamada says, peering into my eyes.

I look down, pretending to know nothing, while thinking, "Yuki is not taking Mr. Yamada's call. Good for her." I want them to break up. I can't help but feel a little angry with my friend for not being strong enough to resist Mr. Yamada, but I have seen first-hand how miserable she's been about her bad choices. I also don't live in her shoes, so I try not to judge. Mr. Yamada probably has no idea she was pregnant. Mr. Yamada disgusts me. Mrs. Yamada is busy caring for their three kids at home: a five-year-old boy and two-year-old twin girls. Poor Mrs. Yamada. At least Yuki is breaking up with Mr. Yamada. I decide to visit Yuki after work.

*　*　*

Yuki's apartment is in Yotsuya. Upon entering her building, I see a familiar figure standing in the lobby. *Oh no!* Mr. Yamada steps into the elevator, and I immediately pull out my cell phone. *I need to call Yuki to let her know he's on the way.* The phone rings three times.

"Hello, Yuki. I just entered your building and saw Mr. Yamada heading up to your apartment," I say hastily.

"Thanks." She hangs up.

I race to the elevator. At the seventh floor, I cautiously peek down the hallway. He's there. *Good. Yuki is not answering the door.* Mr. Yamada starts pacing in the hallway. He pulls his cell phone from his briefcase but drops it. Irritated, he snatches the phone from the floor, punches the keys, puts the phone to his ear, and waits. After a brief conversation, the door opens, and he walks in. *No!*

Why is Yuki letting him in?

More than fifteen minutes pass and my frustration rises to such an unbearable level, I decide to go to Yuki's room. As I approach her door, it swings open, and I quickly step into a corner as Mr. Yamada walks out.

He hunches over as he shuffles to the elevator. I have never seen him in such a miserable-looking state. At thirty-nine-years-old, Mr. Yamada, is not a bad-looking man: medium height and weight, athletic, and he's also smart and successful in the banking business. He'll probably be transferred to a foreign branch one day, as he speaks English quite well. I used to respect him, but after Yuki confessed about their affair, my image of him changed. I don't know how Yuki got involved in a relationship with him. While thinking this, the elevator doors open, and Mr. Yamada disappears inside. I ring Yuki's doorbell.

After a few minutes, she opens the door. I see her eyes are bloodshot.

"What happened?" I demand.

"I told him about the baby," says Yuki, her nails digging into her palms. "I also told him I don't want to see him privately anymore."

"Did he agree?"

Nodding, she says, "He was shocked. He said he wants to talk about the matter when I'm calmer."

I gently wrap my arm around her shoulder to steer her to the dining table.

With my arm still on her shoulder, I try to mollify her. "I'm glad you're ending the relationship with him. I understand it's not easy to break up, especially when you're with someone who is so influential, but I support you, no matter what." Mr. Yamada might shun me because of my association with Yuki. He might even harass me. But Yuki is my best friend and I will stand by her.

Yuki smiles.

"You'd better eat something," I say. "How about going out to dinner? My treat."

She shakes her head. "I'm not hungry at all. Maybe just something to drink."

I hurry down to the supermarket on the first floor and buy two packs of sushi, two bottles of cold green tea, and a bottle of energy drink.

When I return, Yuki is sitting motionless, slumped forward, and staring at the dining table. I place the sushi and tea in front of her. She seems to have lost any willingness to talk or eat.

"Eat something, please," I insist.

"I will," says Yuki feebly.

"I feel so sorry, but you know the baby would have had a questionable life if it had survived. Besides, you don't love Mr. Yamada."

"Actually, I liked him before we became physically involved. He taught me a lot about the business and I even thought he might promote me." Yuki's eyes fill with tears. "I never intended to have a sexual relationship, especially knowing he has a wife and children."

"Then why did you sleep with him?" I ask softly, trying not to sound accusatory.

"You know I play golf. About six months ago, Mr. Yamada started inviting me to golf with the company team," Yuki says, then shakes her head sullenly. "I should have never accepted his invitation."

Yuki's crying turns into sobs. Her shoulders shake. I walk around the table to comfort her.

"I'm sorry," I say, rubbing her back.

"It's my fault. My ambition brought my downfall. I should have known better," Yuki says between sobs. "I was afraid to say 'no' to him."

"Yes, you made a mistake, but Mr. Yamada shouldn't step over the line to victimize you by threating your career," I say in a rage. "Sorry. I didn't come here to upset you."

"I was weak, timid, and stupid." She pulls a tissue from the box on the table, blows her nose, then draws a deep sobbing breath. "Thanks for your concern."

Even with effort, my smile weakens as I observe her misery. "It's late. I should go home. You took tomorrow off, too, right? Are you going to stay at home?" I ask, standing up from the dining room chair.

"I'm going to Enoshima. The ocean sounds good to me now."

"Yeah, I can understand that," I say and shuffle toward the door. "Are you going to be okay?" Her face is puffy from crying.

She nods.

Holding the doorknob, I say, "All right then, enjoy the trip to the beach tomorrow."

"I will. Thank you for checking on me. Good night," says Yuki. Her meek and pitiful appearance does not suit her and makes me feel more concerned.

"I'm glad I came over. Please try to eat something. Good night." I step out from her apartment.

*　*　*

Entering the office, I feel tense about facing Mr. Yamada, but I don't see him anywhere. Soon our manager, Mr. Suzuki, informs us Mr. Yamada will be out today, and our manager will be signing our papers. Angst hits me. Mr. Yamada may be trying to contact Yuki. Right away, I call her.

"Hi, Yuki. Mr. Yamada isn't at work today."

"Thank you. I'm heading to the beach. I won't answer his call, so don't worry," Yuki says in a calm, clear voice.

"Okay. Have a good trip. See you tomorrow," I say, hoping the trip will recharge her.

Upon finishing the call, my computer boots up. I check Yuki's work queue since I will be covering for her. *My word . . . double the usual amount of work and everything needs to be done today.* I sit up straight and determine to finish all of them, I start to process, thinking to skip lunch.

My cell phone buzzes. I open it and see a message from Taka. I read, "Have a wonderful weekend. See you when I'm back." I quickly text him back. "Have a safe trip! I look forward to seeing you again." When I return to the computer screen, I push the "submit" button to transfer funds to an overseas bank and immediately realize I didn't include the amount to be sent. Not only do I feel embarrassed having to point out this mistake to our manager, but this will also significantly slow down my daily tasks. Feeling depressed, I approach Mr. Suzuki and stand in front of his desk with stooped shoulders.

"What's up?" asks Mr. Suzuki, peering up over his reading glasses.

"I'm sorry. I sent a money transfer without entering the amount," I say, and bow deeply.

"Glad you reported without delay. So many numbers and codes, it is inevitable that mistakes will be made, but it's critical to fix it quickly," says Mr. Suzuki, then gives me a tiny smile.

Normally, Mr. Suzuki comes across as stern, impatient, intimidating. To my surprise, this time he is reasonable and even approachable. *What a fair person,* I think. I return to my desk and anchor myself to finish up the work for the day.

* * *

In the middle of mincing onions for a meatloaf dinner, my phone chime echoes through the room. I wipe my hands with a kitchen towel and place the phone to my ear.

"Hello," I answer.

"Good evening, Naomi-san," says Taka in a soothing voice. "I'm on the hotel patio, watching the moon over the ocean. Quite mesmerizing—boats and palm trees with their moon shadows paint a picturesque scene."

"Wow, um, lovely . . ." I nod though he can't see me. "What time is it there?"

"Eleven p.m. I'm unwinding after a long day."

"How did the marine project go?"

"Great. Working with scientists is quite absorbing. We chartered a motor yacht for two weeks so they could study how ocean acidification is affecting marine organisms. I had a chance to dive with them," says Taka. His soft melodic voice tickles my ear.

My voice mimics his. "What did you see?"

"Spiky coral reefs, odd-shaped fish, and green turtles . . . some sea creatures are so luminous they look artificial," says Taka, as if I can see the same picture.

"Really!" I say, imagining a tropical fish aquarium.

"Misa-san swam with a giant turtle."

"Who's Misa-san?"

"Our receptionist."

"That receptionist I talked to?" My voice loses vigor.

"Yes. She dives and speaks fluent English."

All of sudden my heart deflates. "Nice." I try to hide my jealousy.

"I'd like to take you diving sometime," he says. "Oh, by the way, David sent me an email, telling me Yuki-san and he are communicating. How's Yuki-san?" says Taka.

He jumps from taking me diving to David and Yuki's relationship so fast I miss the opportunity to say, "I want to go." I sigh feebly, and answer. "She's fine. Yuki finally told Mr. Yamada she doesn't want to meet him outside of work anymore."

"Glad to hear that. I really hope David and Yuki-san can mend their relationship," says Taka.

David is Taka's good client and Yuki is my best friend. It would be idyllic if we were all mutual friends. While thinking this, I hear a door shut on the other end of the line, then a lady's voice echoes. It must be Misa.

There is a long, strained pause. He usually waits for me to disconnect first.

chapter seven

AUNTIE

IT'S TEN O'CLOCK, SATURDAY MORNING. Tomorrow I meet with my parents to cancel my *omiai*. Maybe I should get some advice from my auntie before meeting with my parents. She is my mom's younger sister, but unlike Mom, she is more liberal and has always been a loyal confidant. I bounce out of my apartment.

As I arrive at her flower shop, she is choosing the most perfect white lilies and lavender-blue hydrangea flowers and placing them in a deep tin container which is already packed full with summer flowers. She is about to leave her shop to deliver the flowers to the Hotel Uehara for their lobby exhibition and asks me to come with her. We take a taxi to Akasaka.

At the hotel, my auntie opens her traditional Japanese wrapping cloth and removes her flower-arranging tools. After spreading the flowers on the table, she cuts the ends of the stems, one by one, before precisely sticking them into the *kenzan*—a cluster of sharp, heavy brass spikes protruding from the bottom of the vase. Watching her, I think someday I want to learn flower arranging. This ancient art has many rules governing the practice; each arrangement is created with particular attention to color combinations, natural shapes, graceful lines, and theme. It thrills me to observe her final creation. Once the pastel-colored flowers are transferred into the large white vase with two red carp swimming across the face, the arrangement stands tall and elegant. Auntie seems happy with her work. After cleaning up the table, she asks me to join her for tea in the lounge. I grin and nod *yes*.

We sit by the window in the commodious lounge. A view of a waterfall and pond melt away my troubles despite the background noise of guests and visitors. After ordering our tea and cake, our talk rambles.

I am about to broach my *omiai* problems with my auntie when she says, "Naomi-chan, why don't you move in with me? I'm not like your parents; you'd be free to do as you wish."

"Auntie . . . you know . . . I already have my own apartment."

"Well, you can save your rent."

I gently let her know I am not interested. The subject goes no further. I wonder if my aunt is lonely.

Her husband is a good provider, but they don't have much in common. They have no children and only one dog which is overweight, obnoxious, and at times, vicious. This white and black cocker spaniel, Momo, is overfed and treated like a baby to the irritation of Auntie's husband. Except for Momo's head, the dog brings to mind a miniature hippopotamus—the result of eating human food and getting no exercise. He knocks me over when he jumps on me. If the dog were better behaved, I wouldn't mind moving in with her as she has a beautiful five-bedroom house. Besides, I love my auntie as a dear friend.

Suddenly, our discussion is interrupted by a loud crash.

Turning to the sound, I see a waitress picking up broken glasses and plates. At that moment, I spot Mr. Yamada and Yuki sitting at a nearby table.

"What are you looking at?" asks my aunt as my gaze lingers.

"My co-workers are sitting near the table the waitress is cleaning up."

"Are you going to say hi?"

"No! I don't want to disturb them," I say. I'm annoyed Yuki is still seeing Mr. Yamada.

"Naomi-chan, are you all right?"

"I'm fine, I just remembered I have an engagement this afternoon."

"Okay," she says, finishing her tea. "Thank you for coming to see me today."

"It was fun watching you arrange flowers."

Auntie's eyes light up. "Come see me again. I'll teach you a lot about flower arranging."

"I will sometime. Well then, I'll see you soon." I decide to leave without getting her advice about my current situation.

At Akasaka station before hopping the train to Shinjuku, I text Yuki to call me back. Her call reaches me while I'm strolling the Shinjuku underground shopping center.

"Hello, what's up? I got your text message," says Yuki.

"I saw you with Mr. Yamada at the Hotel Uehara."

"Eh! You were there," says Yuki. "Well, Mr. Yamada was still bothering me, so I threatened to reveal our affair to his wife if he continues to contact me outside of work."

"Way to go! I admire your courage," I say, the upset feeling I had when I saw them quickly disappearing.

"I don't care if I get fired." Her voice is thick with emotion.

"Good. That's the right attitude."

She chuckles. "Mr. Yamada seems to be scared to death. By the way, I told him not to harass you."

"Thanks." *Mr. Yamada's hold on her is beginning to dissipate.*

"So, where are you now?"

"I'm back home in Shinjuku."

"I want to see you. Where should we meet?"

"How about the west side of Shinjuku Station?"

"I'll be there in thirty minutes. Bye."

* * *

She appears at the station with a glow in her eyes. She must be feeling relieved after her talk with Mr. Yamada. Their six-month relationship is over, and Yuki looks better than she has in a long time. Her heart isn't into shopping, but with each new store she seems happier.

In a shoe shop, Yuki picks up a pair of salmon-colored sandals with double ankle straps. She looks at them for a while before trying them on. The shoes are chic and stylish, and her pretty figure in the mirror projects the girl I used to know. I love seeing her cheery face.

Though I wish I could wear fancy shoes like hers, with the ugly scars on my right foot, I shun them. When I was two, I knocked over a kettle of boiling water that sat on the stove. It isn't as obvious now, because the scars have stretched and faded some, but I'm still self-conscious about wearing open-toe shoes. Instead, I choose a pair of navy-blue pumps with a white rim and a tiny white ribbon clasped by an orange anchor-shaped decoration on the front. I can imagine how well my white dress with its fitted top and flared bottom featuring dark blue and orange floral prints will go with these new shoes. The mere thought of wearing this outfit for my upcoming dinner with Taka makes me grin.

After shopping, we rest at a coffee shop. It has been a long time since we have been able to just sit and talk with each other without distraction. Since our trip to Kyoto, Yuki's and my personal lives have shifted in a new direction. Actually, mine is still in transition until I end my *omiai*, but Yuki's, after the tragedy, seems to be on the right track. Mr. Yamada is on the way out of her life. Although I feel sorry about Yuki's baby, I believe it was better the way things ended. After all, who wants to have a baby from an affair with a married man? Nonetheless, it must be an abysmal experience to lose a child.

I tell her a story about my mom. "When I was little, my mom would take me with her to the *Jizo*-Temple which had many small stone Buddha statues called 'Jizo-san', each in the shape of a child wearing a red baby bib. Each time, she would select one of the statues, clean it with a brush, then place either a toy or piece of candy in front of it. My child mind always puzzled over why she made these ritual visits to the *Jizo* Temple. My mom never explained these visits to me, but at the age of fifteen I found out the reason one day when my Auntie inadvertently slipped up in a conversation and it came out that my mom had lost her only son after a mere ephemeral week of life. The visits were her grieving the loss of her child.

"How about going to a Jizo Temple? You could make a prayer for the baby. I hear many women who have had a miscarriage, stillbirth, or abortion, go to one of these temples."

Rubbing her neck, she says, "Umm . . ." She hangs her head.

"Yuki . . . remember you didn't abort the baby, it was an accident," I say.

"I considered an abortion," she says, looking more dejected. "Maybe my desire not to have the child induced the accident."

"Yuki—"

Yuki lifts her hand, motioning in the air as if warding off a fly. "I know what you are thinking. I'm a terrible person, aren't I?"

"You are not!"

"It was an awful thought. And I feel sorry for the unborn baby, but—" she catches a breath, "to be honest I'm relieved, in large part because the baby would be stigmatized."

I nod. *It is good for her to forget and move on.* An uncomfortable silence surrounds us.

Changing the subject, I ask, "How's David?"

Curving her lips into a content smile, she opens her email on her phone. "Let me show you a video David sent. We stay in touch, you know, through our network of contacts. Look, he recorded his dog, Sam."

I chuckle at the dog. Jumping up and standing on its hind legs, he shows all his teeth like a human who's smiling. I can't help but laugh at his begging pose. Yuki's small smile blossoms into a full-blown laugh.

As Yuki and I visit, I learn David has never married but had a serious three-year relationship with a girl from Boston. The girlfriend found someone else two years ago. Since then he's been single, living with Sam, his Jack Russell terrier, in the Upper West Side of New York. As a commercial magazine photographer, he travels a lot. His two married sisters are continuously nagging him to get married and settle down.

Gazing at Yuki's bright eyes, I recall the time before her relationship with Mr. Yamada when she was ambitious and wanted to become a manager for one of our company's overseas branches. Back then, I wondered if her dream would be realizable with her degree in business administration and excellent English skills. But Japan is such a patriarchal country. It's common knowledge that a woman's potential is often squandered, and a higher education is no guarantee of job advancement. Female *submission is the expected norm. It is a male-dominated country, after all. Yuki's awareness of her challenges likely contributed to her bad decision about our boss.*

Yuki's eyes are still fixed on her phone screen. She looks

content. The pictures David sent must reassure her of his interest. She seems to be more mellow and relaxed after her break-up with Mr. Yamada and her renewed relationship with David. Yuki told me she explained to David how her ambitions lead her into the affair with Mr. Yamada and how she regretted her stupid actions. David accepted that what she did cannot be undone and, despite what happened, restated her importance to him.

Yuki turns off the video and asks in a cheerful voice, "Have you contacted Taka-san since the trip?"

Coming out of my reverie, I say, "Yes, we met once. We had dinner together."

"What did you two talk about?" asks Yuki.

I decide not to tell her the real reason Taka and I met was to discuss Yuki's and David's issues, so I give her the juicy part of our date.

"When he dropped me off in front of my apartment, he kissed me." I shrug my shoulders.

"Eh, he kissed you!"

"Umm . . . it was just a tiny kiss." I grab my orange juice and sip slowly. The pressure of my lips on the edge of the glass reminds me of the sensation of Taka's soft lips. When I refocus, I see Yuki staring at me.

Leaning forward, Yuki says, "Tell me his story."

"Well," I start, "he has four employees. Two are tour guides like Taka-san, one bookkeeper, and a receptionist who makes travel arrangements. Right now, he's in Okinawa and will be back next Monday."

"From the beginning, I knew Taka-san liked you. He's a careful person, so you might miss the clues, but I noticed," says Yuki.

"You like him?"

"Yes! He's smart but modest. And caring."

Suddenly the thought of Taka together with Misa in Okinawa

haunts me. My face must reflect the annoying thought.

"Why the pensive look?" asks Yuki.

"A small thing is bothering me."

"What's that?"

I feel silly thinking about Misa but, hiding my jealousy, I decide to tell her. "Taka-san took his receptionist, Misa-san, because she speaks English well and can dive."

"So?" asks Yuki with a perplexed look.

"Nothing is wrong with that, right?" After a long silence, I continue. "I have a woman's hunch . . . Misa-san likes Taka-san."

"What makes you say that?"

"When I called Taka-san's office the other day, Misa-san answered. I asked her if I could speak with him. It was a bit awkward, as I didn't know his last name," I say. "But I could almost feel the ice in her voice."

"So how did she respond to you?"

"Well, let me see . . . no sooner did I finish giving my phone number, than she said reluctantly, 'okay', then abruptly hung up. I mean it was really abrupt. I heard a bang."

"Well, nothing wrong with that, you know. Some people are rude by nature," says Yuki.

"But she didn't relay my message to Taka-san. I asked her to tell him I called. She either forgot or intentionally didn't tell him," I say, feeling I am defending myself.

"I see. That might be a problem," says Yuki looking troubled.

Observing her concerned look, I become more worried.

Yuki and I leave the coffee shop and part at the Shinjuku Station around four o'clock. I walk home. Images from our chat flood my mind. What it must be like living in New York. David's cute dog, Sam. Then my mind turns to Misa. From what little I know—she speaks English well and scuba dives—she's an intelligent, outdoorsy type of woman. How old is she? Why was she cold when she spoke to me on the phone? My musing continues even after I arrive home.

* * *

After a long night with little sleep, Sunday morning arrives. My anxiety intensifies. Sitting with coffee in hand, I rack my brain for a way to persuade my father to cancel the *omiai* with Mr. Ishida. *My dad will understand how Mr. Ishida's flaws will cause me grief*, I reason. As I consider Mr. Ishida's foibles, an image of his frosty stare is supplanted by Taka's soft, gentle eyes. No matter what, I must end the relationship with Mr. Ishida.

The day is sizzling hot. Blazing sunlight streams in through the rattan blinds. A cicada perched on a ginkgo tree next to my apartment starts buzzing, intruding into my thoughts. I recall a *haiku* I wrote a long time ago, entitled *Passion of Cicada:*

Knowing transient the life

Like a summer love

Crying so loud with passion

How a futile energy is!

I wonder if Taka and I are like a summer love. I've no idea how long our romance will last. A sigh escapes my mouth. *How can I explain to my dad?* I've never had a boyfriend before, now, all of sudden I have two men in my life.

No good explanation springs up. It is almost eleven. I get ready and hurry to my parents' house. Sunday in the city is crowded with young couples. I wish I were with Taka-san.

Inside the temple compound, I see my dad sweeping the garden.

"Hi! You are home!" His smile is as big as a smiling Buddha.

I deflate, thinking about how I must reject the *omiai*, but try to give him a smile as big as his own.

We walk inside the house and I see the table is decked with all sorts of food.

"Naomi-chan, I made vegetable tempura for you," says my mom. I have never seen my mom so happy. "Good to see you." Her voice is tender and soft as if she's talking to a sparrow. "Have a seat."

I face Dad and Mom and see their overflowing joy for my first visit since leaving their home. *How can I disappoint them?*

My chopsticks lay unused next to my rice bowl. While thinking of the timing to spell out my purpose for this visit, I do my best to continue our conversation with small talk.

"Naomi-chan, are you all right? You aren't eating," says my mom.

"Umm." I lower my head.

"What is it?" asks my dad.

With all my courage, I begin. "I'm sorry, but I want you to cancel my *omiai*. Mr. Ishida is just not the right person for me." I bow deep, till my forehead touches the table.

As I raise my face, my dad and mom both stare at me in astonishment.

"I'm sorry." I bow again.

The silence is unbearable. Finally, my dad nods a few times and says, "Don't worry. It's all right. I wish for you to be happy."

My mom looks at my dad with a sad smile, but since my dad asks no further questions, she changes the subject. "How do you like your apartment?"

"I love it. I cook and bake, which I have never done before," I say, trying to make them realize my independence is a good thing.

"Really? Do you need more pots and pans?" asks my mom.

"Thank you, Mom, but I have enough. By the way, I started doing flower arrangements. Auntie is teaching me."

"How wonderful!" says my dad.

My parents' smiles highlight their warm eyes and I smile back.

"Naomi, don't worry about Mr. Ishida," says my dad.

Too moved to say anything, I simply nod.

"Naomi-chan, have some more food," says my mom in her usual jovial manner.

"Thank you." I nod again, reaching for a slice of succulent tomato with mozzarella cheese.

It is heartwarming to eat with my parents for the first time in a long while. After savoring, all my favorite foods, cooked just for me, I leave with a feeling of peace.

chapter eight

MISA

OUR MONTHLY MEETING STARTS AT ten o'clock. Twenty-four employees in the foreign department, wire-transfer section, are convened in a conference room. The ratio of women to men is seventeen to seven. The room has grown noisy with the chatter of women. Our section chief, Mr. Yamada, is already in the room, finishing his writing on the whiteboard. Once everyone has taken their places around the U-shaped table, Mr. Yamada pulls his telescoping pen from his chest pocket before greeting us. Everyone is silent.

"Thank you for coming. Is everyone here?" He glances around the room. "Looks like all are here. All right then, I would like to begin the meeting."

Mr. Yamada extends the pointer to arm's length, stands at a right angle to the whiteboard, and points out the numbers on this month's profit and loss chart.

He periodically focuses on Yuki, but Yuki's eyes are fixed on the whiteboard. It's comical the way he is presenting the data. His halfhearted attempt is obvious as he often points to the wrong numbers. No one says anything, and he seems to be unaware of what he is doing. I try to hide my laughter. But then Mr. Yamada changes the subject and brings up the mistake I made last week. My face and ears grow hot.

"Ochiai Naomi-san forgot to input the amount when setting up a transfer. She realized her error immediately and informed our manager. The system did catch the mistake this time, but we need to be on guard so careless mistakes will be avoided."

I look down, mortified.

At last it's time to leave the conference room. Yuki walks out with me and whispers, "I'm sorry. I shouldn't have taken the day off. Too many people were taking vacation and my absence burdened you even more."

"It's not your fault. I was careless. Don't worry at all; you weren't feeling well," I say, patting her shoulder while thinking about Mr. Yamada. He's pathetic.

"But I feel bad," says Yuki.

"Please don't. No damage was done," I say, wrinkling my nose as I smile to cheer her up. We reach our office. "Talk to you later."

Waiving her hand, she says, "Okay." She drifts to her desk.

* * *

Yuki and I are in the breakroom, having our afternoon tea when I get a call from Taka. He's at the Narita airport. As I flip my cell-phone shut, Yuki asks me about the call.

Smiling, I say softly, "Taka-san."

"So . . ." Yuki waits.

"He's coming here from the airport to take me out for dinner."

"He isn't going home first?"

"He said he has something to give me."

Yuki raises one eyebrow. "Souvenir?"

I shrug.

Before returning to my desk, I run to the washroom to powder my face, apply lipstick, and re-tie my ponytail. I keep looking up at the Tokyo clock above the wall lined with other countries' time-zone clocks and the hands seem to take forever to move.

Just as the clock hits five, I run down to the locker room and change out of the company uniform into my two-piece pink linen suit. Within ten minutes, I stand in front of our office building. A familiar car approaches and stops at the corner. A beautifully tanned Taka, in a white linen shirt with rolled up sleeves, emerges from the silver car. His trendy sunglasses make him appear a little aloof, but once he removes them, his gentle eyes ease my tension. As I smile at him, I notice a lady sitting in the passenger seat. In a second, the lady's long slender legs slide out from the car and she walks towards me, swaying gracefully in her fashionable high heels. Her flared, black-and-white striped summer dress is cut to display her well-rounded bosom.

"How do you do? My name is Misa," she says, greeting me with a pretty smile. "I didn't want to ask Taka-san for a ride, but something happened to my friend and he couldn't pick me up."

Oh no! She is the lady I saw at Izu Ocean Park. Why is she with Taka-san? Does she remember me? My heart races. *I don't want Taka-san to know I was with Mr. Ishida at Ocean Park.*

"Nice to meet you," I stutter, avoiding eye contact.

"Well . . . where do you guys want to go for dinner?" asks Taka.

Wait—is she coming with us? My mood sinks like a lead weight. Taka opens the rear door for Misa, and I slide into the front passenger seat.

"Let's go to Ginza," Misa suggests. "There are some great restaurants there."

"That sounds good," says Taka. "What do you think, Naomi-san?"

"Sounds good to me," I say in a faint voice.

Despite feeling awkward with Misa, whose manners seems occasionally condescending, I smile, trying to act as natural as I can. Nonetheless, her beauty, confidence, and assertiveness are too charming to ignore. My shyness only increases.

"I know of a place in Ginza, a French restaurant that serves nice wine and has wonderful ambiance," Misa suggests.

Looking into my eyes, Taka asks, "Does that sounds good to you, Naomi-san?"

"Yes, that's fine," I respond.

I feel pitiful about not even being able to express any preference when asked. I would have chosen an inexpensive restaurant. But right now, more than anything else, I want to know if Misa remembers me. Meek as a lamb, I follow their lead.

As we drive to the restaurant Misa asks, "How did you and Taka-san meet."

Before I respond, Taka chimes in. "I met Naomi-san at a hotel dining room in Kyoto. It was a nice place with a *Maiko* entertainer." He continues to talk about the *Maiko's* elegant dance in great detail until we pull up to the restaurant.

As I enter the French restaurant, I cannot keep from uttering, "Wow."

I regret it the moment I speak, and bite my tongue.

Misa immediately looks at me, and asks, "Naomi-san, do you like this restaurant?" She stares at me in a peculiar way.

My reaction clearly shows I have never been to such an expensive restaurant and her stare troubles me. My face heats up.

"Your face looks familiar. Have we met before? Umm . . . maybe I'm confusing you with someone else." She tilts her head. "So, do you like this restaurant?"

"Yes," I force a smile, feeling like a cornered mouse.

I can neither enjoy the upscale cuisine, nor focus on the

conversation. Taka seems to realize how uncomfortable I am and takes the lead to order dinner for me.

Luckily, the topic of our conversation remains on their Hawaii trip. I periodically nod, trying to show some engagement, despite feeling pitiful and badly wanting to go home.

When the bill comes, Taka inserts his credit card in the bill-holder. Before figuring out how much I owe, Misa places her credit card on his. With no credit card in my wallet, I pull out some cash.

Taka's hand reaches mine and he stops me. "I invited you to dinner."

"Yes, don't worry about me, Naomi-san. I'm intruding on your date," says Misa, watching Taka's face instead of mine as she speaks.

"You're certainly not intruding. It was fun listening to you speak of your experiences interpreting between the researchers and the locals," I say with utmost courtesy, despite the fact my stomach is churning.

After dinner, outside in front of the restaurant, we decide who will go home first.

"I'll take Misa-san home first," Taka offers.

"Well, Taka-san and I live in the same direction, so it makes sense to take Naomi-san home first, I think," Misa suggests, turning her head towards me and giving me an exaggerated smile.

"I'll take the subway. The station is close. That way we can all get home early," I insist. A moment later, it dawns on me that Misa used his first name. She used his surname when I called his office.

Taka scratches his head, saying, "In that case, I'll walk with Naomi-san to the station. Misa-san, wait here."

Descending the subway stairs, Taka apologizes to me for Misa's intrusion. Upon reaching the bottom of the stairs, he pulls a small box from his trouser pocket. It's a gift from Okinawa. When he hands it to me, his face breaks into a smile. As I smile back, he lightly pulls me toward him and gives me a kiss.

With his hands still on my arms, he says in a soft, suddenly shy voice, "I missed you."

Keeping my eyes on him, I whisper, "I missed you, too."

He nods and kisses my forehead. "Good night. Sweet dreams. I'll call you soon."

As I am about to speak, he turns and runs up the stairs to Misa. I mouth, "thank you for the gift and good night," at his back.

On the platform I see a tiny yellow light growing larger in the tunnel and soon hear the wind rush by as the train comes in. I step in and find a seat. Leaning against the seat, I softly repeat Taka's words: "I missed you." For a while, my mind is occupied. I keep glancing at his gift and am touched by his show of affection, but after passing a few stations, Misa's face starts haunting me. No way could she remember me. The time was too brief. She might remember Mr. Ishida though, as he was constantly staring at her.

I return home, but the disquieting thought lingers. Before washing up for bed, I open Taka's gift. A beautiful pair of oval earrings, pink coral on yellow gold mountings, lie in a velvet box. I gaze at them for a long time. When I finally glance at the clock, it's already past midnight, but my mind is too excited to shut down. Taka is such a special person. He treats me so well, making me feel I'm important to him.

I finally go to bed, but my train of thoughts won't die—they only escalate. Misa's face and Taka's run through my head like mirages.

The alarm clock rings. After too few hours of sleep, I leave for work.

chapter nine

YOSHIYUKI

MY AUNT CALLS THE OFFICE to ask me to drop by her house after work. She wants me to meet my cousin, Yoshiyuki, her husband's nephew.

I leave work for my auntie's house in Aoyama and, as usual, buy her favorite fruit cake on the way. At the gate of her house, I push the intercom button and hear Momo bark.

My auntie unlocks the wooden gate. "Come in, come in . . . Yoshiyuki is waiting for you."

I follow my aunt into the dining room. A tall young man greets me. "Naomi-san, how do you do? I'm Yoshiyuki. Pleased to meet you, I just arrived from Niigata prefecture this afternoon."

"Niigata! Near the Sea of Japan? Please forgive me, I know little about Niigata, other than I hear Niigata produces the finest rice wine in the world."

"My dad was a farmer. He grew special rice for producing *sake*, but recently he passed away. I'm too young to take his business myself," says Yoshiyuki with an amiable smile. "I was overjoyed when my aunt asked me to come to Tokyo to live with them."

"Yoshiyuki and Naomi-chan, have a seat. Dinner is ready," says my aunt, wiping her hands on her apron.

My uncle is already at his chair. Yoshiyuki and I sit, facing each other. Momo lies on his forearms next to my aunt's chair, watching Auntie's every movement. Auntie places an iron pot for *sukiyaki* on a portable gas stove set at the center of the dining table. In the pot, thinly sliced beef, tofu, and vegetables are soaked in a mixture of soy sauce, sugar, and *mirin*. She turns on the stove and takes her seat. In unison everyone says, "Itadakimasu," thanks for the food.

Yoshiyuki straightens his back. "Naomi-san, I cannot believe I'll be living in Tokyo."

I rest my chopsticks on the holder and sit back.

"All my friends moved to Tokyo to look for jobs after finishing high school, but I jumped into my dad's farming business. Growing *sake* rice is quite a bit different than growing the kind of rice we are accustomed to eating and requires a masterly technique. Without my dad's guidance, I won't be able to take over his business. My mom died long ago, and I have no siblings."

"Hmm . . ." I nod sympathetically.

"I had no one close in my home town and I was uncertain about my future. So, I called our uncle and he suggested I move here to help with their floral business. My uncle is helping me out with my dad's debts." He glances at my uncle who is busy eating.

"Good." I offer Yoshiyuki a reassuring smile. I look at our auntie. She looks so content. She must be happy having him here and won't need to ask me to move in with her any longer.

His sweet, innocent look, together with his melodic Niigata dialect, is appealing. Yoshiyuki is two heads taller than I am, of medium weight, and he has the face of a jolly-farmer—fresh and vibrant. His shirt clings to his muscular arms and chest. His skin is brown from working outside all day and his cheeks are red from the cold, biting winter wind blowing in from the Sea of Japan.

I've never seen my auntie react quite like this—I can feel it in my heart. She even forgets her precious dog, Momo. Sitting under the table next to my auntie's foot, Momo whimpers, nudging her leg with his nose, trying to get her attention.

My uncle, the one who took the initiative to bring Yoshiyuki into his family, talks little to him.

"Naomi-chan!" My auntie still calls me "chan" in an endearing way.

"Uh-huh?" I freeze. A slice of beef hangs from my chopsticks and drips sauce onto my rice.

Can you take Yoshiyuki to Shinjuku this weekend, or somewhere else young people go for fun?" asks my auntie in an atypically suppliant voice.

Momo tilts his head and perks his ears, perhaps puzzled by the uncharacteristic tone of auntie's voice. He whimpers. "mmmm . . . ummmmh . . . ummmmh . . ."

My auntie glances at me with begging eyes.

"Yes, sure, I will," I say, pondering how this will complicate the weekend I had planned with Taka.

"Thank you, Naomi-san. It's nice of you. I can't wait until the weekend," says Yoshiyuki. His polite grin blossoms into a full-blown smile.

How can I say no to him? Such a simple farm boy and he has no idea of what Tokyo is like. Although twenty-one years old, I feel a need to look after him.

"Yoshiyuki, eat only what you like, and you may leave the rest," says my auntie, dotingly watching every move he makes.

"Everything is delicious, auntie."

Auntie's glum husband is being neglected. Momo whimpers

intermittently and her husband's rice bowel remains empty. While observing them, my cell-phone buzzes in my handbag. I pull it out to see who the caller is. It's Taka. I excuse myself to answer the call and walk away from the dining room.

"Sorry I wasn't able to answer your call this morning. I was with a client all day. I heard your message. I'm glad you liked the earrings," says Taka.

"Yes, they are pretty. I'm wearing them now. Thank you," I say, bowing even though he can't see me.

"You're very welcome," he says, then adds, "What are you doing now?"

"I'm at my auntie's house in Aoyama,"

"Where in Aoyama?"

"Near Gaienmae Station."

"What a coincidence! My home is about fifteen minutes from there. May I see you after your visit?"

"Well, we're in the middle of dinner right now. But I might be able to excuse myself after dinner. May I call you in thirty minutes?" I say, already thinking of ways to politely leave my auntie's house.

Before my auntie serves cake, I make a trip to the bathroom to phone Taka and tell him I'll be at the Gaienmae Station in twenty minutes or so.

Striding back to the dining room, I say, "I'm sorry, but I've got some urgent business and need to leave right away."

"Oh . . . I was hoping to play a game after dinner," says my auntie, visibly disappointed. "How about some cake?"

I grab my handbag. "No thank you. I've got to go. Glad to meet you, Yoshiyuki-san. I'll see you again soon," I say at the dining room threshold and look at my uncle.

"Take care," says my uncle. I nod and dismiss myself.

Approaching the Gaienmae Station, I notice Taka's Audi just as he is about to park. After parking, he steps from his car, walks to the subway entrance, and stands by a streetlight. His yellow polo shirt and suntanned arms are accented by the overhead light. He spots me and hurries in my direction. I rush toward him. We slow to a stop. Meeting him on the road in the late evening with such short notice sends a tingle of anticipation down my spine.

"Thank you for coming. Would you like to go to my house, or maybe a coffee shop?"

I pause indecisively. "Well, how about that place," he says, pointing to a small shop across the street. "You'll be amazed. I've never been there, but every time I pass I see a slew of pretty hanging flowers and tall planters through the windows."

"Yes, it looks inviting," I say, noticing the cozy orange light emanating from the shop.

As we enter the tea house, sweet, earthy aromas greet us. Flowers are rampant, from the ceiling, on the walls and floors, and even inside the table-top. All the tables are set up as terrariums: through the glass tops, yellow, pink, and orange flowering cactuses, arranged to mimic a desert landscape, can be seen. For a while we study the tea room with its abundant flora that's reminiscent of a British conservatory, taking our time before we glance at the menu of herbal teas. We both order Mango tea.

"So, you were at your auntie's house?" says Taka, stirring a spoonful of honey into his tea.

"She wanted to introduce me to a cousin I had never met. His name is Yoshiyuki-san, and he's just arrived from Niigata prefecture today."

He nods without blinking and has a serious expression like that of a person about to make a big wager on the roulette wheel.

"Are you all right?" I ask.

He continues to stare at me in silence. Under his silent gaze, self-consciousness overwhelms me. I try to break the awkward moment. "This place is such a . . ."

"I've been thinking about you a lot." Taka interjects.

His intimate stare sets off an adrenaline rush and I blush at his words.

"I'm not committed to anyone . . . are you?"

My parents should have canceled the omiai by now. Mr. Ishida is history . . . don't need to mention him.

I shake my head. "No."

"I love you," Taka's gaze intensifies, "and would like to commit to you."

"Me too," I say softly, worrying about whether my parents have already canceled my *omiai. Sure they did. I know they did. They must have.*

Taka's hand reaches out to interlock with mine. He stares at me as if to confirm our relationship is now official. "So, tell me about your cousin Yoshiyuki-san."

The warm thought "there is a person for me now," fills my heart. Feeling I just imbibed the sweetness of life, I begin to explain about my cousin.

I see a waitress flipping the door sign to Closed.

"It's almost ten. I'd better go home." I say and release my hand from his.

"I'll take you."

"I can catch a train. The station is just there." I point out the station through the window.

"I'd like to take you home," he asserts.

We leave the tea house. Sitting next to my newly committed boyfriend, I experience a new intimacy. He plays a pop music CD, my kind of melody, and I silently hum along.

We reach my house. Taka puts his car in park and then slowly leans toward me. My eyes involuntary close and I feel his soft warm lips on mine. Pulling me close to him, his lips press into mine, his hand cradling the back of my head. I lift my hands out of his and pull them up to entwine my fingers in his soft hair. I melt into the moment, Suddenly, he pulls away from me and stares in the direction of my window. I turn and catch my neighbor, the old gossipy woman, staring at us.

He whispers, "I'll call you tomorrow." He gives me a weak smile. "Thank you for coming to meet me. Sweet dreams." He inhales deeply as if to clear something in his wind pipe, then grips the steering wheel.

"Glad to meet you. Sweet dreams to you, too. Goodnight!" I whisper and turn my head to give a dirty look at the nosy neighbor. She ducks away from the window. Reluctantly I slip from the car.

* * *

Taka and I date more frequently. Being in love is a sweet experience. Little things, like having coffee, are tastier when he is around. But love monopolizes one's heart, as I cannot think of anything but Taka. I feel guilty alienating Yuki, but Yuki, too, is developing her own relationship with David, although at a distance.

In November, a great surprise arrives.

Yuki comes into the office, walking directly to my desk, not even stopping to drop off her large red designer handbag, wearing a smile like a kid about to open a present.

"Good morning, Yuki. There is a look of excitement all over your face."

"Guess what?" she says.

"What . . . don't tease me!" Twirling a pen between my thumb and index finger, I pucker my lips. My stare shifts from Yuki's elated eyes to the whirling pen. "Ah ha! David is coming to Japan, isn't he?"

"Yes! You guessed right," she shouts. "He'll be here around Christmas time. It'll be a half business and half pleasure trip."

Her loud voice reaches the people around us. Soon Mr.

Yamada approaches.

"Who's coming here?" asks Mr. Yamada.

"It's none of your business, Mr. Section Chief," Yuki says tersely to her old suitor, yet intones his title a tad softly.

He stares vacantly at Yuki for a moment, then leaves. His shoulders deflate as he sighs wearily. *He wants to be Yuki's friend since he cannot be her lover, but that's too bad. He can't.* I smile at the thought.

Leaning over Yuki's desk, I ask, "Are you going to tell Taka-san?"

"David already contacted Taka-san to serve as a guide for his photography job."

"I want to see him too," I cry out. Immediately I cover my mouth.

"Shush . . . of course," Yuki whispers.

"All right!"

Yuki returns to her desk and I log in to my computer.

*　*　*

In a month, David will be coming, and Yuki is flooded with euphoria, nonetheless she seems to be nervous about reuniting with him. For the first time I've ever seen, it seems she may be suffering from low self-esteem. Understandably, she was hurt by feeling forsaken by David the last time they were together. I think what she needs is some emotional support.

Over the next weeks I shrink my dating time with Taka and meet with Yuki so I can try to make her feel more confident in her relationship with David. I attempt to convince her that she has all sorts of enchanting elements that are the envy of any woman: she's liberated, gregarious, enigmatic, and sophisticated.

On one occasion at our favorite café, I praise her for being such a big influence on me.

"Yuki, perhaps you have noticed that my fashion is trendier." I shrug. "Also, my shyness and easily embarrassed character are slowly improving."

"Yes, I noticed."

"Well, that's thanks to you. And your most valuable influence has been to make me realize I should live my life the way I want."

"I'm not sure I'm such a positive influence. I've been living a selfish life." Yuki lowers her gaze to her coffee.

"No. You are living your life on your terms. And I like that."

She snorts. "I made a terrible mistake."

I slap the table. "Mr. Yamada is history. You were courageous to fix that issue. I admire you."

"Thanks, Naomi. Kind of you."

"You know, if I hadn't met you, I would still be living with my parents, following their monastic life-style. Now I am out of the nest. My spirit of adventure has been ever present in my life and I don't want to suppress it any longer. Life is fleeting."

"I'm glad to hear that."

I hope my words raise her spirits. I want her reunion with David to be successful.

chapter ten

REUNION

ONE FRIDAY EVENING IN THE middle of December, Taka comes to our office and picks Yuki and me up to meet David at the Narita airport. The roads are crowded because of the fast-approaching holidays.

Taka drops us at the south terminal of the airport before parking his car. The arrival board shows David's flight has already landed. Yuki and I hurry to the customs' gate and Taka joins us shortly thereafter.

Within twenty minutes, David's familiar face appears at the sliding doors of customs. With a substantial camera bag slung over his shoulder and a suitcase in hand, he approaches, crying out, "Hey guys!"

"Hi David!" Yuki shouts back, beaming at him from behind the security barrier.

"Welcome to Japan!" I yell, waiving both hands.

He reaches us. "Good to see you guys. I'm in Japan again!"

David extends his hand to Taka and me, then drops his weighty luggage to the floor to hug Yuki. "I missed you."

"Missed you, too," her voice muffles in his chest.

I smile at Taka and he throws an affectionate arm around my shoulder.

We head to the Royal Hotel where David is going to stay. David selected the hotel because Taka's travel agency is next door. Although David is Taka's friend, he is Taka's client, too, so Taka's behavior is not entirely casual. Guiding David along the Keiyo road, he points out all the landmark buildings to David, whose attention is pretty much on Yuki. I hear rustling of paper and Yuki's surprised voice as she says, "Thank you, David."

In the rearview mirror, I see a big smile on David's face.

We arrive at the hotel. Taka and I settle onto a lobby sofa while David checks in and he and Yuki drop off his luggage in his room.

Pulling a computer from his carrying bag, Taka taps his fingers agilely as he searches for a restaurant.

"What do you want to eat?" Taka asks, looking at the screen. "How about sushi?"

"I like that, but Yuki isn't crazy about sushi because of mercury."

Taka laughs. "All right." He scrolls the cursor. "How about this one?" He points his finger at the screen. "Don't worry, this restaurant has all sorts of Japanese food." After a nod of agreement from me, he makes a reservation.

David appears, refreshed, dressed in a T-shirt and blue jeans and carrying a duty-free bag. My eyes are drawn to a ruby on Yuki's necklace. That's her birthstone.

"Thanks for waiting for us," David says.

"I made a reservation close by. I thought you might be too tired to go far," Taka says, showing Yuki and David the menu and some pictures from the restaurant.

"Looks good," David answers. "What do you think, Yuki?"

"I'm fine with whatever you want, David," she answers, as if she has no opinion of her own.

I've never seen her so acquiescent.

The restaurant is on the first floor, facing a bush garden. A waitress escorts us to the table by the window looking out on Japanese maples and holly bushes. Across the room is a section of the Imperial Palace. It is such a welcoming place. David and Taka order sushi, Yuki and I order tempura. David loosens the string of the duty-free bag and takes out a perfume for me and a whiskey for Taka.

"Thank you, David," says Taka, holding up the box of Jack Daniel's whiskey. "I'll relish this."

"Wow, Dior perfume!" I peel off the cellophane packing from the box. "What a beautiful bottle. I'll try some right after dinner. Thank you."

Dinner is brought to our table. Sushi of red clam, eel, abalone, fatty tuna, salmon roe, and more are neatly aligned on a cedar wood plate. An assortment of tempura—a few fat shrimp, a shiitake, thinly sliced pumpkin and eggplant, and a large green leaf—are in a bamboo basket. The aroma of sweet tempura batter wafts around us. Seeing David again brings memories of our Kyoto trip. What a journey we had.

David says, "Naomi, Taka told me you two are dating."

Cheeks hot, but striving to be gregarious like Yuki, I say, "Yes, we are dating." I give a flirtatious look at Taka for his acknowledgement.

Taka grins.

"Naomi is in a dream state," Yuki says to David.

My forkful of food misses my mouth an inch and my face flushes. Wiping my mouth with a napkin, I say, "Yuki! You're the one to talk. Your mind was preoccupied all day with David. You couldn't even focus on work."

David chuckles, and we all laugh.

Around nine, we finish our dinner and walk to the elevators. Yuki will be staying at David's hotel when he is not traveling for photo shoots.

We wait for the elevator. David puts his arm around Yuki's waist. Their faces are radiant. Perhaps their amorous mood affects us; we too cast each other a warm smile.

Taka says, "David, let's meet at my office on Monday at eight. I'd like you to explore Tokyo with Yuki-san this weekend."

"Thank you, Taka and Naomi. You guys have a nice weekend," says David.

The elevator doors open, and there is Misa, standing alone. She is dressed in a black turtleneck sweater, a plaid black-and-white miniskirt, and a pair of knee-high black boots that hug her shapely legs. Her loosely curled hair flows over her generous breasts.

"Taka-san," Misa says, looking straight into Taka's eyes. Then she shifts her attention to David, "Welcome to Japan."

"Are you still working?" asks Taka without waiting for David to respond to her.

"After you left the office, an urgent email from one of our clients popped up. He wanted to advance his arrival date. It's Christmas time, you know. Canceling is easy, but re-booking isn't," says Misa. "I just had a dinner up at the Chinese restaurant, but I'm on the way back to the office to work on the changes on his itinerary."

"It's already past nine," says Taka in Japanese. Before Misa responds, Taka says, switching to English, "You should go home. I can finish his itinerary."

"Okay. Why don't you come up to the office with me so I can show you what I have done so far?" asks Misa.

Taka looks at me.

"Don't worry about me. I can go home alone," I say.

"I'll take you home if you can wait for me. It won't take much time. Please, wait for me," says Taka in a pleading voice.

"I'll wait with you, Naomi," says Yuki.

"No, no, Yuki," I say, "go with David, please. He's tired. He had a long flight."

"Please, you guys go to your room and rest. It won't take much time to get instructions from Misa-san on what I need to do," Taka asserts.

"Sorry, Taka, that you had to drive to the airport," says David, bowing with hands pressed together, a gesture we Japanese use only with close acquaintances when apologizing or pleading. He must have picked this up from some movie or TV drama. Taka shakes his head, patting David's back.

An elevator picks up David and Yuki. Misa follows Taka and I head to the lobby.

The lobby is alive with the twinkle of Christmas lights and red-velvet ribbons hanging from a majestic fir tree. Colorful glass ornaments reflect a sizable crystal chandelier, making the hotel bright and cheerful, but there is no brightness in my heart. My soul is burning with jealousy. I sit on a sofa, facing the dressed-up fir tree as I sulkily observe the guests, mostly couples—happy ones. Christmas is a week away and it seems to be the peak time for the hotel. Watching people is a diversion for a while, but after an hour passes I feel agitated. Ten more minutes . . . if Taka doesn't return, I will go to his office.

Half-heartedly, I finally leave the hotel lobby for Taka's office. There is no receptionist at this time of night, so I look for the directory on the wall and soon find myself standing in front of his door. I knock lightly a few times. No one answers, so I enter. The spacious room has large windows overlooking the Tokyo Tower and city buildings with millions of lights in blue and red. A stunning view steals my attention for a millisecond, but my anxiety snaps back as the image of Misa's tiny skirt flashes across my mind. *Should I say something?* As much as I want to announce myself, my inner voice tells me to keep walking. I see an open door and hear them talking. I approach with cat-like quiet.

Taka is staring at the computer screen. Misa sits lightly on the desk, leaning toward the computer, her hand close to his hand on the mouse, her right breast almost touching Taka's shoulder. I freeze. *I don't want to stay here.* I slink away.

I return to the hotel and take the elevator to the sixth-floor bar instead of going back to the lobby. I need a drink to soothe my ire.

The bar is crowded with young couples and there is no place to sit except at the counter. Two bartenders are busy making cocktails. I order a gin fizz.

"What kind?" asks the bartender. "Kiwi, peach or melon?"

"I'll have melon."

The bartender gives me a quizzical glance. I must look gloomy. I look out at the night view but the reflections of the people in the large window are making it hard to see outside. I turn to the bar and reach for my cocktail, taking no delight in the little pink umbrella poking over the rim of the glass. But there is a tiny piece of paper attached to the umbrella rod, so I open it and read, "Cheer up!" I smile at the bartender's kind gesture.

I'm about to ask for another drink when my cellphone buzzes in my bag. It's Taka.

"Where are you?" asks Taka, his voice high-pitched.

"I'm in the bar," I say.

"On the sixth floor?"

"Yes."

"I'll be right there." Taka hangs up the phone without waiting for me to respond.

In a few minutes, Taka stands in front of me.

"Are you upset with me?" asks Taka, knitting his eyebrows.

Pursing my lips, I try to say something, but cannot think of any appropriate words. Taka frowns.

Trying not to make things worse, I say, "I'm sorry. You were taking a long time, so I decided to wait here. I didn't call because I didn't want to disturb your work."

He leans close to the bar, trying to sit next to me. The bar lights highlight a red smear on his white collar!

Looking askance at the red spot, I wonder what happened after I left the office. I feel nauseous and I need to excuse myself.

"It's late. I want to go home," I say, my eyes downcast.

"I'll take you home."

"I have a couple of errands to run on the way home," I say as calmly as I can, trying not to show my anger, although my face feels tight.

Thrusting his hand in his back pocket, Taka asks the bartender for my check. With a quick nod to the bartender, I slide off the stool. He returns a cheery wink.

Taka walks with me to the nearest subway. He holds my hand, but my body resists his gesture. I let my hand go limp in his.

"I'll call you tomorrow," says Taka, looking into my eyes.

"Good night," I say. I look past him.

*   *   *

The loud alarm clock wakes me up at eight. I make coffee and check the phone. There is a message from Taka. "Call me. I need to talk to you." I pour coffee in my mug and breathe deeply, trying to figure out how to respond. At that moment, the phone rings, and I answer without thinking.

"I couldn't sleep last night. You were acting so strange. Why? What have I done to you?" he asks as if I am the one to be blamed.

As much as I would like to reveal what I saw last night, I can't admit that I snuck into his office so, keeping my voice subdued, I say, "I saw lipstick on your collar."

"Lipstick?" says Taka as if he has no clue. "Hmm . . . on my collar?"

"Yes, ruby red." I raise my voice. My heart pounds fast. "The same color Misa-san was wearing last night."

After pausing for a second, he says, "Aha . . . now I know!" I hear him laughing. "You don't understand! It was a mere accident. When I stood up from my chair, I hit her chin. We were looking at the same computer screen," says Taka.

It was a reasonable explanation, remembering how I saw them sitting so close to each other. I'm still perturbed, but I don't want to tell him what I saw, so I say, "I'm sorry. I misunderstood."

"It's okay. I'm sorry you had to wait so long," says Taka in his usual soft voice. "I want to spend time with you, but I need to do some work this weekend. I'll call you soon."

"It's okay. Please don't worry," I say with an uneasy feeling.

Our conversation ends with me feeling like a fool. I'm not only upset by the lipstick on his collar, but by Misa's mannerisms—sitting on his desk with her legs crossed in such a suggestive way, with her torso almost touching Taka, makes my blood boil. This is *not* my idea of how people should behave at the office. This tormenting image of Taka and Misa is imprinted in my brain.

chapter eleven

SAPPORO

ON YUKI'S DESK LIE STACKS of papers. Her three fingers peck rapid-fire at the numeric keypad. Focused on her work, she doesn't notice me standing next to her.

"Good morning, Yuki. How was your weekend with David?"

"Good morning, Naomi," she says without looking at me.

"What time did you get into the office?"

"Six."

"Six? Why so early?"

With eyes still on the screen she replies, "I'm going to take two days off."

"When?"

"The twenty-third and twenty-fourth, so I can have four days off. David asked me to spend time in Sapporo. Christmas Day, but falls on Saturday this year, so it'll be a special Christmas vacation for us."

"When did you get approval from the boss? I don't see Mr.

Yamada in the office yet."

Turning her head to give me her full attention, she says, "I sent him a text message yesterday." She covers her mouth and whispers, "He owes me a lot. The least he can do is give me a few days off."

"Yeah, I totally agree with you." The moment I say this, I sense someone approaching."Naomi-san, don't disturb Yuki-san," says Mr. Yamada, as he passes us on the way to his desk.

Surreptitiously rolling my eyes, I say, "Good morning, Mr. Yamada," and return to my desk.

Stowing my shoulder bag in the bottom of my desk drawer, I turn on my computer. As the software apps load onto my computer, my thoughts wander to Yuki and David and their impending visit to Sapporo. I have never been to Sapporo, the capital of Hokkaido. This northern island is sparsely populated except for Sapporo city, a former Olympic site filled with tall buildings, ski areas, and resort facilities. The island gets really cold because the Sea of Japan, Sea of Okhotsk, and the Pacific Ocean bring bitterly cold air, but the snow country gets dressed up with fairy lights and decorations during the Christmas seasons. Envisioning David and Yuki in such a pristine snowy wonderland makes me envious. I think the spirit of Christmas and the beauty of winter adds to the magic and romance of a new relationship.

I turn my attention to the computer. In my queue are ten requests for wire transfers waiting to be processed. Some represent outrageously large funds. Nervousness plagues me every time I wire money overseas. After drawing a long breath, I say, "okay," spurring myself to tackle the tasks ahead of me.

At noon, I ask Yuki to go to lunch.

After letting me wait for ten minutes, she finally stands up, grabbing her lunch box. "I'm leaving Thursday and I'm really pressed for time. I am going to cut my lunch time short for those three days."

We hurry to the breakroom.

Untying the handkerchief around her lunch box, Yuki asks, "Did Taka-san return soon after David and I went to our room last Friday?"

Against the clock, there is not enough time to explain what's on my mind, so I hold my thoughts. "I'll tell you some other time. It's sort of a long story."

Biting into her turkey sandwich, she frowns. "Are you all right?"

"Yes, I'm fine. We can talk after you come back from Sapporo."

"Okay, but don't hesitate to call me anytime you want to talk. All right?" Yuki wrinkles her nose and gives me a cute smile, her trademark look.

I nod, fingering the last salmon rice ball from my lunch box.

We return to work. My message light is blinking. One message is from Taka. He wants me to take Friday off to go to Sapporo with him and spend the weekend with David and Yuki. I glance over at Mr. Yamada. He looks up at me and his eyes narrow. *Fat chance. There is no way he will let me go.* I give up any hope of getting vacation time.

I dash to the bathroom and call Taka. "Hello, Taka-san. Thank you for your invitation, but I won't be able to make it."

"It's all right. Well . . . how about coming after work on Friday? I'll arrange for your ticket.

"Um . . ."

"I want you to come. It's beautiful here. I miss you." His voice is suddenly deeper, making me feel wanted.

I look around the restroom and whisper into the phone. "I miss you, too."

"Please come. I love you."

"I love you, too. Okay, I'll come."

"Great. I'll get your ticket and send you the itinerary with other details. By the way bring warm clothes."

"Okay, I will. thank you. See you soon," I say and hang up the phone. I return to my desk, feeling the heat of anticipation as I think we'll be sleeping in the same room.

*   *   *

As the airplane descends into the heart of Sapporo, I peek through the cabin window and see millions of lights illuminating the snow. The plane lands in the New Chitose Airport at 9:05 p.m. precisely. The instant I step from the door onto the gangway, the bitter cold envelops me. I follow a mob of passengers to the gate, and soon spot Taka with David and Yuki. They are hollering my name. I take big strides. Their cheerful voices warm my heart despite the nip in the air.

After an hour's drive, we enter the city of Sapporo. It's amazing. The whole area is vibrant with Christmas lights on tree branches and buildings with spectacular light displays add to the city's own glitter and sparkle. Taka points to a towering building. "That's our hotel," he says.

The hotel, directly connected to the Sapporo station, is tall. The top disappears into low, misty clouds. Once in the hotel lobby, David and Yuki excuse themselves. It is already late. Taka checks with the front desk clerk and receives a package while I remain in the center of the lobby.

Our room is on the thirty-second floor. When Taka opens the door, my body stiffens. *We'll spend our first night together.*

The room is romantic. I drift around the spacious suite, gazing through the panoramic window at the foggy night outside. There is a knock on the door. I turn my head in that direction and see Taka opening the door to let a room service attendant enter. The man proceeds straight to the small round table by the window and sets the table with two wine glasses and a plate with a shining stainless-steel cover.

He places a single rose in the center of the table with a touch of style and opens the cover, revealing well-browned crab cakes topped with greens.

"Enjoy your meal. Hokkaido is noted for its excellent crab," he says with a bow.

Taka thanks him, and hands him a tip before he leaves the room. Taka opens the package he received at the front desk and pulls out a bottle.

"Wine! How nice," I say.

"Have a seat. Remember this wine?" asks Taka, squashing the box and wrapping into the trash can.

"Should I?" I ask, raising an eyebrow.

"This is the wine we had at the restaurant in Ginza on our first date after coming back from our Kyoto trip." Taka tilts his head and gives a slight shrug of the shoulder. "You liked it. The Kofu wine."

"Ah!" I murmur. Surprised by his sentiment, I don't know how to respond. Frankly, I have no recollection of the wine—I was too focused on Taka on that date. But I act as if I am deeply touched. "You remembered! How nice you are." I'm certainly not a wine connoisseur—any wine will do the trick for me if the ambiance is pleasant.

He opens the wine and pours me a glass.

Raising his glass, he says, "Let's drink to our happiness and a Merry Christmas!"

"*Kanpai*," I say, clinking my glass on his.

Large snowflakes begin to swirl in front of our picture window. I press my fork into a crab cake; a subtle scent of the sea wafts from the morsel. "Yum," I say savoring the aroma before dipping it in cocktail sauce. I take a bite of the crispy crab meat, followed by a sip of merlot. "This is delicious. Thank you for doing this."

"Glad, you like it." Taka grins, then turns to look outside. "Falling snow is mesmerizing, isn't it?"

"Indeed." I lean back in the chair and gaze out the window.

"Yesterday," he washes food down with wine, "David, Yuki, and I went to the Jozankei Hot Springs. The springs are at the bottom of a snow-covered ravine with a mountain range in the background. The steam rises from the spring water. Such a breathtaking, serene place. I wish you had been with us. David was fascinated and took photos incessantly."

"Sounds like it's a heavenly place," I say with a sigh.

"By the way, tomorrow I have a place I want to take you," he says, his face suddenly serious. "Just you and me."

"Where?"

"I'd rather not tell you now. Well . . ." he empties his wine glass, "it's getting late. Shall we go to bed?"

My heart palpitates. "I'll take a shower first."

Taka nods.

I step into the shower and turn the silver handle. Water beats down on me and I feel like I am in tumultuous waves. As I wash my hair, I feel cool air and sense Taka coming in behind me. His fingers stroke my neck and my body shivers at the foreign sensation. I drop my arms and shampoo runs down my body. As I turn to him, our mouths find one another, and we kiss. His chest presses against my breasts and I feel his pounding heart. His body, firmly muscled, rubs against mine. The soap and water enhance the wonder I'm feeling.

His kisses are wet and greedy, not like before. With his hands caressing my neck, his tongue slips seamlessly into my mouth. The kisses are deeper. I respond to his passion. Slowly he moves his lips to my ear, then down to my neck while his right-hand traces along my spine. I kiss his shoulder. The water keeps running and I feel it getting hotter.

"Your face is scarlet," says Taka with a dimpled smile. "Maybe it is getting too hot. Let's move to the bed."

I nod.

He tuns off the water and we step from the shower. He wraps me in a towel, then puts a towel around his waist. Taking my hand, he leads me to the king-sized bed.

With our bodies still hot from the steamy spray, our towels drop to the floor and we slide under the satin sheets. He lays on his left side and his slender fingers gently comb my damp hair, then trace my breasts.

"You're so beautiful," he whispers.

I smile and caress his face with my hand. "I love you."

His intense eyes are penetrating. I feel like the rest of the world does not matter.

His hands move all over me and the caress is as light as a feather. Not knowing what to expect, I close my eyes in anticipation. When his fingers trace my inner thigh, my sexual pleasure intensifies.

He lightly lies over me and his fingers entwine in mine. I enjoy his weight, the feeling of being pressed under his body. My eyelids part; I sense he seems a little nervous. Unhurriedly he enters me, and I see a sheen of sweat on his forehead. I close my eyes. A shiver passes through my body, an indescribable sexual ripening arises inside me and my girly nature drops away. I sway rhythmically. Lost in the ecstasy of this new experience, I let myself bask in the totally blissful moment. As I achieve my highest delight, he reaches his, then slowly lays beside me, his chest heaving with each breath. I experience a total bond. *He's mine.*

* * *

A morning service call wakes us at six o'clock, and Taka orders breakfast so we can leave early. The rental car is fitted with snow chains and we drive many hours into a forest where silver birch trees flank both sides of the road. Rays of sunlight stream through the canopy, casting a golden glow over everything. Taka seems a little antsy. His jaw is clenched, and he has been brooding in silence for nearly thirty minutes.

"Look at that brick building," I say, pointing into the distance.

He stares at the premises and I hear him take a sharp, indrawn breath. I wonder what it is that is making Taka so uneasy. "Are you all right?" I ask.

He doesn't seem to hear me. Soon I spot children on a playground. "Taka-san, are we going there?"

He looks at me, nodding. Nearing the building, he slows to a stop. An old lady with an infant in her arms steps from the manor and walks toward the children.

Taka gets out of the car to approach her. He calls to her, "Sister Mari?"

The lady turns to look toward Taka. She doesn't seem to recognize him. He comes up to her and says softly, "I'm Taka."

Her face twists, seemingly in pain, but she soon recovers, and the corners of her mouth rise in a smile. She grabs Taka's arm and holds him tightly. The baby in her other arm begins to squirm and whine, but she continues to hold Taka without words. His eyes close. She releases him, and he smiles as he introduces me to the lady.

"Sister Mari, this is my girlfriend, Naomi-san."

"What a pretty young lady! Nice to meet you," she says to me.

I bow deeply.

She repositions the baby on her hip and bobs her head as she grins. "Come inside! Let's surprise some people you may know."

We follow her. At the entrance, I glimpse a sign on the door that reads "Catholic Church Orphanage." Several children are running around, all bundled in warm clothes against the frigid weather. Walking through the corridor, we pass a large room with many small beds. A man in a white doctor's coat stands next to a steel bed, talking to a toddler.

We enter a large hall—apparently the children's gathering place. Nearly twenty boys and girls—most appearing to be under the age of ten—are standing in a circle. A few kids in their early teens assist the youngest ones in playing a game.

As we stand at the corner of the room, a lady in a white apron stares in our direction, then finally approaches us. She is in her late fifties and has kind features. Under her apron, she is dressed neatly in a white blouse and a long navy-blue skirt. "I'm sorry if I am mistaken, but are you Taka-san?"

Taka immediately recognizes her. "You were my teacher, Mrs. Kimura."

"I recognized your dimples," says Mrs. Kimura. "You have grown so tall."

"This is my girlfriend, Naomi-san," says Taka with a shy look.

Mrs. Kimura bows and I bow back, saying, "Nice to meet you."

"I'm glad I get to meet your girlfriend," says Mrs. Kimura in a cheery voice. "Aha," she says, glancing at her wristwatch, "it's lunch time. Would you like to join us?"

"Yes, I would." Taka turns his head to look at me.

"Yes, I would love to," I say with a steady gaze at his former teacher.

*　　*　　*

We eat lunch with the children. On everyone's Bakelite tray is a small cupcake shaped like a Santa's smiley face. Taka talks with Sister Mari and Mrs. Kimura. I notice he lacks his usual confidence. He's shy in a way I've not seen.

"This place is almost the same as when I left," he says, craning his neck. "The woodstove and the organ are in the exact same spot."

In the center of the room stands a large, round woodstove

protected by a wire screen. A time-worn pedal organ sets in the corner.

"The room is brighter with all the new LED lighting," continues Taka. He smiles an innocent smile, much like the children around us.

The Tomoko teacher says, "It's been over twenty years since you left."

"Twenty-five years. I'm now thirty-five. I left when I was ten." He puts his chopsticks down on the table and turns to me to explain. "I became an orphan at the age of five. My parents died in a plane crash. Having no relatives, I was sent here, where I lived for five years before being adopted by a nice couple, Mr. and Mrs. Taniguchi."

Taka places his hand on mine and I hold his hand, feeling sorry about his misfortune. While listening to him reminiscing about his old days, I observe the children. They look happy on the surface, but I wonder what lies deeper in their minds. The girls' hairstyles are all short bobs; all the boys have uniformly short hair. The children wear light blue smocks. Imagining what orphanage life must be like, I picture a small Taka, dressed in a blue uniform, playing.

My attention shifts back to Taka as he explains about his life after he left the orphanage. I hear how Mr. and Mrs. Taniguchi treated Taka as if he were their own child. They sent him to college in Honolulu to learn international business. Studying abroad was Mr. Taniguchi's idea, as he believed learning English would be key to Taka's future success. Mrs. Taniguchi was not happy sending Taka away because she missed him too much.

"I went back home during my summer vacations, but my mother found many excuses to come to Hawaii to visit me," Taka says with a laugh. "My father was too busy with his business, but he helped me start my tour-guide business when I returned to Japan."

The depth of Taka's gratitude for Mr. and Mrs. Taniguchi must be unfathomable. He calls them Mother and Father. He regards them as his real parents. Sister Mari and Mrs. Kimura appear pleased with Taka's new life. We finish our lunch and leave the orphanage.

As we drive back to the hotel, Taka continues to share stories about himself.

"I have one more surprise." After a long pause, he confesses, "Misa-san is my step-sister."

I turn to look at him, but he continues to look straight ahead.

"Misa-san is Mr. Taniguchi's child from his mistress."

"Misa-san, your receptionist?" My voice hardens.

Taka looks at me and nods.

He explains his adopted parents yearned to have their own children, but Mrs. Taniguchi was unable to bear them a child. After three years of a childless marriage, Mr. Taniguchi became despondent and began drinking in bars in the Ginza area where he met Misa's mother. They grew fond of each other, and a year later, Misa was born. Mrs. Taniguchi discovered her husband's affair two years later and it drove her to a mental breakdown. Feeling guilty about his wife's mental state, Mr. Taniguchi broke off the affair but gave financial support to Misa and her mother. Mrs. Taniguchi's mental condition continued to haunt her husband, so after several years, Mr. Taniguchi suggested they adopt, thinking a child might heal her.

"Have you met Misa-san's mother?"

"Yes, once. Misa-san took me to the bar where her mother worked. Her mother is beautiful. Misa-san looks just like her."

"Why are you working with Misa-san?" My voice sounds petulant to my ear.

"Misa-san pleaded with my father to get me to let her work in my office. I can't say 'no' to my father," says Taka. "I realize Misa-san isn't the office type. She lacks office etiquette. But even though she's flirtatious, she's smart and a hard worker."

I stare at the dashboard.

"Frankly, I don't feel comfortable working with her. Misa-san didn't even live with us. Our relationship is more of a legal formality."

Mustering courage, I say, "I think Misa-san is attracted to you."

"What makes you think that?"

"Woman's intuition," I say, recalling her behavior in Taka's office.

Taka cracks a smile but makes no comment. I realize Taka is in no mood for further talk about Misa.

Our car reaches the hotel around six o'clock. Taka contacts David from the lobby and waits for him to come down so they can plan the rest of our trip. I go up to our room alone. Just as I unlock the door, my cell phone buzzes.

"Hello," I answer.

"Naomi, it's me. I have a big news for you." Yuki's voice rises in pitch, her excitement seeping through the phone.

"What's that?"

Yuki giggles.

"What?" I demand.

"On Christmas Eve, after picking you up at the airport, David proposed!"

"My word! Congratulations!" A warm sensation runs through my whole body and my voice grows thick with emotion. "Yuki, I'm so happy for you."

"Thank you."

"By the way," I say, nodding to myself in acknowledgement of her delight, "we too had an unforgettable time that night."

"Oh yeah?"

All at once we burst into hearty laughter. I hear a door open in the background.

"David is back. I've gotta go," Yuki says.

As I hang up, Taka shouts from the door as he enters our suite, "They're engaged!"

"I know. Yuki just told me."

Taka unzips his laptop case and perches on the edge of the bed. "David wants to take us to dinner. I need to make a reservation."

Sitting next to Taka, I say, "Yuki likes French food."

"All right," says Taka as he searches for French restaurants. "How about this place?"

I peek at the screen and see the fine-looking restaurant. "Perfect!"

"Okay." He calls and reserves for dinner at 7:00 p.m.

We dress and set off for the lobby to meet David and Yuki. They are already waiting for us. As I draw near, the diamond glimmering on Yuki's finger catches my eye. They're so absorbed in each other they don't even see us approach.

When Taka touches David's shoulder, Yuki and David turn toward us, surprised. "Oh . . . you guys are here!"

"Yuki, what a beautiful diamond!"

With joyful eyes, she says, "Thank you."

"Congratulations!" says Taka as he pats David's arm.

David embraces Taka. "Thank you."

While my eyes are fixed on Yuki's ring, Taka disappears to get the car. In a few minutes, he returns, and we leave for dinner.

The night scenery is impressive with festive lighting, but the winding, narrow roads are treacherous with snow and ice. Taka's fingers are curled around the steering wheel. At last he says, "We are here," and I finally relax as he slows down to park.

A grand fir, bejeweled with white lights, welcomes us to a French cottage-style restaurant.

"Such a beautiful Christmas tree!" I exclaim, as we quicken our pace to the front door.

Yuki exhales, creating a patch of fog in the air. "It's bitterly cold, but so pretty."

Inside, a fire crackles and pops in the river-rock-framed fireplace.

"Cool," David says, looking out the window as we are about to sit down. Outside, snow-covered bushes and trees are decorated by gas lights along the paths. "Thanks, Taka. What a perfect place to celebrate our engagement and toast our reunion."

Five months have passed since we met in Kyoto. David orders champagne. Everyone has the same dish, the *Blanquette de Poisson*—fish, a few clams, and sliced carrot covered with cream sauce. Warm stew and a cozy surrounding contribute to creating an intimate time. We nestle in and sip wine late into the night.

The next morning, Sunday, we head to the New Chitose Airport to depart for home. The sky is a clear blue and the air is crisp and cold. The car, bathed in sunshine, is warm inside. I glance at Taka, reflecting on the memorable days we had in Sapporo. The snow country must have sprinkled romantic magic upon all of us. David and Yuki snuggle together in the backseat. Their happiness is infectious.

chapter twelve

BOSOZOKU

ALTHOUGH TIRED AFTER RETURNING from the Sapporo trip, I take my usual evening walk. Bitterly cold weather reminds me of Sapporo and a barrage of memories spring to mind. A sense of apprehension besets me. *Misa-san is Taka-san's step-sister, though they never lived in the same house. She's the child of Mr. Taniguchi's mistress and Taka-san is an adopted son. No wonder Take-san treats Misa-san so courteously. That must be out of respect for Mr. Taniguchi. After all, Taka-san isn't a blood relation of either Mr. Taniguchi or Mrs. Taniguchi. Misa-san's seductive behavior is even more unbearable given the relationship.*

Nearing home, I see a navy-blue SUV in front of the apartment. Someone is sitting in the car. I slow to see who it is. *Mr. Ishida!*

He calls out my name as he steps from the car.

Taking a deep breath, I advance at a trot. "Mr. Ishida, why you are here? I canceled our *omiai*."

"Yes, you did," he says, his face quiet, unperturbed.

"Then what are you doing here?" I frown.

He flashes me a smile. "I'm here because of Yoshiyuki-san."

"Yoshiyuki?"

"Yes, he's in trouble."

Ignoring his smile, I ask, "What kind of trouble?"

"He's involved with a *Bosozoku* group. They are extorting money from him."

"What! How do you know Yoshiyuki? And what does Yoshiyuki have to do with a group like that?"

"It's kind of a long story." He shivers. "It's cold. May I come in?"

"Umm."

Strong puffs of chilly wind blow hair across my face.

"Yoshiyuki-san needs help. If you work with me, we can rescue him."

After a moment of ruminating, I reluctantly unlock the door and let him in. He glances around before seating himself at the dining table. *There's no need to be hospitable,* I tell myself. But I am chilled to the bone, so I turn on the stove to make tea.

Stepping from the kitchen, I press him for details. "How in the world do you know Yoshiyuki?"

"I have to confess. One day, even though you canceled our *omiai,* I yearned to see you, so I drove to your apartment. Yoshiyuki-san was at your door, waiting for you. I told him I was your friend. We chatted for a while, then I invited him to a café for a warm drink. Since then we have become friends."

I shut my eyes, feeling dizzy. The tea kettle whistles. I shuffle to the kitchen, wondering as I do if there is any way I can help Yoshiyuki without Mr. Ishida's involvement. *A Bosozoku gang is pressuring him for money? I can't tell my aunt about this.*

I start to carry the tea to the living room and am startled to see Mr. Ishida leaning against the kitchen door frame.

"You'd make a good wife."

"Mr. Ishida. Please be seated."

He leers, posing in his typical how-can-you-resist-my-charm stance. "Why can't you use my first name?"

I'm annoyed. "Mr. Ishida, I thought you were here to talk about Yoshiyuki?"

I carry the tea to the table. As I am about to place the tray on the table, he grasps my arms from behind.

"Take your hands off me."

As his strong arms twirl my body to face him, the teapot slips from the table. He ignores the spilling tea and forces a kiss upon me. I push him away with all the strength I can muster.

Panting, I shout, "If you don't leave my apartment right now, I'll tell your parents about this incident."

He glares at me, his eyes becoming dark and cold, then utters, "You'll need me."

I stare back at him. "Please leave."

Releasing an audible breath, he trudges to the entry. Before opening the door, he turns to me and, blurts, "I have a pretty good idea where he is."

"Leave."

The door shuts behind him. I rush to the door and lock it. I lean against the door for a moment to gather my wits, then go to the kitchen to get a towel.

With shaking hands, I kneel to clean the mess. *Shoot! What should I do?* Squatting on the floor, I slap the side of my head, wanting to cry, although tears won't come. *I should call Yoshiyuki.* I stand up and grab my cell phone from the TV stand. After one ring the line goes to a recorded message, saying, "subscriber unavailable."

Sitting on the couch, I ponder. *Bosozoku* . . . I saw them once in the Harajuku area near my aunt's house, but that was many years ago. Do they still exist? They have the reputation of being obnoxious, loud motorcyclists who are often involved in petty crimes like pickpocketing, purse snatching, and shoplifting. I don't understand why Yoshiyuki would get involved with that sort of group. I rest my elbow on the armrest to brace my chin in my palm. Ah . . . I see how that could have happened.

I remember a month ago he sported a brand-new motorcycle around, proudly saying Auntie bought him a top-of-the-line Yamaha. As a twenty-one-year-old country boy who recently moved to Tokyo from a small town, his naïveté makes him an easy mark. Perhaps he was riding his new toy around the Harajuku area and saw them. With his foolish curiosity, he may have approached a *Bosozoku* group—or they approached him. I let out a long breath.

* * *

On Monday morning, I rush into the office. I see a few girls chatting around Yuki's desk.

"I wish I had a ring like this," says Kaori, holding Yuki's hand.

Yoko tells her, "If you weren't so picky, you might have a chance."

Patting Kaori's shoulder, Midori says, "Don't worry. You'll meet someone one day."

I break into the circle. "Good morning, girls! Isn't that a pretty diamond? Yuki's fiancé, David, is such a gentleman. And he's so good looking, I tell you."

Yuki is glowing from all the attention and has a smile that stretches from ear to ear.

"Back to work!" says Mr. Yamada, coming out from his office. When he gets near us, he asks, "Are you engaged, Yuki-san?"

Yuki stands up, smiling proudly, stretching her arm out to him to flaunt her sparkling gem.

"Who's your fiancé?" asks Mr. Yamada, frowning.

"David Johnson."

"How did you meet a foreigner?" asks Mr. Yamada, seeming to

forget others are present.

"Mr. Section Chief, I have to get back to work," says Yuki.

Mr. Yamada appears to be surprised by his own remarks. His face turns red and he looks upset. His thick caterpillar-like eyebrows twitch. He snaps, "Get to work everyone!"

The others fade away and I skulk to my desk, hiding my handbag so Mr. Yamada won't notice I came in late. On my desk is a yellow post-it in Yuki's handwriting. The note says, "Your aunt called. She wants you to call as soon as possible."

I call her.

"Naomi-chan, where did you go last weekend? I called you many times," says my auntie, sounding distraught.

"Sorry. What's up?"

"Yoshiyuki is missing," she says, her voice trembling. "He's been gone since Friday."

"Oh no! Did you call the police?" I refrain from worrying her with what Mr. Ishida told me, as there is no need to mention him to her. I already asked my parents to cancel my *omiai* with him..

"I did. Could you please come to my house after work?" she pleads.

"I will," I say and put down the phone.

* * *

At lunchtime, I bring up the matter of Yoshiyuki. I would like to talk to Yuki about my first night with Taka, about his childhood and his relationship to Misa, but that conversation will have to wait.

"My cousin has been missing for a few days. He's involved with a *Bosozoku* group," I say, opening my lunch box.

"*Bosozoku*? Who's your cousin?"

"My cousin, Yoshiyuki, is a former farmer who moved to my aunt's house in Aoyama from a small town in Niigata prefecture.

Apparently, he's being extorted by the *Bosozoku*."

"How did that happen?"

"My auntie bought him a motorcycle. I suspect he drove it around the Harajuku neighborhood. You know Harajuku is a gathering place for punks."

"Umm . . ." Yuki nods, squeezing a ketchup packet over a hamburger.

Leaning forward, I say, "By the way, I learned of Yoshiyuki's *Bosozoku* involvement from Mr. Ishida. He came to my apartment yesterday."

"You're kidding me?"

"No. He's such a scum." I tell her of his brazen behavior. "He tried to kiss me."

"Oh, that's awful. I'm sorry, Naomi. He's stalking you. I'm glad you are okay." Yuki puts her fork down and gazes at me, her eyes full of compassion. "I don't know what kind of information Mr. Ishida has, but I'd never ask him for help. David and I will help you." She rubs her temple in a circular motion with her left hand, causing the diamond to twinkle under the overhead lights.

"I know *Bosozoku* groups were popular in the 80s and 90s, but that was forever ago. I didn't think they still existed, but I've learned they are still active. But those hooligans are mostly underground, so it'll be hard to find the group he's in."

"We'll help you," says Yuki again, fork upright in her hand as if ready to fight.

I appreciate being able to share my burden, especially since David is heading back to the States next week and her time with him is limited.

Lunch is over, and we return to our desks.

*   *   *

It's five to five. While clearing off my desk, I call Taka to tell him I need to see my auntie after work and that I hope I can see him later tonight. There is no answer, so I leave a message.

The subway is filled with commuters in bulky winter coats, making the inside hot and airless. Once I reach the street, the nippy winds accost me. Rushing to Auntie's house, I pass the cake shop where I usually stop to buy a fruit cake.

Momo barks when the door chimes and soon my aunt pushes the door open. She invites me to the living room. As soon as I sit, Auntie asks what I want to eat. Without waiting for my response, she phones in an order of sushi, my favorite.

"Thank you for coming, Naomi-chan," says my auntie. "I don't know what I'd do without you."

"I hope I can help you. Have you reported Yoshiyuki missing?"

"Yes, but they don't take it seriously," says my auntie with disgust. "Your uncle is upset with me," she adds "and blames me for buying Yoshiyuki a motorcycle."

I haven't seen my uncle since I arrived.

"Did Yoshiyuki leave home with his motorcycle?" I ask.

"Actually, the other day a young man banged on the door asking for Yoshiyuki. He was sporting a funny, heavily pomaded hairstyle like that red thing, you know, on a rooster's head, except the color wasn't red, it was yellow. I tell you, I've never seen such a spooky man. A tattoo dragon rolled up his neck and loathsome earrings hung from his ears."

I realize that must have been a member of the *Bosozoku*. "Having someone like that show up at my door would upset me, too."

"I tried to stop Yoshiyuki from going with him, but Yoshiyuki said, 'I'm just going for a ride on my bike. I'll be back soon. Don't worry' and followed the obnoxious man," says my auntie, half crying.

"Did you see any sign or name on the guy's jacket or pants?"

"Umm, let me think," she moans. "Aha! He wore a baggy

black outfit with tall leather boots. On the back of his jacket was embroidered a name in yellow letters."

"What did it say?"

My auntie rolls her eyes, resting her chin in hand. "Argh . . . I remember, 'Mikuni' and at the bottom, 'Rentai.'"

"Mikuni Regiment might be a group name. He must belong to a *Bosozoku* group." I don't tell her how I know this.

"Right! When I watched him leave, I saw others waiting for him who wore the same stupid-looking clothes with the same logo on their backs, all riding outrageous motorcycles." My auntie nods her head many times as if she has just discovered an important clue.

Auntie, now in detective mode, grabs a pencil and paper and begins to sketch the man's face and the dragon tattoo on his neck. The drawing is a bit comical because of his cockscomb hairstyle, but his face is sketched artistically. I wonder where she got her drawing skills. She gives me other information, such as his height and weight. Just as we finish talking about Yoshiyuki, the sushi delivery man arrives. My uncle shows up at the same time. I wonder where he's been but decide not to ask. We eat with little conversation and I leave soon after I finish dinner.

As I step out of my auntie's house, I check my phone messages and see Taka's text: *I want to see you after you visit your aunt.* I decide to call him once I get to the station, thinking it's easier for him to pick me up there. I also see Yuki's message, saying that she and David are at Taka's place.

On the way to Gaienmae Station, I glance at the tea house where Taka took me the last time I visited my auntie. Even in the distance, I can see inside the tea house through the large picture windows. It looks lively, with lots of warm, glowing lighting. After Christmas, the shop is redecorated with the New Year's traditional *kadomatsu,* a decoration of three bamboo shoots combined with pine branches in a straw bundle on either side of the front door to welcome the *toshigami* deity, bringer of a bountiful harvest and bestower of blessings. Twinkling lights frame the large glass windows. The green and red garlands have been put away for next Christmas. On this chilly winter night, the tea house is packed with customers.

I reach the station and call Taka.

"Hey, Naomi-san. Where are you now?" asks Taka, before I have a chance to say hello.

"I'm at the Gaienmae Station."

I'll pick you up in ten minutes."

"Okay." I immediately hear the click as he ends the call. It's as if he does not want to waste a single second.

Soon his car pulls up beside me and I slip in.

After a short drive, we reach his condominium. There are fifteen floors in the modern building and his condo is on the tenth floor. We leave his car in the underground parking garage and step into the elevator. After all these months, I am elated over the opportunity to see his condo for the first time. Taka pushes the door open and I step inside. With a single glance, I am struck with how neatly his house is kept.

"Hi, Naomi!" says David from the living room, an uncluttered, elegant space with stylish furniture—mahogany cabinets, an off-white sofa, and a glass-inlayed coffee table.

"I called and left you a message," says Yuki.

"I'm sorry I didn't get a chance to call," I say, plopping down on a chair. Taka takes another chair to face David and Yuki.

"Did you talk with your aunt?" asks Yuki. "David wants to help find Yoshiyuki-san."

All eyes turn to me. Seeing everyone's concern for my cousin brings a lump to my throat. "Thank you all," I lower my head, overwhelmed by their loyalty.

"Of course. Your problem is our problem." David stands up. "Cheer up! Let me give you a hug."

I stand and can't help but feel like a statue as he gives me a tight squeeze.

"Thank you, David," I say, feeling shy about being hugged by a male friend. Hugging isn't a Japanese custom. Yuki and Taka may be accustomed to seeing people show affection in public since they lived in a foreign country, but this will take some getting used to for me.

"I've some information about the *Bosozoku.*" I show them my aunt's sketch.

"This guy might be the leader of the club. He's about 170 cm and of medium build."

"Wow, your aunt's drawing is excellent!" David says, then laughs, pointing to the rooster-style hairdo and the dragon tattoo on the man's thick neck.

"Contour lines are meticulous," Taka comments, lifting the drawing from the coffee table.

"Doesn't he look like a comic-book character?" I chuckle, then catch myself, realizing Yoshiyuki's situation is a serious matter. Donning a serious face, I continue. "The name of this particular group is the Mikuni Regime."

"Great," says Taka. "Yuki-san told me Yoshiyuki–san met the group in Harajuku."

"Well, I just assumed," I say, shrugging my shoulders.

"It's reasonable, though, if you consider where he lives," says Taka.

David, Yuki, and Taka have already researched the *Bosozoku* while waiting for me. They concluded the best way to find the gang is to drive around the Harajuku, Shibuya, and Shinjuku neighborhoods. Shibuya and Shinjuku are adjacent districts to Harajuku. With Google maps, we study those areas.

Taka leaves the room to make tea and I follow. *What a beautiful kitchen!* His condo, compared to my apartment, is like the difference between a fine wine and a soda pop. The appliances are all stainless steel—refrigerator, dishwasher, stove hood, and sink faucets—gleaming under the soft glow of the recessed ceiling lights. The white cabinets and gray quartz countertops impart a modern appearance to the room. He opens a cabinet and takes out teacups and saucers with silver trim. I place a tea bag in each of them, thinking it would be nice if this were my kitchen.

Taka whispers, "I like seeing you in my kitchen."

As much as I want to say, "Yes, I'd like to live with you," I just give him an ingratiating smile. We return to the others, carrying the tea.

"Why don't we go out and look for that gang now?" David suggests. "I understand they like to cruise at night."

Placing the tea on the coffee table, Taka says, "I was thinking of doing that tonight myself."

I pick up the stack of saucers from the tray and pass them out to each person while Taka places a cup of tea on each saucer. We then take a seat.

"David and I want to help Naomi, too," responds Yuki.

Before I have a chance to thank them, Taka says, "Thank you very much. That's very nice of you, and I appreciate your concern." He leans forward. "Everyone has provided me with enough information about the group—I can take it from here. I worry about something happening to one of you."

Rescuing Yoshiyuki is my affair, but now I feel my problem has become Taka's. Taka emphasizes how worried he is that we might get into serious trouble if things get out of control, and if that happened he says he isn't sure he'd be able to protect Yuki and me. He also thinks it is not a good idea for a foreigner like David to get involved in what could become a police incident.

"I agree," David says. "The girls stay here, but I'll go with you, Taka." With unabashed confidence, he says, "I know how to take care of myself. Photographers travel to dangerous places all over the world. I should tell you my stories sometime." He grins. "After some of the places I've been to, *Bosozoku* don't intimidate me."

"All right then, you and I go, and the ladies stay here," says Taka.

"No, I'm going with you," Yuki demands.

"Me too. I want to go," I say.

"Absolutely not! It's too dangerous," Taka says firmly. "We might come back late, so feel free to use my bed if you get sleepy. There is food in the refrigerator and pantry."

Taka grabs his baseball bat and he and David leave.

Yuki and I sit and talk about our relationships with David and Taka, trying to stop thinking about worst-case scenarios. *Bosozoku* bikers are said to be violent and easily offended if anyone gets in their way—they smash cars and assault people. We become anxious and can't sit still. Yuki finally decides to call David. He tells her they are driving around the Shinjuku area and, although they've seen a few individual bikers, they haven't spotted a group yet.

An hour passes, and it is past midnight.

"Yuki, why don't you lie down? You look sleepy."

"I'm fine, but I'm curious to see the rest of Taka-san's condo." Her eyes light up.

"Me, too," I say, giving her a wide smile. "Well then, let's check it out."

We step into his bedroom and I turn on the light. His bed, a queen size with no frame, stands tall in the center of the room. The bed cover and pillows are light moss green, matching the walls. Yuki passes her hand over the beautiful mahogany desk that stands in the corner of the room. Siting on the glossy surface of the desk are a few manila files, his computer, and a picture in a silver frame. She picks up the picture.

"It's you, Naomi," cries Yuki.

I approach and take the picture from Yuki's hand. It *is* me! I recognize the place: Kiyomizu-dera Temple. I never saw him take my picture.

"I bet Taka-san fell in love with you at first sight."

"You think so?"

"Yes . . . I believe so," says Yuki, eyeing the photo. "You look so feminine in the kimono."

The picture transports me back to that time and I linger in the room.

"Hey, look. His bathroom is stylish."

I realize Yuki has wandered away while I have been reliving my time with Taka. I follow her voice. The room looks bare but streamlined. Only a few items—an electric razor, a toothbrush, and a soap dish—are on the vanity. The bathtub shower is enclosed with transparent glass walls. As I imagine myself standing in the shower, we hear the heavy entry door shutting. Quickly, we dash back to the living room.

"You two are still waiting up for us?" Taka asks.

"Of course," I say.

David comes up to Yuki and takes her in his arms, saying, "Aren't you sleepy?"

Without answering, Yuki asks, "How did it go?"

"We saw a group, but not a *Bosozoku* gang," says Taka. "They were just motorcycle riders."

Putting the baseball bat down beside the couch, David adds, "We'll look for them again in a couple of days."

"Sorry for taking so much of your time. You two must be tired and sleepy," I say, bowing, feeling awful to have put them through all the trouble.

Taka asks David and Yuki to stay the night, but they decide not to and call a taxi. It's almost two o'clock. Taka and I finally go to bed. I lie in bed, wearing my camisole. Taka leaves his undershirt on and slips in next to me. We caress. Our passion begins to escalate. He wraps his arms around me, holding me tight. I kiss him. We indulge ourselves in love until sleep overtakes us.

* * *

With little sleep, I head straight to work from Taka's house. As I enter the building, I am watchful, remembering how I met Mr. Yamada yesterday on the way to the locker room. If he sees me he might notice that I'm wearing the same outfit as yesterday. *No, he isn't that observant,* I think, but it would be terrible if I bump into him. "I hope he's not around," I murmur under my breath. Just before the elevator door closes, Mr. Yamada jumps in. *Oh God!* I close my eyes and inhale deeply.

"Good morning, Naomi-san!" says Mr. Yamada. He nears me and whispers in my ear, "Looks like you didn't go home last night."

I shoot him a vexed look without saying anything, then quickly scan the people around us, hoping they didn't hear his remark.

Once we are out of the elevator, I say, "I was late for work and didn't even have time to get a fresh change of clothes."

"I see," says Mr. Yamada with a sardonic smile.

"Idiot," I say under my breath and dart into the locker room. Yuki is there, changing into her work uniform.

"Hey, Yuki. I ran into Mr. Yamada in the elevator," I say. "He knows I didn't go home last night. He's such a schmuck! I can already tell that today is going to be a long day."

Wearing a sympathetic smile, Yuki says, "Quick, change into our company uniform before the trio arrives. Midori isn't nosy, but Yoko and Kaori are too interested in other people's business."

When we enter the office, Mr. Yamada gives us a wry grin. Yuki shoots him an indignant look.

At my desk, I check my phone messages while waiting for my

computer to boot up. At the end of the year, banks always get busy, so I have loads of work. My attention is riveted on my work as I try to clear my docket. I dash to the copy machine to make copies of fund transfer records. Soon Kaori, Yoko, and Midori crowd around me.

"Naomi," says Yoko, beaming at me. "You have a boyfriend, don't you?"

"Why do you think that?"

"You're wearing the same clothes as yesterday."

"Don't tease her, you guys," says Kaori, watching my reaction. Then suddenly she widens her eyes. "You *do* have a boyfriend, don't you?"

"Kaori, you too? You guys are so nosey. All right, I'll tell you, but not now. I'm too busy," I say, shooting Yoko a dirty look as she chortles.

"Yeah, right. Sorry. Let's go back to work." says Midori.

During my lunch hour, I call my auntie to update her on our search for Yoshiyuki. I tell her my friends' names since they are helping me look for him. Given her curiosity, I realize I'd better share a little bit more about David and Taka. Hastily, I tell her that Yuki and David are engaged, and Taka is my boyfriend, hoping my auntie will not bombard me with questions. But of course, she wants more information than I've just given.

"How did she meet Mr. Foreigner? Is he American? Is he living in Japan?" asks my auntie in a rapid-fire manner, then she takes a breath and jumps with a vengeance on my boyfriend comment. "Did you just say you have a boyfriend?"

"I'm at work, Auntie. I don't have time to—" I start but am unable to finish my sentence.

"So, you have a boyfriend. What does he do for a living? How old is he? Where did you me—"

"Stop, stop, Auntie! I don't have time to explain those things now. I've got to go."

"All right. Thank you for your call. Talk to you soon," says Auntie and hangs up.

I glance at Yuki's lunch box, which is already half empty. Yuki and I have little time to catch up on recent developments. Since David's arrival, many things are happening in our lives. Without time to even touch the surface of all that's going on, we are forced to hurry back to work.

* * *

Even though I work like a beaver all day, I still put in an hour and a half of overtime. As I exit the building, the cold air feels good on my sweaty face. Too tired to cook, I stop by a convenience store on my way home for an instant curried-rice meal.

Before entering my apartment, I check my mailbox and find a makeshift envelope.

Inside the envelope a slip of paper reads:

Sorry for not responding. I need help. I'm being held captive.

I'll be on the Shuto Expressway going to Enoshima around ten p.m. on New Years' Eve.

I asked the lady at a Daily Yamazaki market to mail this. If you're reading, that means I wasn't caught.

Yoshiyuki

I drop onto the couch, wondering why Yoshiyuki didn't call me instead of writing a note. Does he have a cellphone? Maybe one of the gang members confiscated it? Maybe he simply didn't have time or was afraid he'd be overheard. I call Taka right away to give him the news.

"Good! Now I know where to look for him," says Taka, releasing a deep sigh. "Were you okay today? You only slept a few hours."

"I managed okay," I respond, thinking of his sweet touch, "but my boss commented in the elevator this morning, 'You didn't go home last night', and that irritated me all day."

"Forget it. He's a jerk. Our relationship has nothing to do with your work," says Taka, trying to cheer me up. "Can you meet me tomorrow after work? We haven't had much time lately for just the two of us."

"Yes, I'd love that."

"Good, then rest well and I'll see you tomorrow," says Taka. As usual, he waits for me to hang up first.

As I reach for a kettle to heat the instant curried rice, my mom calls. Without any greeting, she abruptly asks, "Why weren't you home last night?" She calls once a week to check on me and, apparently, she called last night. I haven't told my mom about Taka. She is old-fashioned and doesn't like the idea of people sleeping together before marriage.

"I stayed at Yuki's house last night because I missed the last train," I say, feeling a little guilty.

"Good. So, everything is all right with you?" asks my mom in a worried voice.

"Everything is fine. In fact, my life is wonderful," I say with a smile in my voice.

chapter thirteen

COMBAT

NEW YEAR'S EVE ARRIVES numbingly cold, the night crystal clear under brilliant stars with Orion on full display. Tonight is the night Yoshiyuki will be riding to Enoshima with his Mikuni group.

After a long discussion with Taka and David, Yuki and I finally convince them to allow us to come along. As we leave Taka's condo, he grabs two baseball bats. He must have bought one for David. Some of the members of *Bosozoku* are known to carry metal pipes and baseball bats. Just thinking about these weapons makes my stomach clench. Grabbing his binoculars, Taka warns Yuki and me again how violent this gang can be. Covering our heads with stocking hats, Yuki and I look at Taka and nod, showing how serious we are about steering clear of a conflict.

"If any bikers look into the car, avoid eye contact. Keep your faces hidden, all right?" instructs Taka. "If they try to smash the car, call the police. Immediately lock the doors when David and I step out of the car. Yuki-san, since you can drive, you be the driver if you have to make a getaway."

"I understand," Yuki says.

Taka rubs his forehead as if he is still hesitant to take us. "Never, ever, get out of the car," Taka reiterates.

David stares grimly at Yuki.

"Don't worry, David. We'll be careful," says Yuki in a solid voice.

I say the same to Taka.

I suddenly realize rescuing Yoshiyuki may have dire consequences. I feel uneasy drawing my friends into danger.

When the clock on the wall hits nine, we take the elevator down to the parking garage.

The two baseball bats lie between the gearshift and David's long legs. Before Taka steps on the gas, he shoots a glance at David and gives a quick nod. David returns the gesture in kind as if there is a tacit understanding between them.

We drive onto the Aoyama road. The road is jammed with cars going to visit the famous Meiji Jingu Shrine in Harajuku where the deified spirits of Emperor Meiji and his consort, Shoken, sleep. New Year's celebrants, as well as worshipers on the way to their favorite shrines for the first visit of the year, create major chaos. I don't know if we can catch up with the *Bosozoku*. My palms sweat.

Taking much longer than we planned, we finally reach Japan National Route 246. Many motorcyclists are on the street but are obviously not *Bosozoku*. Their wheels are standard, not altered; the riders wear regular helmets and are dressed in normal leather jackets and jeans.

Thirty minutes pass, but we are not even close to the Shuto Expressway ramp.

"May I lower the heater?" Taka asks.

David immediately slides the heater level to the blue zone. The cool temperature feels good.

"Anyone care for water?" David glances over his shoulder and offers a bottle.

Yuki passes the bottle to me before she takes a drink.

The exit sign in the distance reads "Shuto Expressway—Yokohama." Taka bears right and speeds up to merge with the traffic. It's ten minutes of ten and now we are on full alert. I see Taka's and David's busy eye movements reflected in the rearview mirror. Yuki and I scan the road for members of the Mikuni tribe. The Shuto Expressway is still congested, but the traffic thins slightly as we leave the city center, making it easier to see our surroundings.

"I wonder if they are ahead of us or behind us," says Taka, turning his head toward David. "I'll speed up a little."

"Sounds good," David replies.

Leaning forward, I glance at the blue-lit dashboard and read the needle of the speedometer as it approaches 110 km/h, more than thirty kilometers over the speed limit. The Lexus drives smoothly, but I'm feeling tense and stiff. Taka's unusual conduct—exceeding the speed limit—makes my heart pound. I feel awful for putting my friends in danger.

At the Yoga interchange, we enter the Daisan Keihin road, a national highway, leading to Enoshima, the Mikuni's gathering place. More vehicles and bikes appear on the road. Perhaps many of them are visitors heading to the Tsurugaoka Hachimangu, the biggest shrine in Kamakura, near Enoshima.

"I'm so sorry. Could we stop at a rest area?" asks Yuki in a faint voice.

"Sure," Taka answers.

After driving for fifteen minutes or so, Taka turns into a parking area. Yuki and I jump out of the car and scurry to the public restroom while Taka and David wait. As we stand at the sink washing our hands, a thunderous sound pierces the whole area. We look at each other. Without words, we rush back to the car.

Soon a group of ten bikers pulls into the rest area, revving their engines as they cruise to a stop. One of the riders holds the Japanese national flag with the rising sun. Following behind the first group is another gang, also carrying a banner. This one reads VILLAIN in big, red letters. All the riders are dressed in white jumpsuits with skinny black belts. Within minutes, a third group appears in military dress.

The *Bosozoku* bikers show up like a long cargo train, each group like a new car in the rolling chain. The thugs fill up the parking area. The noise from their loud engines and howling voices is deafening. Ordinary folks are leaving, and our car becomes conspicuous. Taka moves the car a distance from the gangs, yet close enough to observe, as more bikers continue to arrive.

"Look," I point out, "there is a girls' group, driving pink bikes."

"They're quite impressive," remarks David.

They are all wearing *happi*, the traditional Japanese straight-sleeved coat. Printed on the back of their coats is the Japanese national red sun, radiating from their team name. None of them wear helmets, probably to show off their long, dyed blonde hair. Inside their coats they wear black tops and jeans and have tight, long, black vinyl boots on their feet. Maybe they look impressive to David, but they look tough to me.

"Notice their half-finger gloves with long brass spikes?" asks Taka.

"Yeah, they look painful." I swallow.

The *Bosozoku* groups are socializing amongst themselves. Most seem to be young, perhaps under twenty. Most of the guys are armed with clubs, baseball bats, or steel pipes. They look terrifying. The thought of Taka and David confronting them makes me feel scared to death.

With so many bikers here and more continuing to arrive, it will be hard to spot the Mikuni group.

"I feel sorry for their parents," Yuki says, breaking the silence. "I bet they have no idea what their kids are doing."

"They remind me of the Hell's Angels, although *Bosozoku* are a lot younger and less organized," says David. No one says anything. David adds, "I feel sorry for their parents, too. Most of them look like teenagers."

I wonder what the Hell's Angels are.

"Hey, look!" Taka cries out and points. "That one, just coming in. He looks like the guy Naomi-san's aunt described. He has black leathers and a punk's hairstyle. I see yellow letters on his back, but it's too far away to read the name."

"Here you go, Taka." David hands him the binoculars.

"'Mikuni' and at the bottom, '*Rentai.*' Also, their bikes' fenders are yellow. They're the ones," confirms Taka, as the lead rider and all his similarly dressed followers arrive.

"Check it out, Naomi-san." Taka passes me the glasses.

I take a look. The gang's hairdos are raised fringe and their boots have long, pointed toes. A guy wearing a leather jumpsuit trails the end of the group. He parks his bike and takes off his helmet. He stands alone because his motorbike is unaltered. His short hair is parted on one side, not like other people of his group.

"Yoshiyuki!" I shout. "That's him at the end of the line!"

I hand the binoculars to Yuki.

"What do we do now, Taka?" asks David.

"We can't do anything yet. There are too many people here," responds Taka. "The Mikuni group came in last, perhaps they'll leave last. If so, we can follow them."

"Right," agrees David, his eyes trained on the Mikuni bikers.

Honking a trumpet-like horn on the center of his handlebar, the lead guy, I assume, starts the procession. Engines rev. Some have no mufflers, adding even more noise to the ear-piercing cacophony.

Leaning forward between the front seats, Yuki points her finger at the lead rider. "Look! The group carrying the national flag is taking off. There they go."

Taka looks back at us and nods in agreement. "Yeah, that was the first group to arrive."

The other groups trail one after the other, revving their engines. They indeed seem to be leaving in the order they arrived.

White smoke blasting from their exhaust pipes fogs the chilly air and the deafening din echoes throughout the whole area. Group by group, the *Bosozoku* dissipate. Within fifteen minutes, half of the gangs are gone. The Mikuni members remain behind, chatting with each other. Yoshiyuki doesn't mingle with the group, instead he stands off to the side next to a light pole.

"Yoshiyuki is looking in our direction," I say, peeking through the binoculars.

"He's probably wondering if you are here," says Taka.

"Look! He's facing this way," adds David.

"Wow, if you can see his face from here, you must have eagle eyes," says Yuki.

"He's walking toward the restroom and looking this way. Naomi, quick, take off your hat and wave to get his attention," says David.

"All right." I slip out of the car and pretend to stretch, reaching my arms into the air. Some of the other bikers are also walking to the restroom.

More *Bosozoku* groups continue to leave after their short stop. Within ten minutes there are only a couple of groups left in the parking lot. It looks as though they are waiting their turn to depart, so they maintain their sanctioned position in the entourage.

Now, the Mikuni gang is getting on their bikes, but Yoshiyuki is still in the restroom. The Mikuni are gunning their engines as if they can wait no longer. A tall, lanky guy starts honking his horn as he rides in a circle.

Finally, Yoshiyuki emerges from the building and walks towards the Mikuni; they are the only remaining *Bosozoku*. Suddenly, the lanky guy drives at high speed directly toward Yoshiyuki. He slams on the brakes and slides to within a meter of Yoshiyuki. He jumps from his bike and kicks Yoshiyuki in the stomach. Yoshiyuki falls to his knees, hunching over and clutching his stomach. The gang hoots in delight.

Yoshiyuki leaps up and, with an uppercut to the chin, sends the lanky man sprawling to the pavement. The man strains to stand up but collapses to the ground. Seven other riders stop laughing and sprint to join the fight.

"Let's go," says Taka to David. They slip from the car with their baseball bats and run toward the *Bosozoku*.

Before reaching Yoshiyuki, David and Taka are swarmed by five of the gang members. The other two *Bosozoku* charge Yoshiyuki.

One of the bikers tries to hit Taka with a billy club, but Taka fends him off with his baseball bat. Another guy comes at him from behind, snatches Taka's bat, and tries to club him with it. When the guy with the billy club comes at Taka again, Yuki lets out a scream and slams her foot down on the gas petal. In a split second we're there and Yuki swerves the car to hit the assailant, flinging him to the side, taking him out of the fight. The guy who snatched Taka's baseball is distracted long enough that Taka can jump on him and take back his bat.

Yuki jams the gear into reverse and aims the car at a guy about to attack David with a wooden stick. I jump into the front seat and fling open my door just in time to broadside the guy.

"Yuki, get out of here!" shouts David.

She spins the steering wheel and turns the car around. Suddenly I see the guy I broadsided standing next to my door. My heart pulses in my throat. He pulls open the door, grabs me, and throws me from the car to the ground. I scream as I roll about three meters across the concrete. A bystander, a large man, rushes toward my assailant, plants his foot squarely in the guy's abdomen and punches him until he is motionless.

Yuki jumps from the car and rushes to me. She kneels and clasps my hand. "Are you all right?"

"My leg." My voice is choked from pain.

The man who defended me shouts to Yuki, "Call an ambulance," then dashes off to help David and Taka.

Yuki shouts back, "I already called 199."

I look around and see another person has joined the fray to help David and Taka. Now David and Taka, with the help of the two bystanders, are fighting three gang members. Yoshiyuki is still single-handedly battling with two guys.

With all my strength, I try to stand up—to no avail. A pain shoots through my leg like a bolt of electricity. "Ouch!" I cry. Soon I hear sirens screaming and see the flashing of bright lights.

A half dozen police cars, along with an ambulance, rush into the rest area.

Police scurry towards the fighting and quickly break up the brawls. Taka drops his bat and hurries to me.

He kneels beside me. "Are you okay? What happened?" He gently holds me in his arms.

"I hurt my leg." I see a stream of blood flowing from the corner of his eye. "I'm sorry, Taka-san," I say, squeezing his hand.

"It's all right," he whispers.

David walks to us, followed by a couple of police officers. Yoshiyuki is still talking to a police officer at the site of the clash.

"David, you are bleeding," says Yuki, rising to her feet. With her scarf she wipes blood from the corner of his mouth.

Everyone makes space, encircling me, as two paramedics arrive with a stretcher. The police start questioning Taka and Yuki.

One paramedic squats down beside me and asks, "Where do you feel pain?"

"My leg," I say, touching my leg lightly.

"Are you able to stretch your leg?" He tries to shift my leg but stops when I cry out in pain.

"All right," says the paramedic, signaling his young partner to help transfer me to the stretcher.

As I lay on the stretcher, the young paramedic asks Yuki, "Miss, are you a friend of hers? Can you come with us?"

"Yes," says Yuki, then she turns toward Taka.

Taka is talking to one of the officers but tells Yuki, "We need to go to the police station, but we'll meet you at the hospital as soon as they finish with us."

Yuki gives him a nod and turns back to me as the paramedics load me into the ambulance. The older paramedic sits down on the bench next to Yuki and places a blood pressure cuff on me. The driver talks with someone on the radio and the siren starts to scream as we leave the area.

"Now it's your turn to be in an ambulance," says Yuki. With tears on her face, she shakes her head in slow motion.

Recalling the accident that resulted in Yuki losing her baby, I say, "Don't worry. My injury isn't that serious." I give her a weak smile as I shift my leg a little. "Ouch!" I scream.

"Careful!" says Yuki, giving me a reassuring rub on the arm.

*   *   *

At the hospital, a nurse rolls me into the ER. While waiting for a doctor, the nurse records my medical history. As soon as the doctor enters the room, he does a quick exam of my leg and asks the nurse to take me to the X-ray room.

When I return to the ER, the physician is already looking at the images. He explains that I have a fractured left tibia.

"The broken ends of the bones are aligned, but to immobilize the limb, you'll need to wear a cast," he informs me.

"How long will my leg take to heal?"

"I would estimate four or five weeks with a cast, followed by a week or two with a plastic boot to complete the healing process."

The nurse pulls in a cart. On it are rolls of bandages, plaster, and a bowl of water. The doctor raises my leg to insert a large rolled towel under my thigh. He positions my leg, then applies the bandage and plaster, occasionally wetting his hands in the bowl to smooth the plaster.

After the doctor finishes the plaster cast, the nurse comes in and transfers me from the bed into a wheelchair.

I thank the doctor, and the nurse pushes me out of ER. Yuki rushes up as soon as she sees me and takes the wheelchair, thanking the nurse. Yuki and I wait for David, Taka, and Yoshiyuki in the dimly lit ER lobby.

"I hope the police finish their questioning soon." I sigh, putting my elbow on the cushioned armrest to rest my chin, and glance at Yuki on the bench in front of me.

"I hope so, too." Yuki nods, fingering her handbag's clasp. I see her worry is the same as mine. Surely David and Taka will be seen as rescuers and not instigators.

I hear the ER entry doors open, then the *squeak, squeak* of rubber-soled shoes on a clean waxed floor and the rapid wobbling of gurney wheels. Someone wrapped in a blanket disappears into an operating room.

"I hope that person will be okay," I say, looking at the ambulance parked in the driveway with strobe lights still flashing. Ambulance lights and siren sounds are getting too familiar.

"Me too," Yuki says.

The wall clock shows it's two-thirty a.m.

"Taka-san and David should have no problem with the police,

I think, but Yoshiyuki-san is another case," says Yuki. "He went with the gang willingly in the first place, so they may consider him one of them."

"I should let my aunt know about him." I realize I should have done this sooner, but the pain of my leg must have muddled my thinking.

"I agree. Call your aunt." Yuki hands me my purse.

I hesitate for a moment, then phone my aunt despite the early hour. Within two rings, Auntie answers.

"Naomi-chan, I'm in a taxi, heading to Enoshima," says Auntie in a hoarse voice. "The police contacted me and said Yoshiyuki is in custody. I heard from the police officer you were taken by ambulance to the hospital. Are you all right?"

"I'm fine, Auntie. Don't worry. I can't talk right now, but we'll talk more, later. I just wanted to let you know we are okay."

"I'm so sorry."

"Auntie, I'm okay. Yuki is with me," I say, doing my best to speak to her in a cheerful voice. "My friends are with Yoshiyuki at the police station. They will help him, so don't worry."

She sobs.

"Please don't cry. Talk to you soon. Bye now." I hang up.

*　*　*

At the crack of dawn, David, Taka, Yoshiyuki, and my aunt show up in the hospital lobby. My aunt rushes to the couch where Yuki and I are sitting. With tears in her eyes she takes my hand.

"Naomi-chan, I'm so sorry. It's my fault this happened. I shouldn't have gotten you involved." Auntie looks around and apologizes to my friends.

Glancing up at the people I care so much for, I say, "They risked their lives to help."

Yoshiyuki stands next to our aunt with his head hanging

down, crying quietly.

* * *

Auntie and Yoshiyuki return home by taxi and Taka drives David, Yuki, and me back to Tokyo. Undeterred by Taka's pleading that he should take care of me, I insist he take me home, thinking it's just a matter of a time before my auntie discloses the story of my broken leg to my mom. When Mom learns the news, she'll be at my apartment in no time.

Once in my apartment, everyone fusses about, trying to settle me in comfortably. I lie on the couch.

"You must be hungry. I'll fix something," says Taka, opening the refrigerator.

Before I can say, "No need," Taka is already grabbing apples and oranges from the fridge.

Yuki is making tea for everyone and David brings a pillow from my bedroom to put under my leg.

Hot tea, a plate of sliced apples and oranges, and the kindness of everyone strengthens my spirit.

"Are you going to be all right?" asks Taka, drawing his eyebrows together in worry.

"I'm fine. Thank you all and so sorry for the whole thing," I say.

After a short conversation, Taka carries me to my bed and tucks me in. "Call me anytime, okay?" He puts my cell phone next to the pillow and kisses my forehead.

A red streak at the corner of Taka's eyes looks fresh and tender. "I'm sorry," I murmur.

Yuki and David step into the room. "Get some sleep. We'll be back soon," says Yuki, and David says, "Sleep tight. Poor Naomi."

My heart is filled with thankfulness.

* * *

The doorbell keeps ringing. I try to answer the door; the knob turns but doesn't open. With all my strength, I shake the door, but it won't budge. My heartbeat quickens. I feel myself starting to panic, then my eyelids part. There's someone knocking at my apartment door. I roll over to swing off the bed. Stabbing pain shoots through my leg.

"Ouch!" I scream, and everything that happened comes flooding back.

I sigh, grab the crutches leaning on the bed, and hobble toward the entry. The doorbell keeps chiming. As I near the door, I hear Mom calling my name.

As I unlock the door, Mom carefully swings it open and steps inside. "Oh, my word!" she cries, wrinkling her eyebrows. "Are you all right?"

"Mom, Mom . . . I'm okay."

With wide eyes, she says, "Your aunt called us at six o'clock this morning. She tried to explain what had happened, but I didn't understand the whole story." Mom places a *jubako*—a special box of New Year's food—on the floor and reaches out to steady me as we move to the dining table. She pulls a chair out for me, then fetches the *jubako*. We settle across from each other.

"What happened?" asks Mom, her visage wrinkled with anxiety.

To avoid worrying her any further, I condense the story and minimize the drama, but Mom groans from time to time, and intermittently utters, "My goodness!"

At the end of my account, her eyes harden, and she shakes her head. "Your aunt shouldn't have asked for your help. I'm so sorry."

"It's all right. I'll get better soon."

She tightens her lips. I reach out to hold her hands.

After a few moments of silence, she unties a lavender cloth with a floral print, revealing a beautiful, lacquered food container.

She says in a tender voice, "Today is New Year's Day. Your dad is at home, waiting for your grandpa and grandma who are on their way from Chiba."

"Thank you, Mom. I'm sorry I caused you and Dad so much worry," I say, sad to miss the holiday with my family.

"You'd better call your Dad soon. He's worried about you."

"I'll call around noon. By that time, Grandpa and Grandma should be there."

She nods, letting her shoulders drop. With no further comment, she walks to the kitchen and puts a kettle of water on the gas stove. I sit quietly.

She comes back to the dining table carrying two plates and two chopsticks. "By the way," she says, "we canceled your *omiai*. Sorry, but we didn't know Mr. Ishida was so rude and arrogant."

"He was." I lower my eyes, thinking it's better not to mention Mr. Ishida's outrageous conduct.

While setting the table she says softly, "How long have you been dating?"

"Since last July," I respond. "Remember when Yuki and I went on the Kyoto trip?"

"Aha . . . that trip." She nods deeply.

"Yes, that trip."

The tea kettle whistles loudly and my mom hastens to the kitchen.

I flash back to the last five months that Taka and I were getting to know each other. The memory is a collage of dramatic events—Yuki's traffic accident, her engagement to David, my first night with Taka in Sapporo, and Yoshiyuki's involvement with the *Bosozoku*.

As Mom carries in a tray of tea, she continues talking, asking, "What does Taka-san do for a living?"

"He has a private tour guide business," I say, reaching for a cup of tea. "He has four employees."

"Is that right? Hmm . . ." Mom nods again and again as if stuck in her thoughts. Then her eyes rest on the lacquered, multi-tiered food box with a gold bamboo leaf design. "Well, shall we eat?" She lifts the lid of the *jubako*. The box is colorfully packed with all sorts of traditional New Year's foods: simmered minnows, steamed fish cakes, pan-fried rolled eggs, creamy sweet potatoes with candied chestnuts, herring roe, sweetened black soybeans, sliced yellowfin tuna, and even more of Mom's home-cooked cuisine.

I rest my chopsticks on the fried rolled eggs and look up at her.

"Don't worry. I saved some food at home for your dad and your grandparents, so enjoy," Mom says, picking up some lotus root.

"You're the best cook."

"I'm so thankful you weren't critically injured." She smiles weakly. "I have to apologize. I'm sorry my sister put you and your friends in such peril." She bows, and I see tears in her eyes.

"No, I'm the one who put my friends in danger." I give her a rueful smile but feel terrible that I've made my parents worry.

A small sob escapes from her throat. Her sadness hits me gravely. Taking a Kleenex from her handbag, she blows her nose. "Your auntie told me Taka-san is a refined person. I'd like to meet him one day."

"Yes, I'd like to introduce him to you." As I smile, big tears in the corners of my eyes flow down my cheeks.

"I also have to thank Yuki-san and her boyfriend," says my mom, handing me a tissue. "So, Yuki-san has a foreign boyfriend. I didn't know that."

"His name is David. A photographer. He's perfect for Yuki. He's smart, gentle, and whimsical."

My phone rings on the dining table and I reach for it and flip it open.

"It's Taka-san." I look at my mom and she returns the look.

Taka tells me he is worried about my leg and wants to come see me, but I explain my mom is here. His tone becomes serious. "Please give my regards to your mother. I'm sorry to have caused her worry. If I hadn't taken you and Yuki-san along with us, you wouldn't be injured."

"Please don't feel that way. I shared the whole story with my mom. She feels terrible and awkward about my aunt asking me for help."

My mom murmurs, "Naomi-chan, please say I'm so sorry to Taka-san."

"Yes, Mom."

Taka heard her, for he says, "Tell your mother not to feel bad about me. Take care and call anytime if you need help. Oh, Happy New Year! See you soon." His tender voice makes me want to see him right now.

We end our conversation, and I turn to see a smile float across my mom's face. She will like Taka, I'm sure.

*   *   *

On the third of January the sky is remarkably clear with almost no pollution, as most Japanese are still enjoying the New Year's holiday and aren't out driving. Taka's car cruises to Narita airport, unimpeded by traffic delays.

"I can't believe I've only been in Japan eighteen days. It feels like a lot longer," says David.

"You arrived last year," jokes Taka.

David laughs. "That's right, I arrived in Tokyo a week before Christmas."

The word "Christmas" triggers memories of the first night I spent with Taka in the Sapporo hotel—snow falling in the night sky, Kofu wine and crab cake, the steamy shower and making love. The vivid images of his firm body and soft eyes float in my mind. I can almost feel his touch and the warmth of his breath, but then in a flash, the sensual images and feelings are crowded out by a flashback to Mr. Ishida's behavior in my dining room. I look outside for a distraction.

"Yuki-san had a big surprise," says Taka, looking into the rearview mirror.

I turn my head towards the back seat. "I'm so happy for both of you. I can't wait until the day of your wedding."

David says, "I called my family and told them about my engagement to Yuki. My two older sisters are anxious to meet her." He teases Yuki, saying, "My dog, Sam, will also love to meet her. He likes pretty women." He smiles at her, then says to us, "We're planning to have our wedding in my hometown of New York—will you both be able to come? You guys are important to us."

"Of course, we'll come," replies Taka as if he and I are one.

When I repeat, "Of course," I meet David's sapphire gaze and it hits me that Yuki will be living in a foreign country, far away from me.

*　*　*

At the departure lobby at the airport, David smooches with Yuki. *How American!* Japanese don't kiss in public. Passengers glance at them.

Still holding Yuki tight, he looks at us and says, "Let's get together soon." His eyes are back on Yuki. "I'll call you as soon as I get home. I'll miss you."

"I'll miss you, too." Unshed tears rim Yuki's eyes.

He walks away from us, looking back over his shoulder every few steps. He soon blends into the crowd, but with his head still towering above the shorter Japanese passengers on their way through security, the three of us watch until he disappears from sight.

chapter fourteen

RESTRAINING ORDER

VACATION IS OVER AND IT'S the first day of work in the New Year.

As I limp to my desk, all eyes in the room turn to me. Kaori, Yoko, and Midori hurry to my side. "What happened to your leg?" the trio question in concert.

Avoiding a possible onslaught of questions about the *Bosozoku*, I say, "I slipped and fell. I'll be fine soon."

Midori takes my handbag from my shoulder and slings it over hers. Gripping my crutches, I totter to my desk, the three of them following.

Kaori pulls my chair out. "Just tell us whatever you need whenever you need help, all right?"

The moment I sit down I see Mr. Yamada striding toward my desk. *Dang!*

"Naomi-san, what happened to your leg?" he asks, meddlesome as always.

"I fell down."

"How?"

Here we go. "My heel got caught in a crack in the road and I lost my balance."

"Sorry to hear that," says Mr. Ishida, his eyes displaying more curiosity than sorrow.

My phone rings and the caller ID displays one of our branches. Reaching out for the phone handset, I glance at Mr. Yamada. With a nod he leaves.

*   *   *

Yuki enters the office thirty-minutes later than usual. She marches directly to Mr. Yamada's desk and hands him a white envelope. My hands hover over the keyboard as I study their faces. He reads her letter, poker-faced. I wonder if she's given him a resignation letter. I expect him to react with sadness, but he doesn't, and Yuki's jaw drops as Mr. Yamada speaks to her. *Why does she look shocked?* Their conversation continues for at least fifteen minutes.

During lunch, Yuki tells me Mr. Yamada is being promoted to manager at the London branch and will be relocating to England with his family this spring.

"Becoming an overseas manager is his dream," she says, staring at her lunch. Then she gives a resigned laugh. "I was ambitious, wasn't I? Mr. Yamada has extensive knowledge about banking and I wanted to learn from him with the hope of one day becoming an overseas' manager myself." She presses her lips into a thin line.

"Yuki, I may be pessimistic, but hardly any women hold senior jobs in Japanese companies. Our society is still not ready for women to be in high positions. At least you might have a chance to become a manager at an American bank in New York. They are more liberal, you know."

"Yeah, right. In any case, I'm so relieved to be out of the relationship with him," says Yuki. She closes her eyes as if trying to wipe the memories of their affair.

I deliberately change the conversation. "By the way, my aunt must have said some nice things about Taka-san to my mom. He spent quite a bit of time with my aunt at the police station," I say, putting down my chopsticks. "Taka-san is a likable person."

Her mouth full, Yuki nods.

"I think my mom no longer sees him as just another one of my male buddies. In fact, she said she wants to meet him." I break into a smile and swallow a spoonful of soup.

"Congrats, no more *omiai*," replies Yuki with a warm grin.

* * *

Sunday, January ninth, starts out to be a nasty day. The heavy rain is unceasing and by late afternoon fog rolls in. Looking through the window, I see the sky is still dark and gloomy. Taka is coming for dinner around six o'clock. I hope the rain dies down. Despite feeling a sense of heaviness, I start to prepare dinner.

When the beef is sliced, the vegetables are cut, and all the ingredients for stew ready for cooking, I realize rosemary and apples are missing. It is four o'clock. Grabbing my rain gear, I leave the apartment and hobble to the grocery store.

In the rain, even such a simple task as going to the store takes twice as much time and energy with crutches. I finally return home. Shifting my weight to the crunches, I climb the concrete stoop, huffing and puffing. The three steps to the front door utterly wear me out.

As my key slides into the door lock, a male voice calls out my name. *Oh, no,* I think, *Taka-san is here already?* I turn around. Shocked, I see Mr. Ishida standing there.

"What brings you here this time?" My tone is cold.

Dripping wet, carrying no umbrella, he walks toward me and asks, "What happened to your leg?"

"Stop! You have no business being here."

"I really want to help Yoshiyuki-san," says Mr. Ishida, staring at my cast.

"There is no need for your help. You said Yoshiyuki and you are friends, but you were just using him to get to me."

His eyes drop for a split second, but his apparent humiliation is short-lived, and he continues. "I know which group he belongs to and where to look for him. Let me help you."

"Too late. He's out of the group, so leave and never contact Yoshiyuki again."

He stares at me incredulously.

Reluctantly, I finally relent and say, "My friends helped me find him."

He advances toward me but stops short of the front steps when I hold up my hand. "Is he out of the *Bosozoku*?"

"Yes."

"How?"

"I'd rather not discuss it."

"Does your injured leg have anything to do with Yoshiyuki-san?"

"I don't want to talk with you any further."

He stares at me in bewilderment, as if mentally lost.

"Please leave," I say in a stern voice.

He continues to stand there, and I resort to the final straw. "If you don't leave right now I'll call the police."

As I am about to drop my umbrella to dig out my cell phone, he runs up the steps, pulls me toward him, and squeezes my arms so tight I cannot move. With only one useful leg I am even more incapacitated.

"Get your hands off me," I grunt.

He lets go long enough to force my chin upward with one hand. "Why do you hate me?"

"You are haughty, egoistic, and narcissistic." Just as I raise my voice, he fumbles with the key I left in the door. "My boyfriend will be here at any moment."

"Boyfriend?" His eyes widen, his grip loosens.

From the corner of my eye, I see my next-door neighbor, Tatsuko, coming from her apartment with a bag of garbage. "Tatsuko-san help! Please help!"

Tatsuko runs to us. Mr. Ishida drops his hands. In his unguarded moment, I push him with all my might. He stumbles and almost falls down the steps.

"Call 119, please!"

"Okay," cries Tatsuko, rushing back to her apartment at top speed.

With a perplexed stare, Mr. Ishida stands there as if in shock. He finally walks down the stairs and vanishes into the fog.

Tatsuko peeks out of her apartment. Seeing he's gone, she moves toward me and picks up my crutches. "Are you all right?"

I grab the crutches and rest my body on the arms. "Thank you very much, Tatsuko-san. If you hadn't come out, I don't know what would have happened. Thank you very much," I repeat. I give as sincere of a bow as is possible with crutches.

A police car arrives with no sirens, just strobe lights flashing. The car rolls to a stop in front of the apartment.

Two officers step out. One officer walks up to me and asks, "Did you call for help?"

"Yes, I did." As Tatsuko begins to explain what she observed, one of the policemen, with an air of authority, interrupts. "Who is the victim?"

"I am." I give them the details of what happened. Over the next few minutes, they place me on an emergency protective order and recommend I file a restraining order. They then leave.

Tatsuko asks, "Why don't you come to my apartment for a

while? I'll make some hot chocolate."

Hot chocolate sounds good now. I nod and follow her. Her apartment looks like an antique shop with years of accumulated things. She immediately brings me a towel and says, "Have a seat. I'll make hot chocolate." She hurries to the kitchen.

Sitting on her couch, I look at her bookcase stacked high with comic books. I think of Taka. I am totally baffled by the whole thing. *What happened to Taka-san?*

Tatsuko brings the hot chocolate in a mug printed with illustrations of sushi and fish. She drags a dining chair over and sits in front of me. "I've seen him before," says Tatsuko, waiving her hand in the air.

"Really," I say, anger flaring.

"I think it was a week ago. When I was at my mailbox, I saw a man getting out of a black SUV. He walked over to your apartment and knocked on the door for a few times. You weren't there."

A chill runs down my spine.

"He returned to his car and waited for thirty minutes or so." She nods to herself, slowly bringing her cup to her nose as she sniffs the hot chocolate. "You'd better be careful."

"Thank you so much for helping me." I bow politely.

"We are in the same position, you know. We are both single women."

"Indeed." I nod deeply.

After finishing my drink, I tell her I should go.

I cautiously return to my apartment and lock the door. I call Taka a few times, but it goes to straight to voicemail. *What's going on?* I lay down on the couch, repeating the same thoughts like a broken record. *What happened to Taka-san? He said he'd come to my place at six. Why doesn't he call?* Tears flow, as I cannot quiet my mind. Late in the night I finally doze off and don't wake until the sunlight comes through the living room window.

* * *

Morning arrives, and I leave for work with a heavy heart. I lumber into the office like a zombie. With puffy eyes, I turn on the computer and open my work queue. There are piles of transactions waiting. I hate Mondays.

Yuki comes to my desk and says, "You look like a deflated balloon."

"Umm . . . I didn't sleep last night. I had a horrible day yesterday. Mr. Ishida assaulted me in front of my apartment, but ironically, I was saved by my nosy neighbor. I won't complain about her anymore! She turned out to be kind and caring."

"What happened?"

Taking a deep breath, I begin. "Well . . . Taka-san was supposed to come around six o'clock for dinner. I rushed to the store to get some items I forgot. When I returned, and was just about to enter my apartment, someone called out my name. I turned to discover Mr. Ishida had gotten out of his car and was heading toward me. He . . ."

Yuki interrupts. "Why did he come to your place?"

"He claimed he wanted to give me Yoshiyuki's whereabouts and the name of the *Bosozoku* group that entrapped him."

Yuki snuffles.

"I know. It was just a trick to get to me," I say dryly. "Anyway, I told him Yoshiyuki was already out of the group. He looked shocked."

Yuki's eyes become narrow slits.

"We bickered for quite some time, then he suddenly dashed up the steps and grabbed me. He tried to open my apartment door. Luckily, my neighbor showed up and he left."

"Yes, you are lucky," says Yuki.

I nod. "I'm going to file a restraining order this afternoon. I'll ask our manager for time off to go to the court."

"Good idea." Yuki pats my arm.

"But you know. . ." I begin, then notice Kaori nearing my desk, so I pull out a file from my bookshelf and open up to the middle section to pretend we are working. I continue in a low voice. "Taka-san didn't show up and didn't even call. He said he would be at my house around six. You know . . . I didn't think about it until now, but I'm wondering if Taka-san may have shown up when Mr. Ishida and I were arguing."

"No, no." Yuki *shakes her* head and gives me a couple of pats on the shoulder. "If he'd been there, he would have rescued you."

"Well, it was almost five o'clock and it was already dark. You know how heavy the rain and fog were yesterday." I lower my eyes to recall the scene. Yuki leans over my desk. "We quarreled for . . . I don't know. . . maybe twenty minutes or even longer. In any case, no matter what I said, he would not leave, so I finally decided to call the police. I had barely gotten my phone from my bag when he grabbed me. Imagine," I add, feeling angry all over again, "I had only one good leg. The thing was, it was a dark and foggy, so if Taka-san was close by he probably couldn't have seen what was really happening. He might have gotten the wrong impression."

"That *is* possible." Yuki nods without batting an eye. "Did you call Taka-san?"

"I called his cell phone yesterday and his office this morning. Misa-san told me he wasn't in the office."

"Misa-san didn't tell you where he is?"

"No." I shake my head.

"Typical Misa-san."

"I'm really upset right now. I'm sick with worry that something may have happened to Taka-san, but then wonder if he somehow misinterpreted what he saw when Mr. Ishida was there. I feel like I'm stuck in a nightmare."

"I totally understand," says Yuki. "Let me know if there's anything I can do."

"Thank you, Yuki."

Yuki heads to her desk and I turn to my screen.

All day long intrusive thoughts of Taka and Mr. Ishida plague me.

*   *   *

Three days have passed since that frightening day. I am skipping dinners and losing weight, which I cannot afford, but I have no appetite. Green tea has been my buddy as it seems to calm me. I hobble to the kitchen to make more. Fumbling through the cupboards, I reach for the container of green tea. Staring at the bottom of the empty tin can, I wonder for the umpteenth time, *Where is Taka-san?* The phone rings and I startle. Maybe it's him!

I snatch my cell phone from the coffee table and see the screen. It's Yuki. "Hi," I say in a flat voice.

"Sorry I'm not Taka-san. By the way, I did call him a couple of times. No answer."

"You called him?" I ask, not knowing whether to thank her or feel like she is prying into my affairs.

"Yes. I even went to his house yesterday, but he wasn't there."

"You checked his house, too!" I gulp in disbelief.

"Maybe something is going on with him. I'll ask David."

"Yuki! I'd rather not involve David. After all, he's Taka-san's client."

"But I regard him as more than David's tour guide. I'm sure David does, too. Taka-san saved my relationship with David. He's our friend."

Grateful for her care, I say, "Yes, I do need your help."

"I'll let you know if I hear anything from David."

Our friendship is getting stronger . . . although sometimes she gets on my nerves.

*   *   *

The next day, during morning break, Yuki relays a message Taka sent to David. "He told David that he hadn't talked to you in four days and that something was bothering him that he couldn't yet articulate. He said he needed more time to digest things before making the next move. He told David to please bear with him, that he'd take care of his own problems. He also told him that he loves you very much."

Pain fills my heart. What is it that he needs time to digest? What's bothering him? He must have seen me with Mr. Ishida. The rest of the day is shot. My mind is on autopilot. I bury myself in my work.

Around four o'clock, a red-faced Mr. Yamada summons me to his desk.

"You sent a half-million dollars to the wrong country," he says. The anger in his voice is paralyzing.

I cover my mouth. A chill shoots through my body.

"Please go see the manager. Now!" Mr. Yamada's loud voice resounds throughout the office.

I limp to Mr. Suzuki's office. He is signing papers as I approach his desk. He pinches the rim of his spectacles, lowering them on his nose.

He looks askance at me. "Aha, Naomi-san . . . ahem.".

"Mr. Suzuki, I'm so sorry," I say, fighting back tears. My heart is racing, feeling like it's nearly ready to explode.

He takes off his glasses with one hand and looks into my eyes as if his stare can melt me. Mr. Suzuki says, "Luckily, we were able to correct your mistake this time. I understand sending the incorrect amount can happen, no matter how careful we are, but to also transfer funds to the wrong country is an even bigger mistake."

His stare is unnerving. Tears well up in my eyes, but I force myself not to cry.

"Is there anything we can do to prevent this from happening in the future?"

Mr. Suzuki pauses for my answer, but all I can say is, "I am so sorry."

"Please be careful in the future. That will be all." He dismisses me with a faint smile.

"Yes, sir," I say, giving him as deep a bow as I can manage.

I head back to my desk, feeling like a complete failure. Mr. Yamada glares at me and I deflate further.

I hit my broken leg on the corner of my desk as I sit. "Ouch!" I cover my face and cry. Yuki darts to my desk, rubs my shoulder, and asks if she can take some of my workload. I nod weakly. She grabs a pile of papers from my desk. My tears splash on the keyboard as I stare at the screen.

"How about I come to your house tonight?" Yuki suggests.

I nod "yes', and say, "Thank you."

* * *

Later, on the way to my apartment, we pick up some sandwiches at a bakery. To have a good companion accompanying me home comforts me, especially when I still need to depend on using crutches. She carries my handbag and soothes my emotional turmoil.

As we enter my apartment, I turn on the heat.

"Thanks for coming to my place. It's good to have you here. Have a seat," I say.

"I thought you could use some cheering up." Yuki draws a chair for me, then sits in front of me.

She has been so supportive since my world turned upside down.

I glance at her face, which seems to be even prettier than usual. People say women get prettier as their wedding day approaches. I guess they are right. I marvel at her flawless complexion.

"I understand making a mistake is painful, but our manager fixed it. Leave what happened behind you," Yuki says, "and in Taka-san's case, just trust him and be patient. He loves you a lot."

"Umm . . ." I rub my neck and don't respond to her comment, having no self-esteem. I change the subject. "Did you choose your wedding dress?"

"Not yet."

"Have you decided on a date?"

"Not yet."

Why do I make myself miserable? My face surely belies the fact that I don't want to hear about someone else's happiness. I feign a smile. Yuki cuts her answers short as if she doesn't want to brag about her good fortune.

Yuki keeps trying to soothe me. "Taka-san must have something going on."

"Maybe so, but why doesn't he call?" I start to sob.

Yuki steps around the table and puts her arm around my shoulder. "He'll call you soon. Give him some time."

"But I need him now," I cry.

"I understand." Yuki says. "Well, I'll make tea. Let's eat." She stands up and walks into the kitchen.

I get up on my crutches and follow her. "Sorry, there's no green tea," I say, and offer Lipton tea instead.

"Just sit down," says Yuki. "I'll serve the tea."

"Okay."

Feeling heaviness in my chest, I stare at the dining table. She returns with tea and tries hard to cheer me up, bringing up some celebrities' silly gossip. I laugh occasionally, and her solace is heartening. When she finally readies to leave, I let her know I'm grateful she made my evening lighter. Yet when I finally lie in bed, troubling thoughts batter my heart.

chapter fifteen

NEW FACES

MR. YAMADA WILL BE HERE another month before transferring to the London office, but his replacement, Mr. Saito, starts working today. Mr. Saito is a short man with thinning hair and rimless glasses. He greets everyone with squinty eyes and a twenty-tooth smile.

Mr. Saito's desk is temporarily placed next to Mr. Yamada's, meaning Mr. Yamada's attention will be on his replacement.

At 9:15 a.m. our manager, Mr. Suzuki, convenes a meeting of the international money-transfer department in the biggest conference room in the building. Twenty-four employees sit around the large oblong table, fidgeting in nervous anticipation. Mr. Suzuki, Mr. Yamada, Mr. Saito, and a new woman sit stiffly upright next to each other at a center table with a large flat TV screen behind them.

Mr. Suzuki introduces the new employees. "Mr. Saito is our new section chief, and Miss Kikuchi is Yuki-san's replacement."

He motions to Mr. Saito, who stands.

"My name is Saito Masao." He clasps his hands below his belt. "I'm from Tokyo. For the last fifteen years, I've been in the Osaka branch office. I'm married to a woman from Osaka and we have three children—three, five, and seven. I'm *really* happy to be back at the Tokyo office. Now my kids can spend more time with their other grandparents."

A few people chuckle when a little Osaka dialect slips into his speech. During his fifteen-year assignment in Osaka he must have picked up some of the Osakan dialect. Osakans are known to have a jolly nature and it is reflected in their language—less formal than the Tokyo dialect. With his congenial smile he squints until his eyes are barely visible. I immediately like him.

He continues. "In the Osaka branch, I did similar work to what you do here. But I'm new to this department and there'll be a lot to learn. Cooperation is the key to our success. I'm available at any time. Likewise, I ask for your support. I'm happy to become a member of your team." He finishes his speech with a deep bow and extends his hand toward Miss Kikuchi, indicating it's her turn to speak.

Miss Kikuchi stands tall, resting her crossed fingers on the conference table. Her fingernails are impeccably manicured— French with glittering red on the tips.

"My name is Kikuchi Aiko. Please call me Ai." She projects self-confidence. "I have seven years of experience in commercial banking. The scale of transactions is much larger here, so this will be a new challenge, but I'm excited about learning new things and happy to be in your group." She bows deeply.

Miss Ai's painted face is in stark contrast to her humble decorum. Her high cheekbones are blushed apple red, and her glossy lipstick matches the shade of red on her fingernails.

As she raises from the bow, a smile spreads over her face. "I live with a lazy two-year-old tabby cat. I sing and play the piano. On a whim, I write music. My other interest is visiting attractions in and around Tokyo and I would love to go with anyone who shares this interest."

Ai seems to have a colorful personality. Definitely, Mr. Saito and Ai will create a different work environment, hopefully a good one. I am elated Mr. Yamada is leaving, but sad Yuki will be gone. Nobody can replace her.

The meeting ends at ten o'clock and we leave the meeting room. Yuki is already chatting with Ai. I mingle with Kaori, Yoko, and Midori to walk back to our desks.

The message light on my phone is blinking. It's Taka. He says he's in Hokkaido and will be back in a week or so after wrapping up some personal business. I start speculating about what he's doing in Hokkaido. Is he alone?

Before tackling my busy day, I hurry to the breakroom. Yuki and Ai are sitting at the table, drinking coffee.

"Hi, Ai-san, I'm Naomi. Welcome to our team."

"Thank you, Naomi-san. This office is a lot better than where I used to work. Yuki-san just showed me the modern cafeteria. What a huge food selection. Lunch will be the highlight of my day," she says with bright eyes.

"Yes," I say, not mentioning that Yuki and I prefer the quietness of the breakroom to the cafeteria.

I pour coffee to the top of my mug from the machine, mix a few drops of cream, then leave Yuki and Ai, thinking I'd rather talk to Yuki about Taka in private.

With all her assigned work and her training of Ai, Yuki is overloaded. Even during the lunch break, Yuki is with Ai and has no time to discuss my personal matters. So, I call her around eight in the evening, but my call goes directly to her voicemail. A few minutes later she calls me back.

"Sorry, I was talking to David," says Yuki in a merry voice.

"How is he?" I pull my legs up on the couch and recline against the back cushion.

"Fine. I need to go to New York soon to plan our wedding," says Yuki. "Can I ask you to train Ai-san while I'm gone? I'm leaving this Friday."

"Me?" My back straightens.

"I know I'm asking a lot of you, but I want to use all my vacation days before I leave the company."

"Uh-huh, I'm willing, but . . . I don't know what Mr. Yamada will think in light of my big blunder."

"I'll ask the new section chief tomorrow morning."

"Okay, I will do it."

"Thanks a lot, Naomi."

"You're welcome. Oh! Taka-san called this morning while we were in the meeting."

"He did?"

"He's still in Hokkaido. He said he has some personal business to take care of."

"Umm . . ." Yuki draws a long breath but doesn't ask any questions.

"He'll be back in a week or so," I say, and swallow nervously.

"Don't worry. He truly loves you," says Yuki, as if she knows what is worrying me.

For more than an hour Yuki quietly listens to my unsettled feelings about Taka's disappearance. In the midst of our conversation I'm overcome with sadness when I think of Yuki leaving. I already miss her. No longer will I have a close friend with whom I can share my dreams, hopes, and heartaches. Tears fill my eyes as she responds to my story with all the loyalty and color that I have come to love.

* * *

A few days have passed since I took over Yuki's duties of training Ai.

The new section chief, Mr. Saito, comes to my desk. "Thank you for covering Yuki-san's tasks in her absence. You're doing a great job."

"My pleasure," I say. I mean it, too. Mr. Saito and Ai are both as nice as I hoped they would be.

"If you need my help, let me know," says Mr. Saito.

"Yes. Thank you very much."

Today feels like a day in the sun. My new section chief actually noticed and praised my hard work. Everyone seems happy to have Mr. Saito here; the mood has already changed—visible in everyone's relaxed and smiling faces. I spot Yoko drinking tea and snacking on sweets while typing. Kaori asks for help from Midori more freely. I, too, frequent the breakroom more often for coffee.

Ai and I work together all day. Although chatty, she gives her full attention when listening and notes everything I tell her.

"It's already lunch time," I say.

Immediately, Ai locks her computer. "I'm ready."

The cafeteria is chaos with hundreds of employees moving around, chatting, and dining. The noise echoes through the lunch hall. A long line has already formed at the buffet. Trays in hand, we chat while shuffling along the lengthy food counter with its mix of Asian and Western foods. The room is packed with tables. Ai and I try, to no avail, to spot Kaori, Yoko, and Midori, in the sea of matching uniforms. We finally resign ourselves to an empty table in the corner.

Ai is a self-assured conversationalist with an odd combination of humble decorum and blunt speech.

Ai says, "If one enters a wrong country code, especially for an undeveloped country, it'd be difficult to retrieve the money. Don't you think so? I hope I never make such a careless mistake."

Taken aback, I hide my surprise. "I actually did that. Sent a half-million dollars to the wrong country."

Ai gasps.

I tell her, "You've got to always be extra careful."

"Yes," says Ai, wide-eyed.

Ai quickly changes the subject. "I'm looking for an apartment near work. Do you have any recommendations?"

The sudden subject change eases the tension over her comment. "The Kanda area is close to work and not too expensive."

"Is that so? I'll check it out. Thank you." With a deep nod, Ai sips at her green tea, clutching the cup with both hands and staring at the cup as if she can stare holes into. Clearly, she's afraid she's insulted me.

After sipping her last drop of tea, Ai resumes our conversation. This time she only sticks to herself as the subject. I listen quietly. She is five years older than me and seems to be wise to the world. Before getting into the banking industry, she had several jobs, which included work in a travel agency, a dental office, and an insurance company. A few nights a week she sings and plays piano at a nightclub. She seems like such a multi-talented lady. I want to listen more, but it's time to get back to work.

* * *

Working with Ai is enjoyable, and I lose track of time. I notice it is almost time to go home. Kaori, Yoko, and Midori flock to Ai's desk.

Raising her eyebrows theatrically, Kaori asks, "How's Naomi treating you, Ai-san?"

"Watch out, she'll burn you out with work." Yoko playfully pushes at my arm while I am holding Ai's mouse, causing the cursor to go off the screen.

Midori says, "Naomi is a good teacher. She is the one who trained me."

"Thanks, Midori," I say, making sure Ai and I have covered all the tasks before logging off the computer.

"Indeed, she is a good teacher," says Ai with respect.

My phone rings and I scoot from Ai's desk to mine.

"Industrial Bank of . . ." I start.

"It's me. Taka."

"Taka-san!" My heart races.

"I'm at the Haneda Airport," says Taka. "Can we meet tonight?"

"Yes, of course!" I swallow hard.

"I'll come to your place. In an hour or so?"

"Okay. I'll be home," I say in a sweet voice, but I'm uneasy about his serious tone.

"See you soon." He hangs up.

I stare into the air, troubled by the weighty tone of his voice, but I'm uplifted by the thought that he's on the way to my apartment. I hurriedly clean off my desk and leave the office.

I limp as hastily as possible with my crutch, heading toward the station to take the train home. The rush hour train is packed like sardines. I hate this time of day. Someone always manages to hit my injured leg. I cannot move, so I stand like a pole, trying not to lean against anyone.

At my stop, I step off the train. Despite all the stairs, I hobble along quite well with crutches. Beads of sweat form on my face as I scurry home, rushing to Taka.

chapter sixteen

BISTRO

Once at home, I hurry to take a half-empty coffee mug to the kitchen, straighten the fashion magazines scattered on the dining table, and sweep the floor before running to the bathroom to wash the sweat from my face and put on some makeup. The doorbell rings just as I'm applying lip gloss. With a surge of nervousness, I open the door.

A stony-faced Taka stands at the door.

"Hi, Taka-san, good to see you. Please come in," I say.

While taking off his shoes, he says, "I see you are walking without crutches."

"I still must use crutches outside the home," I say, trying to read the emotions in his face.

"It's good that it's healing." He gives me a weak grin.

As I turn around, he takes my hand, assists me in walking to the dining table and helps me sit down. He then takes a seat across from me.

He looks straight into my eyes. "We need to talk."

I lean forward and anchor my hands in my lap, wondering if Taka still loves me.

With an unfathomable gaze, he begins. "On the day you invited me for dinner, I left home early to allow for the usual Sunday congestion in the Shinjuku area. It turned out that the traffic wasn't bad at all and I arrived at your apartment a lot earlier than intended." His gaze penetrates mine.

He saw me with Mr. Ishida. I take a deep breath and brace myself.

"You were with a man. I watched for a while. At first, I sensed you guys were just having a serious talk, but when you started kissing, I was hurt."

"We *didn't* kiss." I raise my voice.

He looks at me as if saying "let me finish my story." I shut my mouth, biting at the inner side of my lower lip.

"It was already dark, and it was foggy and rainy. I couldn't see you well from where I was standing, but when he jumped up the stairs and held you tight, I thought you guys were kissing. At that moment rage overtook me as I recalled Misa-san telling me some time back . . ."

"Misa-san remembered me!" I mutter.

"Yeah, she saw you with a man at Izu Ocean Park, I think she said it was about six months ago, but I didn't believe her. As you know, Misa-san tends to fabricate stories for her own good. Seems like she was telling the truth this time, I thought, but your . . ."

"No! It's not what you think!" I raise my voice, shaking my head. "I was assaulted by my previous *omiai* . . ."

"It's all right." Taka gently holds my hands. "I'm sorry he was such a beast."

My tensed shoulders drop, but I wonder how he knows Mr. Ishida is such a bad guy. I frown.

"Yuki told me the whole story."

"You talked to her?"

"She sent me an email, saying 'it's urgent.' So, I called her, and she explained what happened that day between you and Mr. Ishida."

Baffled, I ask, "Why would she email you?"

"When Yuki heard from David that I wanted some time alone, she concluded I was there at your apartment and got the wrong impression."

My jaw drops. She didn't tell me about this.

"Yuki told me you assumed I was there that evening. Right?"

I blink a yes.

Dolefully he continues. "I'm sorry I didn't help you. I'm glad you were okay, and it was smart of you to file a restraining order against him. I'm proud of you."

I let out a breath. "I'm sorry I didn't tell you about Mr. Ishida." I nod, then softly I ask, "Then why did you still need to stay in Hokkaido?" The moment I ask this, I remember our trip to the orphanage.

He gazes into the distance and takes a deep breath. "I'm sorry I ran away from you. After I talked to Yuki-san, I thought about giving you a call, but I realized I wasn't ready."

Taka stares off into space again, then turns to me. "When I saw the guy holding you tight, I felt betrayed. I thought you were intentionally misleading me, making me feel like you cared for me, while all along you had a boyfriend. Seeing you two together transported me to when I was five years old."

I look into his eyes, wondering what he's talking about.

"Remember how I said my parents were killed in a plane crash? Well, that was just what was claimed on the written report kept at the orphanage."

"What?"

"My parents didn't actually die in a plane crash. That was a fabricated story," says Taka.

"Eh?"

"I was abandoned by my mother. My dad died when I was a baby, according to her. In truth, she found a lover whom she cared for more than me."

"I'm so sorry." Tears well up in my eyes.

"I still remember the day she left." His bottom lip quivers. "I was five, too young to understand, but I remember her coming to my kindergarten with a man. She told me a relative would pick me up that afternoon and that I should be a good boy and listen to him. She hugged me, then the man put his arm around her waist and pulled her away from me."

I cover my mouth in shock.

He nods, looking into my eyes. "The man had his arm around my mother's waist, much the same way your *omiai* partner held you."

I feel as if a dagger has pierced my chest.

"Without even a goodbye, my mom walked out of my life. I cried for months."

Tears run down my cheeks. Taka stands up, walks around the table and pulls a chair up to sit next to me. He puts his arm around my shoulder then slowly continues.

"When I saw you and the guy, unbearable feelings flooded my mind. I realized I have a strong fear of losing loved ones."

I look up and see his eyes are closed tight.

"I thought finding my mother could help resolve things."

I can only nod.

"That's why I flew to Hokkaido to visit the relative who took me to the orphanage. I believed he'd know my mother's whereabouts. Since I didn't know his name, I went back to his house near the old apartment where my mother and I used to live, hoping he'd still be there." Taka's eyes are fixed on the table for a second. "He was still there. He gave me her address. She works in an old bistro in a small fishing village."

His voice quivers again. "I found her. She didn't recognize me, but I saw her wrinkled face, prematurely aged, and heard her raspy voice. I felt a lump in my throat. She must have had a rough life. My anger dissipated. I pitied her. I didn't tell her who I was and just made small talk with her. Then I asked her, 'Do you have children?'"

My eyes widen as I ask, "Did she say yes?"

"She told me, 'My boy died.'" Taka's smile is bitter. He then adds, "She looked into my eyes for a long time, not saying a word. Then her eyes filled with tears."

"Did you tell her you are her son?"

"No. There was no need to," says Taka with downcast eyes.

"I'm sorry." My head droops with this jolt of sadness.

"It's all right. I'm okay." His dimpled smile returns, and I grin with relief, hoping our relationship is restored. For a while, we look at each other as if trying to assess our feelings. He cups my face in his hands, and softly places his lips on mine. His gentle touch reminds me of our first night together. He runs his fingers through my hair. We lose ourselves in a long kiss.

When we break the kiss, I look into his eyes and see deep love.

"Taka-san, I'm sorry I didn't tell you about the *omiai*."

He nods slowly.

"Thank you for telling me what happened in Hokkaido."

"I'm just glad we are back together," says Taka, with a smile.

"Can you stay for dinner?"

"I would like to but need to stop by my office. Having been gone so long, I have some urgent business to address." Stroking my cheek with the back of his fingers, he says, "You'll be okay alone? Lock the door immediately after I leave. All right?"

"Mr. Ishida shouldn't bother me because of the restraining

order, but I'll be careful."

"Good."

Taka stands, helps me up from my chair and we go to the door. Taka kisses me one more time before he leaves.

* * *

Today and yesterday are as different as night and day. I let the early morning breeze into the apartment while eating breakfast and catch up on the news. My wall of worries has vanished. I can feel spring in the air.

I arrive at the office earlier than usual.

"Good morning," says Ai gaily when I approach my desk.

Her computer is already on, my chair sits next to hers, and the manuals are open to the page we left yesterday. *Wow*, I think. *It's not even nine o'clock yet. Ai-san doesn't waste any time.*

"Good morning, Naomi-san and Ai-san," Mr. Saito says, approaching us with his friendly squinted-eyed smile. "Already getting started? Capital! Keep up the good work."

We check our queues. There are lots of accounts to be processed. As we prepare to tackle the work, Ai stares at me.

Tilting her head sideways, Ai asks, "Naomi-san, did you have a nice evening last night? You look notably happy today."

"Is that so?"

Ai wiggles her eyebrows in a funny way. I let loose a chuckle. "Yes, I did have a nice evening."

Ai continues looking at me expectantly, as if waiting for a juicy story, but I think it is too personal to talk about my recovered relationship with Taka. "It's already ten minutes past nine. Shall we start to work?"

"Uh, yes," Ai slowly turns to the computer screen and grips the mouse.

Trying to maintain a serious face, I start training Ai but feel distracted by happy thoughts of Taka.

* * *

Yuki is back at work, bringing souvenirs from New York. Boxes of truffles from one of New York City's top chocolate shops go to Mr. Suzuki, Mr. Yamada, and Mr. Saito. Yuki tells Kaori, Yoko, Midori, Ai and me that she would like to give us a gift during our break.

At ten-thirty on the nose we gather at the breakroom. Yuki unwraps a thin square box. Inside, small chocolate balls, covered with ground nuts and cocoa powder, set in the niches of the lattice box. We fill our mugs with coffee and surround the table.

Ai pops one in her mouth. "Oh my! This is insanely rich."

"Americans use a lot of sugar in their sweets, don't they?" Yuki comments, then she peeks into a small duty-free bag. She picks out keychains with "I Love New York" written in bold letters and spreads them out on the table. "I have two colors: red and pink. Pick one you like."

While we are choosing a keychain, Yuki begins to show us pictures she took.

"Her fiancé's eyes look like blue marbles. Pretty," says Yoko.

We all nod. Yuki shrugs with a self-satisfied air, then forwards to the next picture.

"The Statue of Liberty is holding something? Is that a bible?" asks Midori.

"Maybe a bible, I don't know. The cruise guide said something, but I couldn't hear her well."

"You guys were too busy flirting with each other, weren't you?" says Yoko, twirling Yuki's souvenir keychain.

Yuki playfully slaps Yoko's shoulder, then clicks to the next picture.

"Hahaha . . ." Kaori bursts out laughing, pointing to an adorable dog with a biscuit in its mouth and a red bandana around his neck.

"Cute, isn't he? That's David's baby, a Jack Russell terrier named Sam. David spoils him." Yuki laughs as if recalling her fond memories with the dog. Next comes David's picture with his family. We all take a close look and Yuki explains who's who. Yuki and David are in the center, flanked by his parents, his two older sisters, and their spouses. Yuki already looks like she is part of his family.

When lunch time comes, I politely decline Ai's offer to go to the cafeteria. Yuki and I want to eat in the breakroom, so we can catch up on the week's happenings.

As we enter the breakroom, Yuki says, "You look happy."

"I *am* happy. Taka-san and I are back together! Taka-san told me all about your efforts to salvage our relationship. What a trick you played, sending him an 'urgent' email."

One of Yuki's trademark nose-wrinkling smiles appears. "If I hadn't done that, I wouldn't have been able to talk to him."

Putting down my chopsticks, I say with a bow of my head, "Thank you, Yuki."

"That's what a friend is for," says Yuki.

"You are truly my best friend," I say. We nibble at our food for a bit before I say, "So, Yuki, have you decided on a place for your wedding?"

"No, not quite yet." Her smile is so big.

"Are you still planning on April for the wedding?"

"I'm hoping that'll happen. That was our original plan," says Yuki, as if to imply her wedding plans aren't under her control.

I am puzzled. Why doesn't she know more about her own wedding plans?

chapter seventeen

FAREWELL PARTY

TODAY IS OUR DAY TO SAY farewell to Yuki and Mr. Yamada. I glance at Yuki's desk, which is surrounded with pink, white, and yellow balloons. A dozen red roses fill a vase. From Mr. Yamada's desk float two balloons, one white and one blue. Kaori, Yoko, Midori, and Ai stand around Yuki.

"Pretty roses!" I say, sniffing the bouquet.

Yuki grins. "From David."

"Isn't that romantic, to receive a dozen roses?" Kaori's hands cup her cheeks.

Yoko, Midori, and Ai nod and sigh.

Mr. Saito steps over to us. "Tonight, we're having a farewell party at a karaoke bar. I hope to hear you guys sing." He pats Yuki's shoulder. "We're going to miss you."

*   *   *

By seven o'clock, twenty-four team members have gathered at the karaoke bar. On stage stand a digital piano and a large flat-screen TV hanging on the back wall. Everyone seats themselves on sofas spread around the room. The celebrants, Mr. Yamada and Yuki, are seated together. Mr. Yamada's head is turned toward Yuki, but she stares off in the other direction. He looks unsettled and dejected.

Waitresses bring drinks to everyone.

Our manager, Mr. Suzuki, rises from his seat. "Hi all." He clinks his fork against his beer glass.

Everyone becomes quiet and turns to Mr. Suzuki.

"I'd like to extend a big thank you to Mr. Yamada and Yuki-san for all the hard work they've done during their time here. Please, everyone, stand and let's toast to their future!"

"*Kanpai!*" we all shout.

Kaori, Yoko, and Midori, bombard Yuki and Mr. Yamada with questions.

"Mr. Yamada, are you planning to get a car in London?" asks Midori.

"I'll use the subway. Public transportation is pretty good in London."

Kaori asks, "Yuki, are you going to have children soon?"

Yuki taps the table and giggles but makes no comment.

Mr. Saito interrupts the questions. "I heard some of you'll be singing karaoke tonight. Please let's start! Ai-san, how about you first?"

Without hesitation, Ai prances to the stage, sits at the digital piano, and adjusts the mic stand. She sings one of her own songs as she plays the piano:

> *I work for life to get better.*
> *I seek for life to be wonderful.*
> *But life takes its own turns.*
> *I still believe it's worth trying.*

* * *

Ai's voice is pure and vibrant. Everyone is quiet and mesmerized by her performance except Mr. Yamada, whose attention is on Yuki.

Mr. Suzuki rises from his seat, clapping hard. "Thank you very much, Ai-san. You're quite the singer, songwriter, and piano player." He waits for the applause to stop. "Who'll be next?"

Kaori says, "I'll sing."

Mr. Suzuki says, "Ai-san didn't need the Karaoke box, but who'll be in charge of the Karaoke control pad for selecting the songs you guys want?" "I will," Ai volunteers.

"Thank you, Ai-san. Well then, Kaori-san, what's your song?" asks, Mr. Suzuki.

"I'll sing *Onna Minato Machi* by Yashiro Aki."

She starts to sing the Japanese *enka, a* sentimental ballad, with a rich timbre. Her eyes catch the attention of each one of us for a brief moment as she sings with deep emotion; her hands and her body sway to the music, telling the story of the song. Whether she is good or not is hard to judge, but her performance is entertaining nonetheless.

"How about going next, Naomi-san? Naomi-san and I are going to sing a duet," says Mr. Saito, beckoning me.

A sharp clap of hands from my co-workers encourages me to stand. My heart beats fast. The duet idea is Mr. Saito's, as I didn't have the courage to sing alone, even though I love singing. Ai gave me some coaching, and Mr. Saito and I practiced separately. One time during an office break, Mr. Saito and I discussed the choreography of hand movements for the song.

Mr. Saito says, "Our song is '*Stop! In the Name of Love.*'"

Raising our hands in the obvious gesture, we begin singing, "Stop! In the name of love, before you break my heart . . ."

Immediately we command the attention of everyone in the room, even Mr. Yamada, which is a visible relief to Yuki. Mr. Saito's voice, although a bit husky, is quite charming. His hands and hips move rhythmically as he imitates a pop singer. As for me, intent on trying to stay in tune, I am totally out of sync with the body movements. As I raise my hand for the last *Stop!* of the song and as the music fades, I am elated the audience is applauding so loud. I think this is more about how much everyone likes our new boss instead of the song, but I bow in acceptance.

The party ends around nine. Mr. Yamada and Yuki stand near the door to bid everyone a final goodbye. I walk up to them.

"Thank you, Naomi-san, for putting up with me," says Mr. Yamada, giving a warm handshake. He looks as if he is about to cry.

Caught off guard by his uncharacteristic sensibility, I politely say, "I hope you and your family enjoy living in London."

chapter eighteen

FATHER'S BIRTHDAY

Taka invites me to his father's 60th birthday party on the first Sunday of March. This will be my first time meeting his adoptive parents.

The night before the party, I prepare for what I will wear to the event. While shuffling numerous times between mirror and closet for the right outfit, Misa comes to mind. Of course, she will be at the party.

Collecting myself, I try on a bouquet-print dress, but take it off, thinking it has too many colors and is too busy. With a pink silk blouse on, I search the closet for a better match but find nothing satisfying—everything seems either too dull or too bright. After much anguish, I finally grab a white cashmere sweater and a flared navy-blue skirt.

The next morning, I give myself a lot of time to prepare for the party. After a shower, I carefully put on natural looking makeup and slip on the sweater and skirt. For shoes, I settle on an odd combination of walking brace and a flat dress shoe, grateful that I no longer need to use crutches. Before leaving home, I ease the gift I made for Taka's father into my bag and check myself one more time in the mirror.

Taka's parents live in Setagaya, an upper middle-class neighborhood with many modern houses. His parents' house is an elegant two-story Asian-Western structure with a low-pitched roof. The iron gate is open. I walk up to the front door and hear the incessant bark of a dog. Just as I'm about to knock, the door opens, and Taka appears.

"Thank you for coming," says Taka. Behind him, a Yorkshire terrier is bouncing hysterically up and down as if on a pogo stick.

"Thank you for inviting me," I say, worrying that the dog may jump on my injured leg.

Pointing at the dog, Taka says firmly, "Sit! Be quiet." The dog gives a small whimper and sits back on his haunches, tail wagging.

Guests' shoes form a neat line at the entryway. With a rip of the Velcro, I slip off my brace and put it, along with my shoe, in a less conspicuous spot near the far corner, then slide into the pair of slippers setting there for guests. Taka takes my hand and I step inside. The little pooch follows us in silence.

A slender middle-aged lady sticks her head out from the kitchen *noren* curtain, a traditional Japanese fabric divider, as Taka leads me down the hall.

Coming out of the kitchen, the woman says, "Naomi-san, I am Taka's mother. Finally, I get to meet you! Taka talks of you often. He is right. You are so pretty."

"How do you do, Mrs. Taniguchi?" I say and bow politely. So, this is Taka-san's adoptive mother. She certainly has an angelic face and sweet demeanor . . . I can see now where Taka-san gets his warmness.

"I'm so glad you are here today. I'd like to talk to you more, but

I need to prepare the food. Can you stay a bit after our other guests leave?"

I glance at Taka and say, "Yes, of course."

"Good." With a slight bow, she hurries back to the kitchen.

Taka takes me to a roomy living room with a slew of recessed lighting and large windows. "Wow," I utter. Furnished with classy Victoria-style sofas, chairs, and adorned with built-in, tall walnut cabinets, the decor is first class. A large oil painting highlights the ivory-white color of the largest wall.

More than twenty people are conversing in small groups. I glance around and see Misa speaking to an elderly man nearby the picture window. I wonder if he is Taka-san's father. Taka leads me toward them. Trying not to show an awkward gait, I put full weight on my injured leg—but with the strain I feel jerky and uncertain.

"Hi, Misa-san!" I say cheerfully, although I feel awkward since I know she told Taka I was dating Mr. Ishida.

"Naomi-san, glad to see you." Misa touches my arm in a friendly manner.

"So, you're Naomi-san," says the elderly man, giving me a warm smile. "I'm Taka's father."

"Nice to meet you, Mr. Taniguchi," I say, feeling tightness in the throat in the presence of this dignified, tall, solidly-built man.

"Taka tells me you two met in Kyoto. You didn't come with your friend, Yuki-san?" Taka's father stoops to my eye level.

"No, she wanted to come but couldn't cancel her appointment. Lately she's loaded down with work as she is moving to the U.S. to live with David."

"That's right, Taka mentioned her engagement with David. Thanks to David's tour guide request, the best part of that trip was Taka got to meet such a lovely lady," his father says. Despite Mr. Taniguchi's dignified appearance, he is soft-spoken and seems caring. I feel embarrassed, him knowing so much about me, whereas my parents know little about Taka.

While being introduced to Taka's father, I notice Misa's appearance is quite plain compared to how she usually looks. Perhaps because she is with her father? Her hairstyle is a braided updo; her outfit is a high-necked black sweater and Scottish pleated skirt. And she is smiling at me. *Why is she so friendly today?*

As his father asks how long I have worked at the bank, the doorbell echoes into the spacious room, and Misa sprints to answer it.

"Six years," I answer Mr. Taniguchi.

"You must be extra busy since Yuki-san is leaving."

"She left the company," I say, "but her replacement is already working . . ." As I turn to the door to see who has arrived, I see Mr. Ishida hovering at the threshold.

My heart stops. Mr. Ishida gives me a feeble smile, but I don't return it. He lowers his head. I turn to face Taka to see if he recognizes Mr. Ishida. Taka stares back at me as if to ask, *Why are you are looking at me like that?*

Withdrawing my attention from Mr. Ishida, I turn to Mr. Taniguchi and meet his bewildered gaze. I quash my emotions and continue, "Yes, it'll be busy for a while."

"Are you all right, Naomi-san?" asks Mr. Taniguchi, frowning.

"I'm okay, just . . ." I fake a cough. "May I use your bathroom?"

"There is one at the end of the corridor."

"Thank you." I walk away, trying to hide my anger.

Gazing at my face in the bathroom mirror, I ponder whether I should leave now. No . . . I don't want to ruin Taka-san's father's birthday. Not a single alternative comes to mind. I tell myself to act normal, and trudge back to the living room. Taka's eyes are on me as I enter the living room. Misa and Mr. Ishida are now mingling with Mr. Taniguchi and Taka. My stomach in a knot, I resolutely shuffle toward them.

Misa says to her father, "Mr. Ishida is also a friend of Naomi-san's." I notice she is holding Mr. Ishida's hand.

"Is that so?" says Mr. Taniguchi.

I feel my face flush as I worry if Mr. Taniguchi may wonder how Misa and I came to have a common male friend. What can I say if Mr. Taniguchi asks how Mr. Ishida and I met? Am I supposed to answer he was an *omiai* partner for just a few dates. I also fear Taka will now discover this is the man who accosted me that Sunday.

As I force a smile, Taka's hand reaches my waist and he says, "Excuse us. Naomi-san, I've something I'd like to show you."

The instant we are out of the living room, he says, "Is that the guy I saw in front of your apartment? The one who assaulted you?"

I swallow hard.

"Unbelievable. He's shameless! He shouldn't be here," he says, his eyes full of fire.

"Please calm down. I really don't want to ruin your father's birthday."

"I understand, but he's breaking the law."

"I'm safe here. Please act normal, at least while we're in your parents' home."

With his hands clenched in fists, he takes a deep breath. "All right. I'll try my best."

Taka and I return and stand in the corner of the living room. Misa is still holding Mr. Ishida's hand and she starts to approach us. "Please don't try to tag along with us!" I say under my breath with my eyes closed. As my eyes open, they are before us.

"How's your leg, Naomi-san?" asks Misa with a concerned look.

"It's getting better," I say as calmly as I can.

"Mr. Ishida," Taka says in a cold voice. I squeeze Taka's hand, but he pulls it away and continues, "How long have you been dating Misa-san?"

"Umm . . ." Mr. Ishida flinches.

Misa says, "We met at the Izu Ocean Park. He and I . . ."

Mr. Ishida chimes in. "The first time I saw Misa-san was when I took Naomi-san to show her where I dive at Izu Ocean Park. It was our second *omiai* date. Misa-san was there to pick up a scuba tank. I admit I found Misa-san striking and couldn't take my eyes off her." He lowers his head again as if in shame. Slowly raising his head, with a remorseful look in his eyes, he continues. "I saw her again about a month ago at Izu Ocean Park. Misa-san remembered having seen me. We had a nice conversation and I invited her to dinner. That's how our relationship began. My *omiai* with Naomi-san was . . ."

I glare at Mr. Ishida.

"You're *not* supposed to be here," says Taka with a stern look, his voice low, to avoid creating a scene.

"I totally understand. I told Misa-san about my restraining order," responds Mr. Ishida, casting an uncharacteristically sheepish eye at me. "Actually, I'm here to apologize to Naomi-san. My father was outraged over my wrongdoing and almost disowned me. Naomi-san, I'm so sorry about my revolting conduct," says Mr. Ishida in a quiet, steady voice, then lowers his head as if ashamed.

"Please forgive him for my sake," Misa pleads. "It's I who insisted that he come. He didn't want to."

It is strange to hear Misa, who is normally condescending and arrogant, pleading for forgiveness on behalf of someone else. It is hard to switch my mind from indignant to peaceful. There is a long silence before I can say anything.

"Well . . . frankly, I won't forget what happened." I bite my inner bottom lip.

"I absolutely understand. I am so sorry, Naomi-san," says Mr. Ishida, as he gives a deep, prolonged bow.

No one says anything, but Misa's eyes plead for mercy.

With a hesitant breath, I add, "I cannot forget, but . . . I'll forgive you."

"Thank you," says Mr. Ishida in a gentle voice. "I appreciate your kindheartedness." "Thank you, Naomi-san," Misa says, adding her appreciation. She gives me a bow from the waist.

Misa is coming across as warm and ingratiating—something I haven't seen before.

Misa and Mr. Ishida must be in love with each other. They want to smooth the waters for the sake of their relationship and desire my forgiveness. Although I feel dishonored by Mr. Ishida, I'm relieved there will no longer be threats to me. Finally, after all the turmoil, it seems like a fresh page. I can move on with my life.

Mrs. Taniguchi joins us. She seems surprised to meet Misa's friend, but soon breaks into a pretty smile.

"Mr. Ishida, this is Sakura-san, my step-mother," says Misa, extending the palm of her hand to Mrs. Taniguchi then elegantly pivoting her arm toward Mr. Ishida, "this is my friend, Mr. Ishida Norio."

Mr. Ishida puts his feet together and tugs at the hem of his ribbed fisherman sweater. "How do you do, Mrs. Taniguchi." He then slowly bends at the waist. A small paper bag on his arm swings down and almost touches the floor.

Mrs. Taniguchi's eyes follow the falling object for a moment. "It's nice to meet you. Thank you for coming to my husband's birthday party." She bows politely.

"I brought a small gift," says Mr. Ishida in a barely audible voice as he presents the bag to her.

"You didn't have to bring anything," she says. "But it's very nice of you. Thank you."

"What's in there?" Misa looks playfully at Mr. Ishida.

"A pair of I-Imari-ware tea cups," Mr. Ishida stutters.

"I love Imari porcelain," says Mrs. Taniguchi. "You're so sweet."

Mr. Ishida smiles weakly. Mr. Ishida seems to be barely weathering Taka's cold stares.

Misa diverts our attention. "Hey, Naomi-san and Mr. Ishida, Sakura-san is an excellent cook. I love her chocolates. My, oh my, they are so delicious."

"Please help yourself," says Mrs. Taniguchi as she steps away to greet other guests.

Misa takes Mr. Ishida to the table where an impressive buffet is laid out and Taka and I watch them. Taka is still leery of Mr. Ishida, even though Mr. Ishida apologized. I am grateful Taka is so protective of me.

After Misa and Mr. Ishida fill their plates with Mrs. Taniguchi's handcrafted food, Taka and I take our turn. With plates in hand, Taka takes me to his room, which Mrs. Taniguchi still keeps the same way as when he left. On the azure blue walls hang western movie posters and pictures of family trips. A photo of his high school soccer team sets on a sun-faded desk. The team stands in two rows, all smiling with fresh faces. Taka is in the center of the second row.

We perch on the edge of his bed. I laugh at the bedspread printed with soccer balls.

"My mom treats me like I'm still a kid," says Taka shyly.

I can see from his room how much his adopted mother loves him.

Glancing around, I spot a few picture albums on the bookshelf. I take down one of the quilted albums, likely handmade by Mrs. Taniguchi, and we perch on the bed. Leafing through the photos, I notice he is not smiling in any of his younger pictures. Even though he's surrounded by toys, his face is impassive. In one picture, he stands next to a blue bike, wearing a blue helmet. He looks content, but expressionless. He doesn't start smiling in his pictures until junior high, around the time he joined the soccer team.

As I turn the last page, I feel a warm hand on my shoulder. Taka gently pulls me into his arms and starts to kiss me. From the corner of my eye, I see the pattern of soccer balls. A sweet image of Taka playing soccer forms in my mind. The moment we lie down upon the the bed, I hear a knock on the door. Taka rises and opens it to see Misa standing at the door.

"Taka-san, are you coming? We're going to cut the cake."

"We'll be there soon," answers Taka, straightening the collar of his polo shirt.

We return to the living room. All the guests are around the dining table. His father is holding a knife poised over a cake decorated like a golf course. The main part of the cake is green, representing the grass, and a golfer figurine stands, ready to tee off. A blue lake is edged by a white sand trap, made of fluffy frosting, and nearby stands a tiny, plastic red flag. His father awkwardly begins cutting the cake. Mrs. Taniguchi takes the knife and begins slicing in even cuts.

Her slices reveal ice cream inside. She hands Taka and me each a plate. The cake tastes decadent. I hear other guests praising its deliciousness.

Taka's relatives and his father's work and golf friends are in the living room chatting when we move to take a seat there. Mrs. Taniguchi's brother comes to us and introduces himself as Taka's uncle. Taka's step-uncle nostalgically tells me about taking Taka fishing when he was a teenager. Soon he and Taka engage in a lively conversation.

Mrs. Taniguchi calls everyone for opening presents. At the table, surrounded by guests, Mr. Taniguchi's smile grows bigger as he opens his first gift which is from Mr. Ishida—a pair of vintage Imari tea cups and saucers, hand-painted in blue, red, and gold. They are quite impressive. Indeed, Mr. Ishida has sophisticated taste.

"Wow, they're beautiful," says Mrs. Taniguchi, picking a cup from the paulownia wooden box, and showing it to Mr. Taniguchi, who is smiling at Mr. Ishida and Misa.

Mr. Ishida smiles bashfully, and Misa suppresses a smile.

A happy face on Misa must mean a lot to Mr. Taniguchi.

Mr. Taniguchi picks up my present, gives me a small grin, then unwraps the box. "Ohhh, did you make these?"

I nod.

He delightedly holds up three knitted golf club covers with pom-pom tassels with two-tone colors of lime green and navy blue. "Thank you. These even have my initials. That's amazing."

Mr. and Mrs. Taniguchi seem impressed, but Taka is more surprised than anyone else.

"Wow, I didn't know you knit," says Taka.

"I'm not really a knitter." I shrug my shoulders but can't keep a small smile off my face.

"Such a thoughtful gift for my father. Thank you, Naomi-san," says Misa.

Thrown off balance by Misa's comment, I can find no other response but to bow.

One after another, Mr. Taniguchi opens his gifts as Mrs. Taniguchi busily rakes away the wrapping papers to tidy up.

After opening gifts, many of the guests remain. Taka and his uncle resume their reminiscence. I glance around, looking for Mr. Ishida and Misa. I approach the large picture window that opens to a view of a peaceful landscape. An umbrella-shaped maple bends over the edge of a small pond where red, gold, and silver carp swim, flexing their bodies back and forth.

Misa and Mr. Ishida come into sight. Each of them holds a glass of wine and Misa and Mr. Ishida lean against each other like lovers.

Taka steps my way. I turn to him and beckon him to look outside.

Taka comes up to me and looks outside. "They look happy." Taka turns to me and says with a wry face. "It still bothers me that he assaulted you."

"Forgiveness is healing," I say, echoing my father's teachings.

The instant I say this, I think of Taka's sad saga. It must be difficult for him to forgive his mother for abandoning him. I am grateful his Hokkaido trip gave him a chance to begin to heal.

Misa sees us and waves. I wave back.

Taka takes me to his step grandparents—they are Mrs. Taniguchi's parents. They are soft spoken, just like Mrs. Taniguchi. It is obvious how much they love Taka—their smiles are nonstop when they talk about him. When I am laughing heartily, Misa and Mr. Ishida appear and announce they are leaving. I feel strange and awkward, but I say, "Good night." Taka follows me in a terse voice. "Goodbye." Mrs. Taniguchi's parents in unison give a warm "see you soon."

Taka and I continue talking with the step-grandparents, but after a short time we decide to head off.

When we leave the house, Mr. and Mrs. Taniguchi and the Yorki follow us to the entry hall. Their Yorki barks at our feet.

Mrs. Taniguchi says, "We really enjoyed having you, Naomi-san. Please come again. I'll make dinner next time."

"Thank you. I'd look forward to that." Taka puts his arm around my shoulder. I add, "It was a wonderful party. Again, happy birthday, Mr. Taniguchi."

"Thank you. It was very nice of you to make me such beautiful golf club covers. I'll cherish them." He grins, waiving his hand to stop their Yorki from barking, but the dog ignores him.

Taka tells the dog to be quiet and he stills.

Mrs. Taniguchi scoops up the raucous dog. The little dog acts like a curious baby in her arms. "I'll look forward to having dinner together."

"Thank you very much. I'll look forward to that, too," I say then think, *here comes the awkward moment.* I step down and put the brace on my foot.

"What happened to your leg?" Mr. and Mrs. Taniguchi ask in tandem.

Of course, they would ask. With no good explanation, I repeat what I told my coworkers. "I slipped and fell onto the sidewalk." Taka covertly covers his mouth to hide his smile.

"Oh no, that must have been a nasty fall," says Mr. Taniguchi in a warm voice, pulling the inner parts of his eyebrows together.

"It's not so bad. I'll get back to normal soon," I say, strapping the Velcro together in haste.

"Please take care," says Mrs. Taniguchi, stepping toward me. The little dog in her arms comes to my eye level as I am bending over.

I smile at the dog and it sniffs my face.

It's around eight p.m. as we leave. The night sky is full of dazzling stars.

As Taka drives me to my apartment, I reflect on how much he seems to have changed since he was adopted. It's obvious his adoptive parents provided him a better life. In his photo albums, he looked like a doleful child, but over time the images start portraying confidence, cheerfulness, and contentment. I like his family, though Misa is still a mystery.

"What are you thinking, Naomi-san?"

"I'm thinking how nice your family is."

He smiles, and I can see his dimples even in the darkness of the car.

We reach my apartment. He turns the engine off and opens the moonroof. He pulls me close and we kiss under the starry sky for a while.

He releases his arm from my neck to gaze into my eyes. "I feel so close to you."

"And I to you."

"Thank you for coming to my father's birthday. I'll see you soon. Good night and sweet dreams."

"I enjoyed meeting your family. Sweet dreams to you too."

When shutting the door, Taka says, "Count the days."

As I slip into bed the words "count the days" keep me awake.

* * *

On Monday, Yuki calls the office to ask me to have dinner with her, saying, "Let's catch up." There is little time left to see Yuki, so spending any time with her is precious. We meet at the curry restaurant where we used to go after work.

Surprisingly, Yuki is already there. "Sorry I'm late," I say, feeling strange as this is usually Yuki's line.

"No problem," says Yuki, pouring me a glass of wine. "Thank you, Naomi, for coming."

"Of course. My pleasure. Did you already order food?"

"No, just wine. Are you going to order the usual?"

"Yeah, sounds good."

We order a beef curry with mango chutney.

With a gleam in her eye, Yuki initiates the conversation. "David is so relieved you and Taka-san are back together. Lately, he seems to be communicating with Taka-san a lot."

"Please say thank you to David for helping us get back together. How is he?"

"He's great," says Yuki, wrinkling her nose and giving me a cute smile. "He's practicing Japanese now."

"Really? When are you guys getting marri—"

Yuki interrupts. "How was Taka-san's father's birthday party?"

"Guess what? Misa-san brought Mr. Ishida to the party. Can you imagine? I was shocked. Despite the restraining order he had the audacity to show up there."

"Oh my, Naomi. That's terrible! How did you handle that?"

"Well, it turned out better than I could have hoped. Mr. Ishida apologized and there was no embarrassing confrontation. I have to say, though, Taka was furious with Mr. Ishida at first."

"I can understand why Taka-san would be so angry. At least Mr. Ishida apologized." She gives me a serious look as she says, "You know how Misa-san is . . . what if Mr. Ishida becomes your brother-in-law?"

"Yuki! Don't assume too much. Taka-san hasn't proposed."

"I'm intuitive. Will you be all right in that sort of atypical family? Can you tolerate Misa-san?"

Putting down my wine, I say in a determined voice, "Yes, I can. I love Taka-san way more than you can imagine. I'd tolerate anything to be with him."

"That's what I wanted to hear."

Yuki seems relaxed. Our favorite dinner comes, and our talk becomes livelier, just like the times we used to have here at our favorite restaurant. Our subjects tend to jump in many directions: work, New York, David, and, of course, Taka.

chapter nineteen

CHERRY BLOSSOMS

On a Sunday in April, Taka shows up at my apartment just before noon to take me to Ueno Park—one of the prettiest areas in Tokyo for viewing cherry blossoms.

Sporting a navy-blue suit with a light blue shirt and a two-tone burgundy-navy blue tie to match, he looks so handsome. Glancing down at my outfit, I say, "Give me a moment to change."

"You look pretty as you are."

"Please come in and wait." Wondering why he is in a suit, I scoot into my bedroom to switch from my sweater and jeans to a peach-colored wool dress.

After a thirty-minute drive, we reach the popular park. Taka grabs a blanket from the back seat and we start strolling the central path, which is lined with nearly a thousand cherry trees. The lawns on both sides of the path are filled with revelers enjoying the day drinking their *sake* and eating scrumptious foods. Everyone is in such a festive mood, playing their favorite popular music on boom boxes and singing, totally immersed in their own blossom-viewing party.

We find a free spot under a gracefully arching cherry tree and Taka spreads the blanket.

"Save this spot! I'll be back with food," says Taka.

"Eh? I didn't know this was a picnic date. I could have made sandwiches or something."

"Don't worry about that, just enjoy the view." He takes off in the direction of his car.

He returns with a brown paper bag on his arm and a wrapped cake box in his hand. He sets the box on the blanket first, then kneels to stick his hand in the sack to take out cheese, ham, and some rolled sandwiches. Lastly, he grabs a bottle of champagne.

"Thank you for all of this. Wow, you even bought a cake?" I smile at him.

He picks up the box and hands it to me.

"It's awfully light for a cake." I raise my eyes and study his face. I slowly unwrap the paper and lift the lid, revealing loosely-filled packing peanuts. "What is this?" Taka remains silent. As I paw through the box, my fingers clasp a small object. I wiggle it to shake away the Styrofoam popcorn. It's a jewelry box.

He takes the box from me and stares into my eyes. I feel paralyzed. The ribbon slips away as he opens the case in front of me. A sparkling gem transfixes me.

As I finally raise my eyes, he asks, "Will you marry me?"

The noise of the other picnickers fades, and I feel as if I am under water. Inch by inch my senses return. I cry, "yes", the emotions surging out of my heart.

Taka reaches for my left hand and slips the beautiful diamond onto my finger.

"Congratulations!" says someone from a nearby group. Suddenly, more people join in, shouting choruses of good wishes.

With champagne in hand, we kiss under the blossoms. Warm sun shines through the pale pink petals. I feel so blessed.

"I need to tell my mom, my dad, Yuki, and everyone I know."

"Well . . . that may not be necessary." He puts his arm around me. "Actually, your parents and aunt already know I was planning to propose. Yuki and David are also in on the plan. We wanted to surprise you by having a double wedding."

My cheek muscles seem locked in a perpetual smile.

Raising my eyes from the diamond, I say, "Aha! That's why Yuki didn't look for a place in New York for her wedding. Now I understand her strange behavior and why my aunt and Mom have been asking questions like, 'What do you think would be an ideal wedding venue for Yuki-san if she decides to wed in Japan?'"

Taka throws back his head and laughs.

"When did you decide to have this surprise wedding?"

"Remember when Yuki-san invited you to dinner after my dad's birthday party?"

With an affirmative nod, I respond. "Yuki acted as if she knew your wishes and probed me about my feelings toward you and your family members . . . many hypothetical questions such as: Would I be able to get along with Misa-san? What if Misa-san got married to Mr. Ishida—could I deal with him as a brother-in-law?"

Taka snickers. "Yuki-san did a good job. I know you love me a lot, but marriage is different. You can choose your spouse but not their family. I was deeply concerned about Misa-san, knowing of her egotistic attitude, but more so about Mr. Ishida if they marry. Fitting into my family dynamic could be quite challenging." He pauses to study my face.

I give him a reassuring smile. Taka releases a long, deep breath.

"So, how did you get permission from my parents?" My eyes bounce between the diamond and Taka.

"I arranged to meet your parents to receive their official consent. They invited me for dinner one night."

"They didn't tell me."

"Your father apologized about the *Bosozoku* incidence. Apparently, your aunt explained the episode to your parents. Your father went on to talk about your *omiai*. He explained how you weren't interested but were trying to comply with their wishes. But the nightmare with the restraining order woke your father up to the realization that they have been controlling your life and he felt terrible. By the way, your father mentioned Mr. Ishida's father was deeply sorry after learning that his son received a restraining order."

"Well . . . a few weeks after I filed the restraining order, my dad phoned me. He felt extremely guilty and upset about having introduced Mr. Ishida to me. My dad's usual calmness was utterly gone, I tell you. He said 'sorry' so many times. I thought monks never lost control," I say.

"He's human."

I chuckle. "By the way, on the night of your father's birthday, I called my dad to explain Mr. Ishida's appearance at your parents' house and how he apologized for his indiscretion. There was a long pause, then Dad asked if I would be able to forgive Mr. Ishida. I told him I already had expressed forgiveness and Dad seemed relieved."

"Good. After all, your father is a Buddhist monk. Forgiveness must be important to him. In any event, your father was impressed by your wanting independence. He admires your self-reliance."

"Really?"

"Yes," Taka says with a deep nod. He takes my hands in his. "Your parents were happy about my proposal. I saw tears in your mother's eyes."

A wave of joy envelops me.

"By the way, your aunt said she wants to help with the wedding arrangements since she has so many connections with large hotels. She mentioned that it would be a great honor to be able to return the favor of you rescuing Yoshiyuki-san from the *Bosozoku*."

"Now it all makes sense."

"You need to let your aunt know what kind of wedding you and Yuki-san would like to have."

"Yes, I will. My choice is a western-style, I simply would love to wear a dress, not a kimono."

"That'll be pretty on you. I'm fine with either way as long as you are happy."

I kiss him. As our lips release, my gaze shifts to the fresh blossom petals above.

*   *   *

The next morning, I inform Mr. Saito about my engagement and request a week off for my honeymoon.

"Congratulations!" Mr. Saito exclaims.

My co-workers look at us curiously. Ai, Kaori, Yoko, and Midori migrate to Mr. Saito's desk.

"What's going on?" asks Midori and Yoko in unison.

Kaori spots my ring. "Look!" she says to the others, pointing at my ring. "You're engaged?" she says to me.

Midori takes my hand, swallows, then utters, "Wow."

"Hey, you guys. You have so many questions for Naomi-san, why don't you save them for break time?" suggests Mr. Saito in a light voice.

*   *   *

At our lunch hour, Ai, Kaori, Yoko, Midori and I meet in the cafeteria. As soon as we sit at a table, Yoko says, "So, you too are getting married?"

After finishing her bite of spaghetti, Kaori frowns and says, "What's going on with Yuki? I haven't received a wedding invitation yet."

I giggle, covering my mouth with a napkin.

"Why are you laughing?" asks Yoko. "By any chance, are you two thinking about getting married on the same day?"

Glancing at everyone around the table, I nod and smile.

"What!" exclaims Midori. "Didn't I hear Yuki is getting married in New York?"

"She changed her plans, so we can have a double wedding. My engagement just happened yesterday, so I haven't had a chance to talk to Yuki yet. I'll call tonight and ask her what kind of wedding she wants. I definitely want a western style. Even if she chooses a traditional Japanese wedding, we'll celebrate with a shared reception. You will all be invited."

"How did he propose to you?" asks Yoko in a lilting voice.

My smile is wide. "He took me to the Ueno park to view the cherry blossoms. He had a surprise picnic all laid out." Momentarily my ring steals my attention.

"Yeah and . . .," Kaori says impatiently.

"He brought me a cake box and inside—"

Midori cuts in quickly and quips, "The cake morphed into a diamond."

I giggle and shrug my shoulders.

Ai's perfectly mascaraed eyes widen. "I'm happy for you guys."

"I can't wait to see your and Yuki's future husbands," says Kaori.

"We're getting married on Sunday June fifth," I say.

"I'm amazed you guys could get ready so fast," says Midori.

"I know. We're lucky to have a lot of support," I say.

Poking a meatball with her folk, Yoko asks, "Do you think David will bring his friends from New York?"

Kaori slaps her hand on the table. "Are you thinking about finding an American boyfriend?"

"Could be . . . what's it to you?" Yoko retorts.

I look down at my watch. "It's five to one. We need to go back."

The four of them continue chatting as we return to our desks.

* * *

After work, I meet Yuki at a desert shop in Shinjuku. Without even exchanging greetings, I burst out laughing. Yuki immediately understands and chortles loud enough to draw looks from other patrons.

Wagging my finger at her, I say, "Crafty you! I heard the whole story from Taka-san."

Playfully she grabs my finger and pulls it near her. "Finally! Now you are on the same page with the wedding plans."

As I nod, she looks my ring over. "Wow, how beautiful. Congratulations!"

"Thank you. I really appreciate your efforts to save my relationship with Taka-san."

Glancing up from the ring, she says, "Of course. I care about you and Taka-san. David and I are happy for you guys."

"By the way, you need to decide which style wedding you want to have so my aunt can make the arrangements. Ours will be a Christian-style wedding."

"David wants to wear a *kimono*, so ours will be Shinto style."

"Okay, I'll let my aunt know."

My name is called, and we follow the waitress to a seat by the windows that overlook the main street. It's swarming with pedestrians and vehicles leaving work. The pathways are filled with myriad umbrellas in all colors, bobbing down the streets.

The instant we settle in the chair, Yuki asks, "May I take a look at your ring again?"

"Of course."

Yuki takes my outstretched hand and compares my ring to hers. Hers is a cushion cut, square, with lots of small diamonds surrounding the center stone. "A round solitaire. I like it. Simple but elegant. I like how the two smaller diamonds sandwich the solitaire. It's interesting that Taka-san and David have such different tastes."

"They do." I finally raise my head from looking at our rings. "So, how is everything going?"

"Everything is crazily busy; there's no time to put my feet up before the wedding."

Yuki explains she needs to get all the proper paperwork together for her and David to get the marriage certificate, plus find the requirements for an immigration visa.

"You are overloaded!"

"Tell me about it. In addition to this hectic schedule, I need to clean out my apartment and coordinate my wedding with David via phone and email."

"If you need my help, packing is one of my fortes."

"I'd love to have you help me pack—that way I can spend more time with you."

Yuki and I spend the rest of the evening indulging in excited conversation about our weddings.

* * *

A few days later, Yuki and I meet at the hotel where my auntie is arranging our weddings. Auntie chose this hotel as David wants to wed in the Shinto style and this hotel has both European style and traditional wedding venues.

Before entering the hotel, we explore the garden with its three-story wooden pagoda. There's a small Shinto shrine on the other side of an arched red bridge that crosses over a pond.

"This place is perfect for you and David. It reminds me of our Kyoto trip," I say.

"It surely does."

Upon entering the hotel lobby, our wedding coordinator, a middle-aged woman, awaits us. "How do you do? I'm Honda Rie." She greets us with a well-timed formal bow.

"Pleased to meet you," I say. "I'm Ochiai Naomi and this is my friend, Okada Yuki-san." Yuki and I bow together.

"So, you are Naomi-san. We greatly appreciate your aunt's artistic flower arrangements. Her centerpieces for receptions and bouquets are always exceeding our customers' requirements and expectations. Helping with your wedding is a way to show our gratitude for your aunt." She gives us each a reassuring smile.

"Thank you, but it's we who are grateful to you. I know the waiting list here can be over a year long."

"You are most welcome." Giving a brief nod, Miss Honda continues. "Shall we start?" She beckons us to follow and we trail after her.

As Miss Honda pushes open the chapel doors, my eyes are nearly blinded by the white pearl floors and walls. A large window behind the alter frames a lush green bamboo forest. *How divine!* An image of Taka and me standing before this altar flashes to mind. In the moment, oblivious to the presence of others, my mind is absorbed with one thing: Taka and me. Yuki pulls my elbow, nudging me to follow Miss Honda.

The next venue is a small replica of a Shinto shrine.

Miss Honda says, "Only the bride, groom, and their families are present at the ceremony inside the shrine. Afterwards, they welcome the guests in the reception room."

"By the way," I ask Yuki, "how do you plan to have David's *kimono* and *hakama* pants ready before the wedding?"

"I took his measurements when I was in New York."

Miss Honda assures, "Yuki-san already gave his measurements to us."

"Good thinking," I say.

Miss Honda asks, "Are you free this afternoon? You could look for your wedding dresses. You don't need an appointment."

"Yes, we'll do that, Miss Honda. Thank you very much for showing us the beautiful wedding venues," I say.

"You're most welcome." Miss Honda bows politely and leaves.

We descend to the lounge for a quick lunch, then head to the bridal room.

The bridal room is dazzling with opulent lighting. Immediately, the lady at the reception desk rises to welcome us. Once we mention the name of Miss Honda, she escorts us inside and finds someone to assist us.

Yuki walks away with her sales person and I follow my assistant. In no time I pick one from a wall display. I enter the fitting room and my assistant brings me the silk ball gown; the ruche bodice of the dress is embroidered with hundreds of tiny pearls in intricate swirls over the bust. Feeling like a princess, I step out of the room.

My assistant comes forward. "You look stunning," she says. In a jiffy she uses pins from the cushion pillow on her wrist to pinch out the excess fabric. "This dress compliments your figure. Let me help you set the veil in place."

I nod. With her help, a two-tier-lace veil sets in my hair. I feel a lump in my throat.

Yuki decides on a *shiromoku*, a white-silk kimono, and a white hat called a *wataboshi*. The headpiece is traditionally worn during a Shinto ceremony to veil the horns of jealousy, ego and selfishness. Since a kimono is basically one size, adjustable with many strings hidden inside a sash, a fitter will dress her on the day of the wedding.

After we finish our fitting, the next task is to meet another coordinator to decide on the lunch menu. Our reception room is already reserved for our sit-down service, so we just need to select food for the two-hundred-fifty guests. Since foreigners will be attending, we choose French cuisine with a fish and meat selection.

Yuki and I are impressed with the service we're receiving. Everything is moving smoothly, thanks to Auntie's excellent arrangements.

chapter twenty

WEDDING

YUKI'S AND MY BIG DAY FINALLY arrives: Sunday June 5th. The night before the wedding I stay at my parents' house. Before heading to the ceremony, there is one more custom for me to perform: I need to thank my dad for his life-long guidance and unconditional love.

In the morning, I go from room to room and finally find him sitting alone in a living room chair, his torso straight as he peers out the window.

I rest on a settee to face him. "Dad?"

He turns. "Yes, my dear."

His eyes are tinged with tears. A sudden squeezing sensation overtakes my heart and the words I practiced last night elude me. Taking a long breath, I begin. "Thank you for being a good dad. You've been so supportive."

He gives me a weak smile. "I almost ruined your life."

"No! Please don't think that way. If you hadn't thought it was a good match, you wouldn't have arranged the *omiai*."

"You have matured a lot. I'm proud of you. I won't commandeer your life any more. It's your life and you should build it the way you want. Mr. Ishida called and told us he's attending your wedding. You're good at forgiving and I'm awed by your compassion."

"You instilled in me many values to help me be a good person."

Eyes shimmering with tears, my father says, "I'm grateful to have you as my daughter. As you know, I'm a monk's son and all I have ever strived for is to be a monk. Perhaps I was too strict, but you were always compliant and never complained."

Shrugging my shoulders, I say, "Well, not always compliant. Once in a while I would sneak out to have drinks with friends."

He laughs. "Your mom covered for you well then." His smile fades away. "I'm happy for you. I like Taka-san. He seems to be a kind person. I'm confident you two will build a solid foundation together." His warm eyes melt my heart.

Tears run down my cheeks. I hear my mom coming into the room. With the back of my hand, I wipe the tears away.

Patting my father's shoulder, my mom says, "Naomi-chan, you need to get ready."

"Yes, get ready." My dad's pitch rises, lightening the mood. "We'll be leaving soon."

*　　*　　*

My dad pulls the car from the garage to the driveway, and Mom and I get in. I glance back at the house for a moment. *From now on, when I return to this temple house, it'll be as a visitor.* A surge of sadness fills my heart.

As instructed, we arrive two hours early so my hair can be styled, and my makeup done, and of course to then slip into my stunning dress. Stepping into the lobby, my sadness turns into eager anticipation, I quicken my gait. My parents scurry to keep up.

I spot women in *montsuki*—black kimonos distinguished by a white round crest on each shoulder, embellished with ornate gold embroidery on the bottom that are usually worn by older or married women for formal occasions. Young ladies in colorful, formal, long dresses talk with men in black tuxedos. I wonder which of all these people are attending our wedding.

"Naomi!" someone shouts.

I turn and see Yuki and David coming in with their families. I count ten foreigners, including David. We all congregate in the center of the lobby. As Yuki starts introducing David's parents, his two sisters and their husbands, and his friends, Taka appears with his parents and grandparents. Our crowd grows like a swarm of bees, and the hotel's guests shoot us curious glances. Yuki and I excuse ourselves to go to our bride's room, leaving Taka and David in charge of the crowd.

Yuki and I separate to get dressed. My team members, a hairstylist, cosmetologist, and fitter create a Vogue-like wedding model out of me. My hair is styled in an updo with small crystal accents and sprigs of baby's breath on top and my makeup is light but perfect. As soon as I'm tucked into my ruched-bodice gown, I waddle to my parents' waiting room.

The escort eases open the door for me. My dad, a tea cup in hand, straightens his back, "Wow, what a lovely bride!" He walks up to me.

"Naomi-chan, you look so beautiful," says my mom. She releases a deep, satisfying breath then gingerly lowers my veil— the last act before giving her daughter away.

I place my hand on my dad's arm, ready for him to escort me to my waiting bridegroom. The chapel doors swing open, and the wedding march emanates from inside. Over the music, I hear a baby's squeaky cry from somewhere in the packed room.

My dad and I proceed down the aisle. The prelude of the

Butterfly Waltz excites me, but then a lump forms in my throat and my breath becomes quicker and more shallow. The veil obstructs my view, making everything blurry. When we reach the altar, my dad gently releases me and with care I lift the hem of my flowing gown and ascend the stairs to my groom. The music ceases, and the hall becomes silent.

I face Taka and Taka lifts my veil. His eyes widen, and his lips part slightly. I try to grin, but my lips twitch. The minister gives a slight nod and begins the service. Time seems to stop. I have difficulty following the minister's words. Taka squeezes my hand.

I repeat after the minister in a quivering voice. "I, Naomi, take you, Taka-san, to be my husband . . . I promise to be true to you . . . in good times and bad . . . in sickness and in health . . . I'll love you and honor you all the days of my life."

We exchange rings. Taka holds my shaky hand firmly, but I sense a subtle tremble in his, too. As the glimmering silver ring settles on my finger, I hear the minister say, "I now pronounce you husband and wife. You may kiss your bride." Joy and light fill my heart.

I see Taka's eyes are bright with love. He gives me a soft kiss.

He looks so handsome.

I sigh with contentment. Taka takes my arm, and we walk back down the aisle amidst a storm of applause.

* * *

After the ceremony, Taka and I wait outside the reception room for David and Yuki.

"Here they come. David, your kimono sits well on you!" says Taka, scanning David from head to foot. "You two look like Emperor and Empress *hina* dolls."

"Well, I don't know what *hina* dolls are, but I feel goooood." David opens his arms and spins around, smiling, then looks at us.

"You two look stunning. Naomi, how lovely you are."

Leaving not much time to admire each other's appearance, an employee of the bridal service ushers us briskly into the reception room. We're immediately caught in the beams of spotlights. David and Naomi are at the forefront. The spotlights follow us to the head table amidst the echoing sound of applause over the music of Yiruma's *River Flows In You,* my choice.

The ballroom is set banquet-style. Candles in tall, wrought-iron holders, decorated with white lilies and roses, adorn each table. The tables are covered with a lilac-purple satin overlay. A large oval crystal chandelier at the center of the hall hangs over a small dance stage. The dance stage was David's idea. Typically, dancing is not part of a Japanese wedding.

As we reach our table, the room lights come on and we are bombarded with a barrage of camera flashes. Yuki and I sit next to each other, our grooms on either side of us. Many in the audience raise their cameras or cell phones to take our picture. The room is clamorous with all sorts of hurrahs, clicking devices, and moving chairs. It's quite overwhelming.

Clapping, the emcee stands. "Presenting Mr. and Mrs. Johnson and Mr. and Mrs. Taniguchi. Aren't they gorgeous? We could stare at them all day, but then we'd miss the congratulatory speeches." The audience becomes quiet. "The couples decided the first speaker and guest of honor will be Yuki-san and Naomi-san's boss, Mr. Saito. Since it's a double reception, the order of speech was decided by a flip of the coin. Naomi-san speaks after Mr. Saito, followed by Taka-san. Yuki-san and David-san will speak last."

Mr. Saito strides to the microphone and begins in English. "To our guests from America, the family of Yuki-san would like to extend their appreciation to you for making the long journey to be here for this special day." He glances toward David's family and friends, then switches to Japanese. "I'm honored to stand in this place on such a special day for Yuki-san and Naomi-san's wedding. How rare that two co-workers and best friends marry on the same day and that their grooms are also good friends. Yuki-san and Naomi-san met their grooms in Kyoto last summer, such a momentous trip to an ancient city."

"Bravo!" someone shouts. "I'm going to Kyoto!" announces a male voice.

A burst of laughter erupts from the audience.

Mr. Saito grins and finishes his speech. "Naomi-san is next." He bows and returns to his seat.

I stand and take the microphone. As I glance around, nervousness overtakes me, and my knees feel weak. Shifting to a more comfortable stance, I take a deep breath and begin.

"All my life I have smelled incense and have listened to my dad chanting sutras with his singing bowl. Even after I moved from my parents' home in the temple compound, my dad's chanting still echoed in my ears. I always feel his presence watching over me." I shoot a grin at my parents. "Dad, remember, when I was little, I loved the ocean and always scared you and mom?" I turn to address everyone. "One time, at the age of five, I sprinted to the edge of the ocean to retrieve a beach ball. A big sneaker wave engulfed me and pulled me far from the beach. When my dad saw me, he immediately jumped in and swam like crazy to catch me as the current pulled me further out. He finally managed to reach me and take me in his arms. He told me later, 'my heart was pounding so hard I didn't know if we would make it back. But you were floating like a buoy, splashing and laughing, unaware of the seriousness of the situation. You've always been fearless, and I like your adventurous spirit.' Well, I'm not sure I'm any less reckless now, but don't worry Dad, I have Taka-san." I turn towards Taka and smile, then turn the other way to look at Yuki. "Because I am a monk's daughter, I have had a traditional upbringing, but since

I met Yuki, almost four years ago, my true nature has emerged. Yuki's brave, open-minded, and courageous way of living always fascinated me and has influenced me a great deal. I embrace the adventurous life."

My dad is crying. Seeing his tears, I choke up, so I hurriedly pass the microphone to Taka.

Taka begins. "I first saw Naomi-san and Yuki-san in a hotel in *Gion* where David and I were staying. I was immediately drawn to Naomi-san."

Taka bows to my parents. "Father, yes, Naomi-san has a cheerful and adventurous disposition, and I, too, highly value that quality. Father and Mother, I'll do my best to protect your precious daughter."

My parents give Taka a synchronized bow. He turns to face his parents.

"I'd like to thank my father and my mother who adopted me when I was ten."

The audience becomes quiet, their faces motionless.

Taka continues. "My parents have given me unfathomable love. I cannot describe how much I appreciate all the things they have done for me." He turns his gaze upon Mrs. Taniguchi. "Mother, when I first moved into your house, I cried out in my sleep for months. You always hurried to my room and cradled me in your arms until I fell back asleep. Thank you, Mother. I'm truly blessed to have such loving parents."

Mrs. Taniguchi's head is down, her shoulders heaving. Taka looks at Yuki with his wet eyes. She stands up and takes the microphone with her little finger delicately arched upward.

Yuki greets David's family in English. "First of all, I'd like to thank David's parents, sisters, their spouses, and friends for coming all the way to celebrate our wedding." She bows. "When I flew to New York, David's family accepted me immediately. I was touched that my future father-in-law got up early one morning to make cornbread for my breakfast. On the last day, before coming back home, my future mother-in-law and David's sisters threw a big party for me. I already felt like I was a member of his family. Thank you very much." She turns to me and switches to Japanese.

"Although excited to move to New York, parting from Naomi is almost like losing my soul. I've never met anyone with her patience, kindheartedness, and such a buoyant nature. My life has been enriched by her presence. I'll miss her so much." She pauses. "Let's keep our relationship as strong as it is now." I nod deeply, and Yuki turns to face her parents. "Thank you, Dad and Mom, for accepting my way of living. New York is only fourteen hours away. We'll be coming to Japan often, so we can see you and our best friends Taka-san and Naomi."

Her parents are nodding. Yuki hands the microphone to David.

David begins by addressing Yuki's parents. "*Arigato Oka-san and Oto-san. Yuki wo shiawase ni shimasu.*" He then looks at his family and translates. "I said, 'Mother and Father, thank you, I'll make Yuki happy.' Well, that's the extent of my Japanese. From here, Yuki will interpret." David gives a chuckle before he starts. "The Japanese often say if your wife is *Kakadenka*—extremely overbearing—peace will reign in the house. So, I encourage Yuki to be *Kakadenka*."

Yuki translates, and the guests laugh hysterically. David's speech is brief and witty. At the end, he thanks his parents, his sisters and their husbands, and his friends for attending the wedding.

With the speeches behind us, I can finally relax, sit back, and observe our guests while eating. The trio—Kaori, Yoko, and Midori—look beautiful in their lovely kimonos, presenting a striking appearance unlike what I am used to seeing when we're all in our company uniforms. Each one's individual taste is apparent from the kimono's they are wearing. Kaori's is purple. I chuckle. Most of Kaori's belongings are purple: her handbag, watch band, even the jewelry she wears. I do not know what that reveals about her personality. Yoko's kimono is red with a floral design in white, yellow, and green—conspicuous and peppy, which shows the flashy side of her character. Midori's kimono shows her modest personality. It is a light green silk with a silver river embroidered on the bottom; simple yet classy.

It is time for *Oiro-naoshi,* changing of the wedding dress. David was surprised to learn the bride changes her dress two or three times in the course of her wedding day.

In the changing room I slip on my floor-length, form-fitting pink evening dress. The side slit shows off my legs. I felt self-conscious when I made the choice, but decided to wear it, swayed by Yuki's compliments.

After a short time, Yuki emerges from her changing room, transformed back to the Yuki I know, having removed her weighty wedding kimono and shed the white porcelain look. She's redone her makeup. Her red V-neck open-backed dress hugs her Barbie-like figure.

When Yuki and I return to the banquet room, Taka is holding an electric guitar, David has a microphone in hand, and behind them, Ai sits at the electric keyboard, ready to perform.

"David–san will sing Luther Vandross's *Always and Forever,*" announces the emcee.

Taka starts strumming his guitar. David, standing in his traditional Japanese kimono, begins singing with a Rod Stewart-like husky voice and immediately draws attention. Many of the guests' mouths are agape. David's friends whistle. When he comes to the lyrics, ". . . baby . . . baby, always love you forever . . ." he slowly turns to Yuki and me with his arms open wide. Yuki and I grin. Kaori, Yoko, and Midori are watching with their mouths half open. Yuki sways in rhythm to the music. I notice Misa's eyes are fixed on Taka. A tinge of jealousy hits me, but I remind myself Misa has Mr. Ishida now. I divert my eyes to Ai's tight canary-yellow dress, displaying her plump hourglass-shaped body. I smile at her daring style.

"A great performance!" Mr. Suzuki and Mr. Saito say in unison, coming to our table as David and Taka are about to sit down.

David's sisters scurry up to David and one of them says in a high-pitched voice, "We didn't know you could sing."

"Well, I did it for my wife," says David, peering into Yuki's adoring eyes.

Yuki flashes him a smile.

Ai appears at our table and stands in front of Taka and me. "I had so much fun performing with Taka-san and David-san."

Taka bows. "Thank you, Ai-san. You did a wonderful job."

Yuki and David walk around the bride and groom table to our side to join the conversation. David drapes his arm over Ai's shoulder. "Thank you, Ai, for playing the piano for us. It wouldn't have been as enjoyable without you."

"How did Ai-san get involved in this?" I ask.

"I heard from you," Taka answers, "that Ai-san played keyboard in Yuki-san's farewell party, so I called your office and asked her for this favor."

Ai smirks.

David's three friends show up and David introduces his bride to them.

Misa and Mr. Ishida greet us. Misa is elegant in a black, knee-length cocktail sheath with an off-the-shoulder neckline and sheer lace sleeves. Her hair tumbles over her bare shoulder and she steals the attention of many with her big Amerasian eyes, full lips, and flawless tan skin. Mr. Ishida looks handsome in his well-fitted, tasteful suit.

"Congratulations, Taka-san and Naomi-san. I'm truly happy

for you two," says Misa.

"Both of you look stunning," says Mr. Ishida with soft eyes. "I'm grateful to be able to attend your wedding. I wish you a lifetime of love and happiness."

Taka pats Mr. Ishida's shoulder. "Thank you. Please take care of Misa-san."

Mr. Ishida responds in a serious manner, "Yes, I will," then he gives a bow of agreement.

"Thank you for your blessings," I intone with all seriousness.

Mr. Ishida and Misa bow.

As Misa and Mr. Ishida withdraw, Yoshiyuki squeezes in along with my aunt. A fresh-faced young girl with no makeup, in a navy blue, knee-length dress stands bashfully at his side.

"Congratulations, Naomi-san!" says Yoshiyuki.

Before introducing his girlfriend to us, Yoshiyuki looks over at Mr. Ishida and whispers to me in an accusatory tone, "Why is Mr. Ishida here?"

"It's a long story. I'll explain to you some other time," I say.

He nodes quietly and with a lightened voice says, "This is my girlfriend, Ayaka-san."

"Thank you for coming."

"Congratulations," Ayaka says with a shy smile. "I've heard nice things about you."

"Really?" I gently pat Yoshiyuki's arm. "Your life must be going well. I'm happy you have a lovely lady in your life."

Yoshiyuki says, "If you, Taka-san, Yuki-san, and David-san hadn't rescued me, my life would be—"

I interrupt him. "We're just so glad you're back on the right track." I notice his eyes tearing up, so I say, "How did you two meet?"

His serious face transforms into a smile. "Ayaka-san ordered flowers from our aunt's shop and I delivered them to her."

"Aha-ha! Lucky you," I say and pat his back.

Yoshiyuki's face begins to flush.

I then turn to my proud-looking auntie and talk quietly with her for a few minutes.

A half year has passed since the *Bosozoku* incident. Yoshiyuki is more sophisticated, though his red cheeks and dialect divulge his country roots. His hand, tightly clasping that of his girlfriend, suggests a close relationship. I look around for my uncle and see him eating alone at a table. I wonder how Yoshiyuki has influenced my aunt's relationship with my uncle.

Yoko, Midori, Kaori, Taka's friends, and David's friends all crowd around us. Yoko says in English, glancing at David's friends, "How romantic that David-san sang for Yuki. I think I'd like to have an American boyfriend."

"Yoko, you are audacious," says Kaori in Japanese, shooting her a rather scornful glance.

"Would you like to be my girlfriend?" says one of David's friends, stepping into the circle.

"No joke, she take serious," Midori says in broken English.

Yoko hits Midori's arm lightly. Two of David's other friends laugh, but the one who asked to be Yoko's boyfriend is locked in a warm stare with Yoko.

The cake cutting starts. Two identical three-tier cakes, decorated in white buttercream frosting with a yellow ribbon around the bottom of each tier and yellow gerbera daisies cascading down one side, are rolled in on a cart. Four employees of the hotel set up two round tables for the cakes.

Each couple stands by a cake and waits for the coordinator's signal. People are snapping pictures. Taka stands behind me with his right hand over mine on the knife. We cut a small piece at a snail's pace, remembering to pose for the camera before releasing the knife. Taka lifts a piece and steadily holds the cake as I lean forward carefully.

Mr. Saito rises to his feet with champagne in hand. "Please stand and raise your glass. *Kanpai* to the two beautiful couples' happiness."

Everyone shouts. *"Kanpai!"*

Taka and I toast. People start chatting at their tables while guests trickle over to our table to wish us well.

* * *

Before the dancing starts, David disappears, then returns in a white tuxedo. He looks relieved and visibly animated after changing out of the unaccustomed kimono.

The emcee invites the brides and their fathers to the dance floor. The lights darken, blue lights flash, and the stage floor sparkles with white lights like hundreds of fireflies rendezvousing.

Yuki and I stroll to the stage and our fathers join us.

My dad stands like a cornered animal, oddly cute. He must be feeling uncomfortable. After all, he's wearing a newly tailored suit, not his usual monk's robe, and is about to dance in public. Never in a million years did I think my dad and I could dance together like this. I love him for doing this for me.

"Thank you, Dad," I whisper in his ear.

"I'm happy for you. Come visit us when you can."

A flood of memories burst into my mind. With blurry eyes, I follow his steps.

As the father-daughter dance ends, the emcee asks the grooms to bring their mothers to the stage. Mrs. Taniguchi looks as if she is about to cry. Taka's eyes are red. He must adore his mother so much. I tell myself I will be a faithful daughter to his mother.

David and his mother's dance are entertaining. His mother twirls and twists, kicking her legs high in a joyous mood. I can't help but laugh quietly. How very American.

Finally, David and Yuki and Taka and I face each other on the stage. Our song, "From This Moment On," fills the room. Taka holds my hand and puts his right hand on my waist, slowly leading me across the floor. Although my left leg has recovered from the New Year's Eve's *Bosozoku's* combat, he holds my body tight so he can shift my weight, enabling me to move smoothly. Intoxicated by the romantic music and the mood, I feel like I've fallen into a realm of fantasy. I glance at Yuki and David. They, too, are dancing as if in another world.

Our music ends, and another slow song starts. Our guests join us on the dance floor. Yoshiyuki and Ayaka stand on the stage. They look so young. She puts her chin on his shoulder, clinging her arms around his neck, and Yoshiyuki starts leading the dance. He firmly rests his cheek against her head, as if no one can ever tear him away.

Yoko dances with David's friend . . . the one who asked to be her boyfriend. I smile when I think they might become a couple because of the wedding.

Mr. Ishida brings Misa to the stage. With his face pressed against her cheek, he draws her closer. Misa closes her eyes and a relaxed smile fills her face. *She finally has found a person who satisfies her longings,* I think.

The emcee announces the arrival of our limo. Guests line up from the dance floor to the door.

David, Yuki, Taka and I flit from guest to guest, saying our goodbyes. The crowd's cheers and applause resound throughout the ballroom.

"*Itsu made mo oshiawase ni!*"

"Happy Forever!" someone shouts to be sure David's friends understand.

"*Arigato!*" I say.

"Thank you!" adds Taka, his smile wide.

My hand in his, I turn and meet his soft eyes. They so reflect his gentle, agreeable, personality. How fortunate I am to have Taka and I'm so grateful the whole *omiai* ordeal is behind me.

David and Yuki are greeting guests while Yuki translates for him. *"Arigato,"* David says repeatedly. They will be a good couple. Soon Yuki will be living half a world away, but I am confident our connection will always be close, and our true loves we found in ancient Kyoto will last forever.

David and Yuki, Taka and I climb into the limo. We give everyone one last wave as the limo pulls away. As I sink back into the white leather, I realize my new life with Taka has begun. My heart couldn't be more full.

ACKNOWLEDGEMENTS

I SINCERELY THANK my publisher and editor, Linda Stirling at The Publishing Circle. I could not have written this book without her mentorship, inspiration, expertise, and patience.

I also thank the remarkable members of SW WA/OR *Write to Publish*, a writers' club, who gave me their thoughtful ideas and critiques.

Very special thanks to my caring, loving and supportive husband, Steve Olson, who helped me throughout the entire process.

ABOUT THE AUTHOR

KUMIKO OLSON, a native of Tokyo, Japan, earned a degree in English literature from Japan's Chofu Gakuen Women's Junior College (now known as Den-en Chofu University), then began a career teaching Japanese to foreign students. In 1984, at the age of thirty, Kumiko immigrated to the United States. She holds a Master's degree from Portland State University in Conflict Resolution. Using her bilingual skills, she worked as a translator at various companies, including the Sony Corporation and Fujitsu Global.

Kumiko also authored *From Tokyo To America: Seven Times Down Eight Times Up*, a memoir of young love, marriage, immigration, divorce, and the pain of starting over in a new land. After its publication and warm reception, and inspired by the work of her great-uncle, Kanji Kunieda, the highly regarded Japanese novelist and playwright, she became a full-time writer. *A Kiss in Kyoto* is her first novel.

She resides in a rural town on the outskirts of Portland, Oregon.

PLEASE LEAVE
A REVIEW

Dear Reader,

I hope you enjoyed my novel, *A Kiss in Kyoto.* If you did, please do me a favor and leave a review at the website of the bookstore where you purchased your copy.

Independent authors have a much better chance at being successful when our readers share with others how much they enjoyed the book. The more reviews we get, the more visible we become.

Thank you for reading *A Kiss in Kyoto,*
and thank you for your kind review.

Kumiko Olson

Also by Kumiko Olson

FROM TOYKO TO AMERICA:
SEVEN TIMES DOWN, EIGHT TIMES UP
A MEMOIR

七転八起

*"Seven Times Down
Eight Times Up"*

———————

a Japanese proverb

PREFACE

"STOP IT! HE IS CRYING. Eru is just a puppy!" Mom shouted from a sliding corridor window that faced the backyard. I dropped Eru. He hit the ground and dashed into the crawl space under the floor. I sat there. In a moment, Mom showed up and squatted face to face with me. Grabbing my arm, she said mournfully, "How can you be so mean? That poor puppy. You can't throw your tantrum on the dog. I've seen you swinging him around in the air many times!"

I kept quiet. When Mom could no longer wait for my apology, she left and went inside the house.

With not much reflection, I soon reached my tricycle. As I flung my leg over my bike Mom returned, holding a brown sack. I thought it must be filled with candies. She thrust the bag at me, saying, "I can't have such a mean child in this house! You can go live at the train station. Here is some rice. You can ask the stationmaster to cook your meals."

Instead of crying, I bit my lip, clenched my fists, and then crossed my arms over my chest. I stood in place, not moving, but Mom carried me outside our gate and set me down. The gate shut in front of me.

With a fluffy pink infant's hat squeezed onto my four-year-old head, and the sack of rice in my hand, I started off toward the train station in Ohanajaya. I wasn't sure how to get there, but knew the general direction. *Station people wear blue clothes and blue hats*, I recalled. A vision of stern-looking people came to mind. I halted. *I don't want to go!* I glanced over at the flower field that ran alongside the road—white butterflies and blue dragonflies hovered over the mustard-flower field. I wished to be there, instead. As I turned my head, I saw Mom in the distance, racing towards me. She couldn't keep up the ruse. Out of breath, she scolded, "Silly child." She lifted me off the ground and perched me on her hip. "Will you behave yourself now?"

I leaned my head on her chest.

Despite her frustration, Mom popped some sweet rice into my mouth as soon as we got back inside the house.

Mom was worried about my conniption fits and seriously wanted to stop them. I was a stubborn child, and if things didn't go my way, I sulked. That was why my two brothers left me alone. In my childhood, I did not play with the neighbor children much at all. I followed my mom as if I were her shadow.

One of my best buddies was my dad. For countless hours, I would sit next to him in his workshop, watching as he hammered with his steel tools. Half of his shop floor was covered with tatami mats. We would sit on a cushion in front of his workbench. Dad would put goggles on me to protect my eyes. He told me funny stories while he sculpted metal to make prototypes of European plastic doll's eyes that opened and closed. He often said, "Little one, what are you doing here when you could be playing with the other girls?" But a stubborn child will sit for hours.

My parents never gave up urging me to play with other children. When I was enrolled in kindergarten, my parents held great hope, but other children bored me. They aren't likely to be good playmates, I thought. I preferred solitary play: to draw or read. My lack of social skills made kindergarten difficult.

Shy and withdrawn, I only made a couple friends during my school years.

A few years before entering college, I began to consider which major to pursue. I was good at artwork. While still in elementary school, my calligraphy had been hung in the National Museum of Western Art, and my watercolor painting of a Buddhist temple received a silver award from the Katsushika School District.

So one day I said, "Dad, I want to go to an art college."

"Ummm . . . not a bad idea, but an artist's life is full of hardship," he said.

Dad had an antisocial friend who was well-known for his paintings of tigers, but he often recounted to my dad how difficult it was to be an artist. Dad didn't want me to have such an arduous life, but he was concerned about me becoming more aloof and shy around other people, living in my own world. He never said, "No," outright, so I finally asked him to share his thoughts.

"Well . . . it's sort of a solitary life. You won't be as exposed to other people like you would be in a corporate job. Besides that, you can't expect money to come in always, which limits what you can do."

When I heard his words, I said to myself, "Hmmm . . . but I am a woman. I am not thinking about making money. I will marry and not need to make a living." This was typical thinking for Japanese women in the seventies.

But Dad's words resounded in my ears. I didn't want a solitary life.

In the back of my mind, I had often thought it would be cool to speak English. I imagined myself speaking to foreigners, whose hair, eyes, and skin colors were all uniquely different from mine. How internationally sophisticated I could become! I expressed this thought to my dad.

"Good! You can meet all kinds of people. The world is getting smaller. You are now living in an era where learning English is important. It can open new horizons for you," he said.

"Dad, I want to travel to foreign countries."

"If I were young like you, I wouldn't mind doing the same thing." He grinned, happy about my decision.

So I enrolled in a private junior women's college that specialized in English. A few of my classmates had been kaigaishijo (children of Japanese expats) in the U.S., and those ladies painted their years in America as the most wonderful time of their lives.

* * *

My first job after finishing school was to work in the foreign department of the Industrial Bank of Japan. My co-worker and friend, who often visited Vancouver, Canada, raved about how beautiful that part of the world was. My dream of going abroad grew stronger. I saved money, left the company, and went to England to go to school. But a few months after I was enrolled in a technical college, while I was strolling on the sidewalk near Piccadilly Circus, a drunken driver in an English Austin taxi hit me. Luckily, my only injuries were a few cuts and bad bruises, but I was bedridden for a week with severe pain in my back and neck. This accident discouraged me from staying in England any longer.

Returning home from London, I soon found a job at a language school as a Japanese teacher. In the school, I met my future husband, Thomas, who was working in Japan as an English teacher. We married within two months. After three years, we moved to his hometown in Florida. Our decision to move to the U.S. was a dream come true. Although I had expected to experience cultural differences, I had never anticipated that so many life changing events would await me. My story unfolds the day I landed at the Orlando Airport in Florida.

chapter 1

Melbourne, Florida

DREAM LAND

IT WAS MIDNIGHT ON August 10, 1984. After a month of separation, I was rejoining Thomas to start our new life in Melbourne, Florida. As I stood at the doorstep of the airplane that had just landed at the Orlando airport, damp air streamed onto my skin. Walking a few steps further, I saw my husband standing by the door, smiling radiantly. He must have persuaded the airline people to give him permission to come inside the passenger dock. *It is very you,* I thought to myself. He always liked to surprise me.

"I missed you," said Thomas.

"I missed you too." I said, lowering my eyes, then looking up at him from beneath my lashes in the manner I'd learned he appreciated.

"Ken is here, waiting outside in the pick-up lane to welcome you."

"That's very nice of him," I said, fuzzily recalling Ken's small, oblong face. I had met him once, two years before, on our belated honeymoon. Ken was Thomas's high school friend.

"Hi, Kumiko. Welcome to the U.S.!" Ken bent over me and hugged me lightly. He was standing still, but his upper body moved like a tree nodding in the wind. With his short, wiry body and scant hair, he reminded me of Woody Allen.

Ken opened his old station wagon door for me and I hopped in. As the car cruised down the highway, the spotlighted palm trees lining the highway gave me a tropical feeling. I'd felt fatiqued, but having my husband back and being in his arms helped my mood and I perked up considerably. Although I had neither a strong knowledge of the American culture, nor enough English to feel comfortable, I believed our new life looked promising. An hour-and-a-half later, we arrived at Tomas's parents' house in a suburb of Orlando. We thanked Ken and wished him a goodnight.

Thomas unlocked the door of his parent's house. We had stayed for a week during our one-year-late honeymoon in September of 1982. Once inside, we tiptoed through the dimly-lit hallway into the room that had been Tomas's bedroom when he was a child. Though no lights were on, I recognized the house by its faint but distinctive smell, a smell that instantaneously took me back to my first visit. We stepped into his childhood room and Thomas turned on the lights. As I glanced around, I saw his self-portrait drawing, a large world globe, and his high school speech trophy and I could tell they evoked nostalgia in my husband.

"I'm glad you made it," he said with a relaxed smile.

"Me, too," I said, smiling back.

"It's 2:00 o'clock. You must be very tired. Let's get some sleep," he said.

As I slipped between sheets that had been chilled by air-conditioning, I felt cold, but his soft kiss and gentle touch ignited my passion. In closing my eyes, his smell, absent for a month, intensified the love, and I felt ecstatic.

*   *   *

The next morning, I woke up with the sun. I was anxious to see Tomas's parents, Jacob and Sophia, but I gave myself plenty of time to do my makeup. While I was putting on my makeup in the bathroom, I saw something familiar: a large, flat case with a partitioned shelf that rose as the lid was lifted. I remembered from our previous visit that the aqua-colored case held numerous cosmetics. It had impressed me a great deal because I had never seen such a pretty multi-layered cosmetic kit. I opened the lid and gazed at the pink, red, plum, and many other shades of lipstick. The eyeshadows, too, came in a full selection of colors. I was tempted to use them, but realized it would be safer to stick with my own cosmetics, so as to be myself in front of Tomas's parents.

As I came out of the bathroom, I saw a light on in the living room. I took a deep breath to gather my nerve, then exhaled slowly as I walked toward my father-in-law to say, "Good morning." He gave me a big hug with a tiny kiss on my cheek. Sophia was reading the newspaper. She took off her glasses and stood up to give me a warm, friendly hug.

Thomas joined us a half-hour later.

"Good morning, son. I made cornbread. Hope Kumiko will like it," his father said.

We shifted into the dining room. The table was already set for breakfast. Once we sat at the table, Sophia poured coffee and fresh orange juice, then served us eggs, sausages, and cornbread. To show Thomas's father appreciation, I tried his cornbread first. The melted butter deepened the canary-yellow color of the bread and the aroma stimulated my appetite. I took a bite.

"It is delicious, Father," I said.

"I'm glad. It's a southern-style cornbread," he said.

My heart warmed from his family's welcome.

Soon after breakfast, Thomas and I left for our new home in Melbourne. He had told me earlier that he had found the apartment while staying at his parents' house. As he drove, he explained it all to me in a confident and subtly showy manner, for this was his home ground. Although my eyelids drooped and my head operated in a fog from lack of sleep, I felt overjoyed at the sight of rich-looking Mediterranean-style houses with landscaped yards filled with all sorts of both tall and short amusingly-shaped palm trees . . . and the crystal clear sky—so beautiful, unlike the polluted Tokyo sky

As our used 1982 Toyota Cressida passed through the gate of our apartment complex, I saw the name, "Whickham Village," carved on an oblong wooden board. A few lanky palm trees and a dense growth of tropical caladiums with pink spots, charmingly planted in the small flowerbeds in front of the gate, adorned the two-year-old apartment complex. As the car neared our apartment, my heart started pounding fast with glee to see my American home.

Right away, I caught sight of a swimming pool surrounded by a tall wire fence. Inside the pool area were a few overweight old ladies lying on reclining chairs by the pool in their flamboyant swimwear. There were a few young blonde moms playing with their small children in water that reflected the blazing sun. No one had a private swimming pool on their own property in Japan, at least not to my knowledge. If there were any private pools, I imagined they must be few in number and that they would be owned by wealthy families. Next to the swimming pool, there were two green tennis courts, not being used. I felt rich and elated.

Thomas parked the car in a wide space in front of the

apartment. He opened the door with a key on a chain that had no other keys attached to it yet, and let me in first. I took off my shoes, a Japanese habit, and felt the coolness of the floor tiles. The entrance led to beige carpeting that spread over into the rest of the rooms. This thousand-square-foot two-bedroom apartment had many windows as it was located at the end of the row, but vertical blinds blocked the daytime heat of the scorching Florida sun.

First we entered the master bedroom. A dominating tall king-size bed in the center of the room astounded me.

"Is this the waterbed you were talking about on the phone? It's huge," I said, recalling the conversation we had before I came to the U.S.

"Yes, lay down and check it out," he said.

As the height of the bed came up to my stomach, it was a bit hard to do so. Instead, I placed my hands on it, then pressed down on the mattress.

"Wow . . . it's soft," I said, wondering if it would make me seasick.

"You'll sleep like a baby," my husband assured me. I walked into the bathroom. I stroked the countertop of the double-vanity with two shiny faucets, then looked up at the large mirror. Smiling, I thought, *I will enjoy using this room a lot.*

The kitchen fascinated me, too. A huge refrigerator, a dishwasher, and an oven—typical Japanese households didn't have an oven, and used a gas stove with an integrated broiler. I thought I could adjust to this new living style effortlessly and agreeably. Everything I had been experiencing so far was like being in paradise, where no reality intruded. This was America and everything was big and wonderful!

*　*　*

Later that evening, lying on the unfamiliar waterbed, I thought back over the day. I realized Thomas had worked very hard. He had to have been extremely busy all month preparing countless things, finding his job and our apartment, and getting our car and waterbed. He fell asleep holding my hand, but, having jet lag, I stayed awake for hours, my mind traveling back over all the things that had happened since I had met him. The three years in Tokyo with Thomas had passed very fast. I could not believe I was in the U.S. I remembered the first day we met . . .

* * *

The first time I saw Thomas, he was in the teachers' break room of the language school. He stood out, as he was 6'4", a brunette with blue eyes, a slender, handsome young American who wore a well-cut brown business suit. I didn't want to stare at him, but because of his height and appearance, I couldn't take my eyes off of him easily. A few days later, he approached me with the school manager when I was chatting with other Japanese teachers in the break room.

The manager said, "Kumiko-san, this is our new English teacher, Thomas-san. He has suggested that you and he tutor each other in your own native languages."

I thought his approach was a little presumptuous, as we had not properly met each other, but I could not refuse my manager.

* * *

In my first English lesson, Thomas started drawing the outline of the U.S. map on the blackboard, then he filled in each of the state's border lines as if this was a geography class. When he finished drawing, he pointed to Orlando, Florida with his slender finger. "This state is my home town. My parents live here," he said, then he shifted his finger a little north. "This is Georgia. My college is in Atlanta, the capital of Georgia."

For the entire forty-five minutes he rambled on about his personal background. At the end of the class, he abruptly asked me if I could show him around Tokyo that weekend. His boldness amazed me, but I agreed, thinking about how hard it must be to live in a foreign country.

The following week, he asked me out on a date. Although I still thought he was conceited, I had noticed how caring and sweet he was when we were walking around Tokyo. He walked on the street side of the sidewalk, while listening to me attentively. His sensitivity appealed to me, so I agreed to a date.

He took me to the Disney movie, *Fantasia*. He thought we both would enjoy it, but I fell asleep in the middle of the movie. Classical music and slow-paced movies have a hypnotic effect on me and often put me to sleep.

After the movie, he invited me to dinner at his place. The menu was salmon and stir-fried vegetables. He spiced the curry pilaf with all sorts of unfamiliar seasonings (cumin, oregano, basil, and other unfamiliar things) and raisins. The curried wild and brown rice mix with raisins was spicy and sweet, but also quite savory.

After cleaning up the table, he served a fruit cup of apple, orange, and banana. I realized how thorough and thoughtful he was, and his kind gestures gave me the impression he was a good person. When he saw me off at the station, he asked me to meet him the next day after our classes.

We started seeing each other daily. The following Saturday, we visited the National Museum of Western Art, where we played a little game.

He said, "Let's choose four paintings that we like from this room. After we choose four paintings, we'll tell each other what we chose."

"Anything I like?" I clarified.

"Yes, anything you like."

I moved like a crab, sideways, observing one-by-one the European paintings on the walls. I took more time than he did. While waiting for me, Thomas stood at the center of the room that held over fifty paintings. Knowing his eyes were following me, I tried to deceive him by staring at some of the paintings I had no interest in a bit longer.

Forgetting about being in a museum, "I'm done," loudly as I walked toward him.

He mouthed, "All right", and waited for me to come to where he was standing. Then he said "You go first."

I told him of my selections. He was flabbergasted. We had chosen exactly the same paintings.

*   *   *

Within five weeks, Thomas had decided to marry me. Even though we had only been dating for a little over a month, I didn't hesitate to agree to marry him. I liked his caring personality and proactive approach. In order to receive my parents' permission to marry, he immediately changed jobs and became a technical writer at an electronics company, to prove he was capable of earning a respectable income and being a good provider. As concerned as he was about my parents, he only called his parents to announce he was getting married. I was surprised, but glad his parents were happy about our engagement.

We were married within two months of the day we met. His parents flew from Florida to Japan to attend our Shinto wedding. Traditionally, the religious wedding ceremony is held at a shrine, and in our case, the shrine was located inside a hotel. A Shinto priest always conducts the ceremony, which is attended by only the close family members of the couple. In keeping with this, only his parents and my family were there. In the ceremony, following the Shinto rites, we drank *sake* using a special cup, and we took turns taking three sips each of three different bowls of *sake*, each one larger than the last. Thomas was in *hakama* (Japanese traditional clothing) standing next to me. He, especially in the *hakama*, reminded me of Richard Chamberlain in the movie *Shogun*. I was in a red silk kimono with a crane design, when we took our vows. His eyes were on me, while my mind was focused on the priest's words. Thomas remembered the whole oath; my parents were greatly impressed, and I, too, was pleased.

*   *   *

After our marriage, my life became busier. Thomas had already learned some Japanese and knew about Japanese culture before arriving two months earlier. Even so, living in another country demands a higher level of communication skills, and he needed my help.

Thomas had become a member of a *Go* club before we married, and had been playing the game in his spare time. But a few months after we got married, he found a new hobby and spent less time playing *Go*. His boss, a fellow American, had built a computer from scratch, and he helped Thomas build his own computer. For a while, we spent every weekend in the Akihabara District. Tomas's Japanese wasn't good enough to shop by himself for specialized items that required detailed knowledge, so I had little time for myself on the weekends.

Akihabara, known as Akihabara Electric Town, is famous worldwide as the center for electronic and electronic goods. A visitor to Akihabara will be overwhelmed by the buildings lining the main street, whose walls, roofs, and windows are covered with all kinds of colorful shops' names and signs. Walking into the alleys, one finds small shops that specialize in electric parts, wires, and tools. We spent many hours there looking for computer parts such as chips, registers, capacitors, and circuit boards.

I also helped him do painstaking jobs like using a soldering iron to place memory chips onto a motherboard. This was a task I disliked. One early afternoon while sitting at a table soldering memory chips, I placed the soldering iron next to me on the floor pillow on which I sat. While I was intensely involved in doing my job, I smelled something burning. I glanced down at the cushion. The hot tip of the soldering iron had penetrated the cushion, making a sizable hole. I jumped up and beat the fire out with a magazine.

The incident stressed me so much that I was haunted by a dream later that night. I dreamt about burning a bunch of holes in a cushion with the soldering iron.

The next morning, Thomas looked at me with a curious face and asked me, "What about your dream last night? In your sleep you said, 'It's big. Be careful.'"

He thought I was having an erotic dream about a giant penis. I had to disappoint him by telling him the dream was about a soldering iron burning a big hole in a cushion.

"Eh? Ah, Sou" (is that so?) he said, with the subtle nuance that he was a bit disappointed.

* * *

To my great relief, after six months, he finally finished building his computer.

Using his own self-built computer, he started to learn programming. His first program was a horseracing game. He tried to teach me programming, but his learning pace was faster than mine, and soon he wanted to be a professional. However, his realization that he would not be able to find a job as a software programmer in Japan led him to look to his own country, where the software industries were way ahead of the curve. Thomas decided we would move back to the U.S.

* * *

The jet lag, the excitement of a new American home, and the sinking sensation of the soft waterbed kept me awake for a long time. Despite getting only a few hours of sleep, I woke up with a fresh mind, ready to take on the day. Our new life in Florida had begun. After breakfast, Thomas took me to a grocery store called Albertsons.

As I entered the huge supermarket, enormous vegetables piqued my curiosity. I had never imagined that they could grow that big. Onions, eggplants, cucumbers, green peppers, and potatoes were giant-sized, easily three or four times bigger than the ones grown in Japan. Moving to the fruit section, I was amazed by the wide variety of fruits. In Japan, imported fruit prices are very high because the Japanese government protects its own industries from foreign competition. Inside Albertsons, there were fruits like mangos, lychees, star fruits, durians, and passion fruits I had never seen before, but even fruits I recognized, like apples, came in many varieties. They were colorfully compartmentalized in sections on the counter like apples on parade. *They must be imported from all over the world. How lucky Americans are,* I thought.

Another eye-opener was the meat section. The big slabs of pork and beef were lavishly laid in the large window case. The amount in the packages, I thought, could serve a dozen Japanese people. Everything in the supermarket looked oversized, including a great number of the Floridians whose colorful shoes and clothes didn't cover much. Pushing the shopping cart, I heard Thomas saying behind me, "Are you gonna be here all day? I want to go home." He didn't mind explaining to me what things were, as my face was beaming with excitement, but after showing me practically everything in the market, he finally got tired. The shopping cart was heaped with enough food for a week or more. I felt as if we were stocking up for an emergency; most Japanese homes have small refrigerators and the majority of people shop for groceries daily.

* * *

Thomas's work started a week after I arrived in the U.S.. I had not even recovered from my jet lag when he told me I'd need to get a driver's license because he would be taking a two-week business trip soon, and I would get hungry if I could not get out for food. Although I knew I would need a license, I felt stressed that I had so little time to practice before the driving exam.

I had already had a couple of driving lessons with my oldest brother, Shohei, before coming to the U.S.—just enough to be able to move a car forward and backward at a slow speed. My brother was patient, and kind enough not to shout at me, although one time he commented that I had slow reflexes. It hadn't been easy for me to learn how to control the amount of pressure to apply to the brake or gas pedal.

"Easy . . . easy, don't stop abruptly," my husband said in our first lesson.

"I know. I'm sorry," I said, but in a second, I did it again.

I noticed the strained look on his face. I didn't blame him though, because his car was brand new. All I wanted at that point was to grip the steering wheel, to at least get some idea of how cars maneuvered, even if I didn't fully understand everything.

The next Saturday, Thomas took me to Winter Park, Orlando, near his parent's house, to teach me how to parallel park. On the way there, he had me take the steering wheel on the highway. I had only the minimum skill gained in the forward and backward practice with my brother at ten or fifteen miles per hour on an empty road near my parents' house. Driving on a U.S. highway was terrifying! When I was driving, I felt the speed was two times faster than if I was a passenger, and my heart seemed to beat twice as fast as well.

At Winter Park, Thomas showed me how to park a car by a concrete curb. He picked a place where there were two oak trees overhanging the roadway, just far enough apart for me to practice parallel parking between them.

Sticking out his head from the window, telling me how to cut wheels, he said, "Are you watching me?"

"I AM WATCHING YOU," I said impatiently.

"Okay, it's your turn," he said coming out of the car.

In spite of his instruction, I had in my mind how I would park. I tensed up, knowing that if I didn't park the way he showed me, he would lose his temper.

I moved the car very slowly and cautiously, past the big tree, far enough, I thought, and started to back up to park in that space, but his strident voice broke my concentration. All I could hear was his shouting. "Cut the wheel sharply! Not that way! Don't go that way!" I decided I would be a lot better off if I learned by myself.

Early the next morning, I got up before Thomas woke, so I could practice alone. No one was on the road; only a few cats dotted the edges. I started the car and eased forward at a slow speed, then made many circles around our apartment complex. I had already purchased a thick blue cushion at Kmart, to raise myself up so I could see well. I drew the seat as far forward as I could, leaving minimal leg space, so I could control the pedals without stepping on the wrong one. In the evening I practiced as well, but I realized I didn't have enough time to complete my lessons. I asked Thomas to take me to his office, so I could use the car while he was working. He was a little hesitant, but kind enough to agree.

The next morning, Monday, I put on walking shoes and grabbed the blue cushion, (which became my security blanket), and two brown Albertsons' paper bags. He took me to his office building. As he disappeared inside, I began practicing parallel parking between the two bags. After about ten or fifteen minutes, people started coming out from the building and moving their cars away from the area where I was driving.

One night a few days after Thomas had started taking me to his office for my driving practice, he said, "Let's go get your driver's license tomorrow."

"To-to-tomorrow?" I whined.

The DMV office was not crowded after one o'clock on a Thursday, so my name was called quickly. When I was directed by an officer to go outside, I went out and scanned the area to look for my examiner. A tall woman stood next to my white Toyota, so I assumed she was my examiner. As I got closer, I noticed her physique was manly and she looked stern. I was already nervous, but her formidable manner made my body stiffen. Remembering I was a brand-new immigrant, I approached her with my best manners to try to open the passenger's door for her, but she scowled me down, saying, "Get in your car." Intimidated, I forgot about being kind, and focused on listening to what she instructed me to do.

Incredible! I passed the driving test!

* * *

In the same month I moved to the U.S., I had a great opportunity to see a space shuttle launch which was originally scheduled in June, but had been delayed three times. In the early morning of August 30th, taking scenic A1A Highway, Thomas and I headed to one of the off-site viewing locations (the causeway over the

Banana River Park) near the Kennedy Space Center. We reached the site around at 7:30 a.m., and there were already many people anxiously waiting to see the shuttle. About ten minutes before nine, I heard someone shout, "The launch is soon." A few minutes later, I saw a white cloud bellow from the rocket engines, momentarily followed by an immense blast of noise as the shuttle lifted off and sputtered skyward. I was emotionally taken by the smoke, fire, and the ground-trembling noise. This was an event I had never imagined being able to witness.

*   *   *

Although two weeks had passed since I got my driver's license, I hadn't driven anywhere alone except to the grocery store. One evening before we went to bed, Thomas said, "By the way, you have a dental appointment next Monday."

"What?" I asked.

"I heard you complain that your tooth hurt. Remember? You said your back tooth hurt when you ate dinner last week."

"You're gonna take me there right? 'Cause I don't want to drive by myself," I protested.

"It'll be good practice for you. I'll teach you how to read a map."

I had some difficulty reading a road map. Like most Japanese, I had never used a road map to navigate. In most of Japan, streets are not named except for the main roads, and blocks are numbered. Mailmen have to know the area well. Japanese have to know the city, the name of the ward, and the block number in order to find a place. Beyond that, most Japanese ask for directions. When you ask for directions, people usually give you some landmarks. You'll hear something like this: "You go straight that way for three blocks and at that intersection you take a left turn. There is a tall white building. Pass that building, and in a distance of ten feet, you will see an elementary school on your right. Pass it, then turn right into a small alley, then follow it for a while . . ." In any event, I studied the directions before I took off for the dentist. But even though I had looked at the map, it was quite a challenge to drive to an unfamiliar area. I surely had a guardian angel.

Thankfully, I managed to get to the dentist a few minutes before my eleven o'clock appointment. *My word! Is this a dental office?* I thought. The waiting room looked like a small-scale hotel lounge. As I finished the paperwork, filled with a great deal of consent forms, an assistant took me to one of the rooms. Unlike a Japanese dental office, the patients' rooms were all individualized. The room I was taken to was equipped with all sorts of hi-tech machines. *A decade ahead of Japanese dental technology,* I thought, and felt good about receiving treatment. But when the dental assistant said, "We have to take X-rays of all your teeth first." I was troubled.

I said, "I know which tooth hurts. I pointed it out."

"We have to take pictures of all your teeth. I'm sorry, but that's our policy," she said.

"Twenty-three times!" I cried out in surprise.

Feeling helpless, I let them take the X-rays. Not only did I have to bear the pain of having X-ray films pinch my relatively small mouth each time, but I also dreaded being exposed to so much radiation. In a strange way, I discovered in myself a resistance to following the American way. Nonetheless, I realized I simply needed to adapt to the U.S. system in order to fit in.

There was another thing I had difficulty adapting to. When nearly two months had passed, Thomas wanted me to pay bills and balance our checkbook. That was a struggle. The majority of Japanese people use cash and don't write checks except for business purposes. Even fewer carry credit cards. Even to this day, many Japanese people prefer cash. Consequently, I found it difficult to manage money using plastic cards or checks. I needed to learn how to pay bills from scratch.

I told Thomas, "I don't like carrying credit cards."

"Too bad . . . you are in the U.S.," he said.

"But the risk of getting into debt is high," I snapped back.

"Unfortunately, if you don't use credit cards, you can't establish your credit here," he said.

Japanese highly value saving money. I liked the idea of using cash because you could see visually how much money was in your wallet. The virtue of saving money and the virtue of borrowing money to build credit are totally different concepts. I didn't know which system was sound, but since Thomas told me to use credit cards, I did so, regardless of my concerns.

*　*　*

As autumn came to an end, there was an incident that drove me to look for a job quickly. Normally a jar of orange juice sat in our refrigerator, but there wasn't any one day and Thomas wanted some

He said angrily, "Can't you make orange juice? You have nothing to do all day!"

"Sorry! But you don't need to get upset like that," I snapped back.

It was true I had nothing to do. I was kind of swimming around like a Beta fish does when it is poured into a bigger fish bowl from the tiny see-through container from a pet shop. But his complaint made me ready to take action. I said I was sorry, but almost at the same time, fuming, I yelled, "I'll find a job TOMORROW!" Perhaps he wasn't that angry, perhaps he was just tired, but I was a very sensitive person and didn't take reproach lightly.

The next morning, I drove to the Melbourne shopping mall and roamed the inside of each shop. At each place, I asked of any salesperson who was available at the moment, "Can I apply for a job here?" Many of them looked at me as if to say, "What are you talking about?" but I wasn't hesitant, and continued to search for a place to make a strong appeal. Though I was a genetically shy person, when the time came to achieve something, I became adamantly persistent. My smiling face and a conservative, but chic, outfit helped me to finally get the attention of a manager of the Jordan Marsh department store. He was standing at the main door, amiably greeting the customers. I didn't know who he was until he took me to his office. He sat in his executive high-back leather chair, leaned back, and loosely folded his arms.

"Have a seat. How can I help you?"

"I would like to work at this department store."

"Any experience working at retail stores?"

"In Japan," I said confidently, back straight, hands stiffly crossed over my lap.

"How long you've been in the U.S?"

"Two months."

He rested his elbow on the armchair, held his chin in his hand, then looked at me, knitting his eyebrows a bit. His eyes were riveted on me, but for a long moment, he was silent. I felt awkward under his stare.

He finally said, "Okay, leave your resume, and we'll let you know soon."

I bowed deeply and left the office.

* * *

I waited for his answer each day. A week passed then another, finally in the third week, I received a call from the Human Resources Department, asking me to come back to take three days of training. I was exulted as I had almost given up all hope of getting the job.

I showed up in the classroom at 7:45 a.m. with a bulky Sony tape recorder, sat down in the front row, and nervously waited for the instructor to come in. Register machines had already been set on our long narrow rectangular tables. Until our teacher showed up, fifteen people—a few old, chatty women, several young ladies, and a few young men—talked with their neighbors. But I was quiet, so quiet I could even hear my own heart beating noticeably faster than its usual pace. I hoped the instructor would be nice and understanding.

A petite young woman in a short, tight navy blue skirt and white silk blouse, with a thin red bowtie ribbon around her neck, stepped lightly into our classroom.

"Good morning, everyone! My name is Susan," she said enthusiastically.

"Good morning Susan," we said in chorus.

"We have a three-day training. It's important for you guys to show up for the classes on time and learn all the procedures," she said in a serious voice, then added, "If you fail to learn all the transactions taught in the class, then you'll need to take another class."

No one said anything. My heart started racing even faster. I was starting my first job in this country!

* * *

Every so often, Susan stood behind me to make sure I was following the procedure. For two nights I reviewed the tape recording to catch up for the next class. I managed to pass the training and was first assigned to work in the gift-wrap department around the busiest time, the Christmas season. In a dimly-lit back room, I had no contact with customers except when my co-worker needed to take a break. All day I wrapped boxes that held all sorts of different items inside. Odd shapes of boxes significantly slowed my work and made my fingers weary. This was the most boring job I had ever worked. Only soft rock music playing from my co-worker's radio sustained my mind.

"I wish I could work on the floor and not back in a dark room," I said to my husband one day.

"Oh, you know, I had called HR to get you in there because they had been taking time getting back to you," he said, then added as if he just remembered, "They said they had been waiting to find a suitable position for you."

I recalled they took a long time to get in touch with me, and I had been peeved and often took out my vexation on Thomas. I nonetheless hadn't asked him to do anything. He thought he had done me a favor, but I reproached him saying, "I can handle those things by myself, just as I found the job without your help."

Towards Christmas, the manager of HR came into the room where I was rushing to wrap a whole bunch of boxes piled up around me. He made his way around the tables to my place while looking around the room as if he were counting the boxes.

He said, "Hi Kumiko. You are doing a great job! You know, soon you'll have a chance to get on the floor." He tapped my shoulder lightly in a gesture of approval.

"Thank you very much," I said, and bowed.

* * *

Finally my day came to work on the floor. I started out in the "dresses" department. Though unfamiliar clothing brand names overwhelmed me in the beginning, I hastily familiarized myself with them. What scared me most was answering calls from customers who asked me to check to see if we had a particular item. I listened very carefully to the descriptions and jotted them down. For instance, a customer would ask, "Can you see if you have Dockers pants? Khaki Style and Slim Fit . . . cargo style. My size is fourteen. By the way I'm looking for tan." I would puzzle . . . *What is Khaki Style? What is cargo?* I had to at least attempt to find the item. I detested running around like a chicken with its head cut off. I often ended up looking for another salesperson and showing them my scribbled notes. A lot of times I managed to run away from the phone calls, but at times I was assigned to work on the floor by myself. When I stood alone, I kept a low-profile, hiding myself among the hanging clothes, far from the telephone.

It was sometimes a challenge dealing with customers. One evening when I was in the lingerie department, I was shocked to have to deal with a middle-aged woman in a muumuu dress who brought in a gigantic bra to return. The bra, once white, looked worn out, and she told me she wanted to exchange it for a new one, because it simply didn't fit. I was perplexed and stared at it for a while, but as I looked up and saw the customer's impatient countenance, I suddenly remembered I wasn't supposed to argue with a customer if the price was less than fifty dollars. I processed it as damaged goods.

In Japan, I had worked in the dress department of a large department store during my junior college summer vacations. No one brought me a return. Returning items is rare in Japan unless they are damaged or broken at purchase. In general, dealing with customers is easier because most Japanese pay cash. An important attitude in the Japanese retail business is to treat the customer like a god. At large stores, when you arrive at the opening time of 10:00 a.m., sales people are standing in a line to great you. While bowing slowly and deeply, they all say in unison, *"Irashai mase,"* (welcome) in enthusiastic voices.

* * *

In early May, fortunately or unfortunately, I fell down a staircase inside the mall as I hurried to the parking lot after work. I thought the injury wasn't bad, but I couldn't walk. Thomas immediately took me to a doctor. The doctor said I had a greenstick fracture in my right shinbone. I ended up using crutches for almost a month. I quit the job, feeling justified in doing so, because I couldn't work on crutches. Frankly, I wasn't prepared for that sort of job, so I was perfectly happy not working. I felt relieved. *Well, it's time to rest!* I reasoned. But my injured leg made even simple tasks unimaginably hard and tiring. Even bathing wasn't easy. I had to lean forward to hold up my upper body, and hang my left leg over the rim of the tub to wash. *Well, then again,* I thought, *it could be worse if I had damaged my right leg, in which case I wouldn't be able to drive a car.*

Towards the end of the treatment, I mentioned to my husband how uncomfortable I was about the way my doctor had been treating my leg.

"I don't like my doctor, Dr. Chan. He always soaks my foot in warm water to give it a massage. But often he raises my leg up high, trying to look up my skirt. You know I can't wear pants because of the cast," I complained one day.

He rubbed his chin and frowned, then asked, "How long have you been going?"

"About a month," I responded.

"You know, Kumiko, you'd better be checked by another doctor," he said.

The next evening after work, Thomas took me to an orthopedist. The new doctor removed the cast. The X-ray showed the tiniest hairline fracture. When the new doctor told us that I hadn't needed a cast, I got agitated, and Thomas was furious. When we got out of the office, he cursed. "I'm gonna call that quack doctor tomorrow and chew him out!"

My leg muscles had atrophied. When I tried to stand, my knee couldn't carry the weight. If I tried to use my knee, I thought I would topple over. I immediately started to rehab my leg by swimming—breaststroke, dog paddle, and backstroke for many hours. It took days to be able to use my right leg in a normal way. I learned by this experience that the human body is meant to walk. "Use it or lose it." After swimming, I sat in a Jacuzzi and rubbed my legs. I saw the bubbles streaming up from the jet ports, and this triggered an image of a hot spring. My thoughts then turned to my parents. *Ah . . . almost a year has passed since I left Japan.* I remembered my mom saying many times, "Your dad and I want to thank Thomas-san's parents in person. You know they came all the way to Japan to attend your wedding." So that night, I asked Thomas about inviting my parents to our house. Thomas thought it was a great idea.

* * *

They visited in late July—just about a year after we had moved to the U.S. On their arrival day, I was anxious, as there wasn't a direct flight, and they needed to catch connecting flights twice, one in Atlanta and one in Orlando. Thomas and I hurried to the Melbourne International Airport a little earlier than their scheduled arrival time. But as we proceeded toward the gate I saw my parents already walking towards the baggage claim. I immediately recognized my mom's blue-striped dress, which I had bought using my employee discount when I worked at the Jordan Marsh department store.

I called out, *"Otosan! Okasan!"* which means Mom and Dad in Japanese.

When they saw us, they grinned as if their facial muscles

couldn't stretch any wider. Dad raised his right hand up to his shoulder. Mom stooped a little, attempting to make a greeting gesture. We trotted towards them.

When we met, my dad let out a big sigh of relief and said elatedly in Japanese, "You know Kumiko, when I saw the clock in the Atlanta airport, I noticed the time was different than on my watch. For a while I didn't understand." He took a quick breath and continued, "But I soon realized the time difference between Japan and the U. S. I adjusted my watch there, and hurried up to catch the next flight. If I hadn't realized the time difference, I tell you, we wouldn't be here."

"Oh-oh, I didn't even think about the time differences. Sorry. I am very glad you noticed," I said.

Proudly, Mom said, "I just followed your dad. If I were alone I would never, ever be able to come to the U. S. Your dad can read English, you know."

Changing planes in Atlanta and Orlando must have been quite a challenge for them, I thought, recalling my own travels. I was glad my dad was travel savvy.

We arrived home. I was tickled about showing my parents around.

"Wow . . . it's cool inside!" Mom said.

"Central air conditioner is on," I replied.

Mom started roaming around. Dad and I tailed after her.

"Wow . . . the rooms are spacious," she said.

"It feels good walking on the soft carpet," Dad noted with pleasure, as if the carpet could take away his leg and foot fatigue from their long journey.

In entering the kitchen, I remembered to explain how dangerous the garbage disposal could be. When I turned the switch on, they threw their heads back in astonishment.

After showing the kitchen, I took them to one of the bathrooms to show them how to use the shower over the tub, because the layout of Japanese bathrooms and western ones were quite different then. In the U.S., a bathroom is usually a single room with a toilet, a washbasin, and bathtub or shower. However, in Japan, the toilet has its own separate room. The actual bathing room has a tiled floor with a drain and it is equipped with a sink and deep tub. The previous apartment Thomas and I had lived in had a hand-held shower fixture that was hooked up to a waist-high attachment on the wall in the washing area, but the shower hose wasn't long enough for us to stand up, so we used the shower while we squatted on a little stool. When I lived in Japan, quite a lot of people didn't have bathtubs, especially the ones who lived in apartments. They went to a communal bath house, called a *Sento*. We used to have a *Sento* near our home, but our traditional cultures have faded away and there aren't many of those public baths nowadays.

The next day was a big day for my parents. The main purpose for their trip was to return the honor to Tomas's parents who had crossed the ocean to attend our wedding. They carefully carried a Hakata doll of a Samurai figure (traditional Japanese clay doll) in a glass case that was twice as big as a man's shoe box. Trying not to bump the box against anyone or anything, they had been watchful all the way from the time they left their home in Japan. My mom said that at times they needed to put the doll on their lap in the airplane. They hadn't relaxed until they finally saw Thomas's parents opened the package. The Hakata doll was in perfect shape. Another of my parents' gifts was a vintage ivory necklace for Thomas's stepmother, which wasn't a good idea as she was a high-school biology teacher and didn't like the idea of wearing ivory because of elephants being an endangered species. Of course my parents hadn't been aware of that, and handed it to her as an honorable gift. But Thomas's parents showed great appreciation, so my parents felt a great release from their obligation to say, "Thank you," in person and relief that all had gone well. Japanese are tangled with *Giri* (moral obligation.) They won't feel comfortable until they return a favor, whatever it might be.

* * *

Before my parents came to the U.S., Thomas had told his boss, Steve, how much my dad liked playing golf. Steve was kind enough to ask his father, Roy, to play golf with my dad. One weekend, Roy took my dad to the membership-only country golf club in Melbourne to which he belonged. On that day, the four of us appeared at the golf course in the early morning and we met Roy. Thomas introduced us to Roy, and then Roy introduced the couple of friends he had brought along. Thomas and Roy chatted in a light mood for a while before Roy turned to speak to my dad. Roy had a chiseled, tanned face and stern look, but when he talked to Dad, he softened his expression and very slowly enunciated, "Hi, Kiyoshi, do you like playing golf?"

"Yes, he does," I answered reflexively.

"Well, shall we start playing golf?" Roy said gently to my dad.

"Yes," Dad said in English, without waiting for my translation. He understood "play golf" and his facial muscles relaxed after he realized the ritualistic conversation was over.

As Thomas, Mom and I were leaving, I turned and glanced to see how Dad was doing. He was laughing. I can vividly recall when we first entered the golf course. My dad's wide eyes had scanned the whole course. He said, "Wow . . . how beautiful the landscape is! I cannot wait to play." But it wasn't the golf course that caught my eye first. I was looking at the white houses. Along one side of the golf course, there was a line of Spanish-style houses. They were very striking with whitewashed walls and terracotta-colored roofs. Because I was facing the houses while talking to Steve's dad, I pondered if the golf balls might hit the houses. This was my first strong impression, but the course was picturesque. On the manicured green grass, there were soaring spindly palm trees standing around the small lakes. The course looked tropical and paradise-like under the sapphire sky.

*　*　*

When Thomas, Mom, and I returned to the golf club, the group had already finished playing golf and stood waiting for us. Dad had barely noticed us walking toward him, when he ran to me. Hastily, he asked me to translate how impressive the golf course was, and how thoughtful they were. When Roy and his friend caught up to us, Dad turned his head back to give a big thank-you smile to them.

As soon as I finished translating, Dad jumped into our conversation before letting Roy respond, "Roy-san sang an old Japanese love song, *'Shina No Yoru'* (China Nights) and we both sang together."

When he said this, for a moment I wondered whether or not they had evoked the memory of World War II. *Well. . . I hope not.* After all, Dad was in seventh heaven with joy. Tapping on my dad's shoulder, Roy-san praised him. "Kiyoshi is very good." Roy's two other friends flattered my father further, saying, "He's a Japanese Arnold Palmer." Scratching his head, Dad smiled bashfully.

This memory of the golf outing was strongly imprinted on his mind. He sent me a thank you letter to give to Roy after they went home. I translated his long calligraphy, and gave it to Thomas's boss along with Dad's formal letter.

*　*　*

During the month of their visit, Thomas took us my parents to Epcot Center, Kennedy Space Center, and Vero Beach. On weekdays, I took my parents to all the places I could think of. One day, I took them to St. Augustine. I had been there with Thomas before and that memory of the historical Spanish architecture with brilliant shades of red was ingrained in my mind. Striking Renaissance architecture buildings sprawled across the landscape and the moss-draped oaks were ubiquitous; the timeless art in the Colonial Spanish Quarter utterly captivated me. Much to my regret, we had only three hours to spend there and needed to head home.

On the way home from St Augustine, there was a frightening moment. I stepped on the accelerator with the transmission in reverse after waiting for a traffic light to turn green. It took us back at top speed for roughly thirty feet. I immediately stepped on the brake. *Why on earth had I put the transmission in reverse!* That sensation was unnerving and nauseating. My heart pounded vigorously and my hands trembled. Luckily, there were no cars behind us. My parents did not utter a word, but looked at me questioningly. I didn't say anything and only thought *are they gonna trust me to drive further?* They didn't express any concerns about my driving, but they were quiet all the way home.

Despite the fact I scared them, they enjoyed riding with me till their departure day. Having fulfilled their mission to return their obligation and carrying loads of treasured memories, my parents returned safe and sound.

*   *   *

After my parents returned home, I became homesick. Many times, gazing out the window of our living room and looking at the sky, all I could think about was my parents. Thomas worried about me.

One evening, he said, "I got this address from my co-worker. This church has activities and non-Christians, like you, can join there too. They do cooking and have arts and crafts projects, so I heard." Since he strongly encouraged me to go there, I used the Toyota during the day and visited the church. Nearly twenty people gathered for church activities. Mostly, they were immigrants like me. There were Chinese, Italians, and some Puerto Ricans. We each took our turns demonstrating how we cooked our national cuisines. Cooking foreign cuisines with the locals was quite entertaining and an eye-opening experience. Fried Plantains (fried banana) with creamy aji amarillo sauce (yellow hot-pepper paste mixed with mayonnaise) was *delicioso*. The twice-weekly meeting stirred my interest. November soon arrived and the intense sun softened. Life in Florida was becoming pleasant, but then one evening I heard Thomas grumble, "Why am I the one who needs to go to counseling?" His company was sending him there due to his bad behavior. I already knew about his discontent because he had been telling me how rude his coworker was—his coworker's chair was always left in his way, like a shopping cart parked in the middle of the aisle. Contorting his face with anger, he said, "It's annoying I need to move it aside all the time." Knowing his aggressive self-righteous temper, I had suspected something might happen. *Here we go*, I'd thought when he'd first complained to me. He had finally kicked his coworker's chair.

No . . . that's the wrong approach, I thought to myself. In any case, at first I deemed needing the professional help of a counselor to be shocking and shameful. However, after some reflection, I began thinking that there might be a slight chance for him to better control his hot temper if he took enough counseling sessions. But a month or so later, another incident occurred between the same coworker and Thomas. This time, the company decided to dismiss him. He was furious, and I was disappointed.

This episode reminded me of several incidents that had happened in Tokyo. Whenever he spotted a smoker in a movie theater, he would get out of his seat, march over to the smoker, grab him by the arm, and point him to the door. Because he knew that smoking was prohibited, it greatly annoyed him. He would also become vexed when he saw people trying to cut in front of a line. He stepped towards the people and said in poor Japanese, *"Yamete kudasai!"* (Please don't do that!) He had no tolerance for what he thought was not right. But he was not a policeman: he only embarrassed me.

I had always been worried that his audacious behavior would get him in trouble. In odd contrast, however, he did many altruistic things. I saw him picking up soda cans, Styrofoam cups, and litter on roads. He often handed money to female panhandlers. Once he saved a stray cat. He had the cat washed, neutered, and given vaccines before finding its owner. After he found its home, he even visited to see if the cat was treated well. He didn't kill spiders or bugs wandering about in our house, but caught them in his hands and released them outside. In fact, I learned Eco-consciousness from him. I started doing little things like carrying my own grocery bags.

He had shown me many acts of kindness, but I remembered that at the beginning of our marriage, he was oppressive. I knew his intentions were good, but it was unbearable being told no coffee, no alcohol, no junk food, no red meat, no trash magazines, and no high heels. He even tried to get me to jog every weekend. After a while, he gave up on the idea of trying to change my eating habits and preferences because he realized some habits can never be changed.

In any case, we needed to make a living, so he had to find another job. He suggested to me that we move to Atlanta because he had gone to college there. Moving to a different place didn't inconvenience me at that time since I didn't have friends or anything to tie me down. In fact, I thought it would be rewarding to get to know the different parts of the U.S. Right away, he looked for a job in the Atlanta area.

www.ingramcontent.com/pod-product-compliance
Lightning Source LLC
Chambersburg PA
CBHW062022190726
48284CB00014B/1966